A figure strode into the firelight.

At the sight of him, Brigid started violently. Her heart seemed to skip a beat, then began to pound again. Against the dancing flames, surrounded by the small, dark people, the man stood out with vivid distinctiveness.

He smiled with a terrible beauty, repellent but magnetic. He wore black leather knee boots, black leggings and a red shirt with billowy sleeves. He smiled broadly, white teeth gleaming against pale skin, contrasting with a fall of black hair. His yellow-green eyes were magnificent and invoked in Brigid a desire to please him.

The swampies crowded around him, and he reached out and touched them as if bestowing benedictions—or stroking his pets. He radiated more than charisma; he exuded an aura of evil—absolute, unregenerate, charming and desirable evil.

Other titles in this series:

JAMES AXLER

OUTLANDERS™

SHADOW SCOURGE

A GOLD EAGLE BOOK FROM

WORLDWIDE®

TORONTO • NEW YORK • LONDON
AMSTERDAM • PARIS • SYDNEY • HAMBURG
STOCKHOLM • ATHENS • TOKYO • MILAN
MADRID • WARSAW • BUDAPEST • AUCKLAND

First edition May 2000

ISBN 0-373-63826-4

SHADOW SCOURGE

Special thanks to Mark Ellis for his contribution to the Outlanders concept, developed for Gold Eagle.

Life itself is but the shadow of death, and souls departed but the shadows of the living. All things fall under this name. The sun itself is but the dark *simulacrum,* and light but the shadow of God.
—Sir Thomas Browne, 1605-1682

The Road to Outlands—
From Secret Government Files to the Future

Almost two hundred years after the global holocaust, Kane, a former Magistrate of Cobaltville, often thought the world had been lucky to survive at all after a nuclear device detonated in the Russian embassy in Washington, D.C. The aftermath—forever known as skydark—reshaped continents and turned civilization into ashes.

Nearly depopulated, America became the Deathlands—poisoned by radiation, home to chaos and mutated life forms. Feudal rule reappeared in the form of baronies, while remote outposts clung to a brutish existence.

What eventually helped shape this wasteland were the redoubts, the secret preholocaust military installations with stores of weapons, and the home of gateways, the locational matter-transfer facilities. Some of the redoubts hid clues that had once fed wild theories of government cover-ups and alien visitations.

Rearmed from redoubt stockpiles, the barons consolidated their power and reclaimed technology for the villes. Their power, supported by some invisible authority, extended beyond their fortified walls to what was now called the Outlands. It was here that the rootstock of humanity survived, living with hellzones and chemical storms, hounded by Magistrates.

In the villes, rigid laws were enforced—to atone for the sins of the past and prepare the way for a better future. That was the barons' public credo and their right-to-rule.

Kane, along with friend and fellow Magistrate Grant, had upheld that claim until a fateful Outlands expedition. A displaced piece of technology…a question to a keeper of the archives…a vague clue about alien masters—and their world shifted radically. Suddenly, Brigid Baptiste, the archivist, faced summary execution, and

Grant a quick termination. For Kane there was forgiveness if he pledged his unquestioning allegiance to Baron Cobalt and his unknown masters and abandoned his friends.

But that allegiance would make him support a mysterious and alien power and deny loyalty and friends. Then what else was there?

Kane had been brought up solely to serve the ville. Brigid's only link with her family was her mother's red-gold hair, green eyes and supple form. Grant's clues to his lineage were his ebony skin and powerful physique. But Domi, she of the white hair, was an Outlander pressed into sexual servitude in Cobaltville. She at least knew her roots and was a reminder to the exiles that the outcasts belonged in the human family.

Parents, friends, community—the very rootedness of humanity was denied. With no continuity, there was no forward momentum to the future. And that was the crux—when Kane began to wonder if there *was* a future.

For Kane, it wouldn't do. So the only way was out—way, way out.

After their escape, they found shelter at the forgotten Cerberus redoubt headed by Lakesh, a scientist, Cobaltville's head archivist, and secret opponent of the barons.

With their past turned into a lie, their future threatened, only one thing was left to give meaning to the outcasts. The hunger for freedom, the will to resist the hostile influences. And perhaps, by opposing, end them.

Prologue

Louisiana, the time of skydark

The distant booming of drums almost smothered the rustle of swift and stealthy feet in the clearing.

Falconer whirled to see a small figure lunging at him from the moss-shadowed arch formed by the intertwining boughs of two cypress trees. Although the light of the noonday sun could not penetrate the vast clouds of pulverized dust overhead, nor the leafy canopy of the bayou, his eye implant afforded him a clear glimpse of a fierce, dark face and the glitter of steel in an upraised hand.

Twisting his body, Falconer avoided the down-sweeping edge of the machete. Before the attacker recovered his balance, Falconer brought his own heavy blade down on the swampie's forearm. The razor-keen steel sheared through flesh, muscle and bone.

The arm dropped to the marshy ground, fist still clenched around the handle of the machete. Blood spurted in a crimson arc from the hacked-off stump just below the swampie's elbow. It almost immediately became a trickle, as if a spigot valve had closed.

Falconer wasn't particularly surprised, since the briefing jacket he had studied in White Sands footnoted the swamp mutants' conscious control over their double circulatory system.

He whipped his eighteen-inch knife up and around in a horizontal sweep. He felt the shock of impact vibrating in his Teflon shoulder socket, then the swampie's head tumbled from his squat neck, seemingly propelled by a scarlet fountain.

The creature's body trembled for a long moment, then toppled forward. Falconer stepped aside to avoid being doused by the flow of blood from the severed carotid artery. Foliage rattled behind him, and he pivoted on his heel just as the underbrush disgorged the *houngan,* Mama Minuit.

Her lilting voice, pitched to a husky amused whisper, said "Done tol' yo' there be guards. Good t'ing he not one o' *les morts-vivants.*"

It had taken Falconer several days to focus past her Creole accent, liberally sprinkled as it was with debased French slang. He turned his snort of derision into a grunt and nudged the disembodied head with a foot. "One of the undead or just another mutant, he's still not regenerating a new head."

The heat-sensitive cell in his right eye socket showed him the decapitated swampie's expression, frozen in a fierce death rictus, lips pulled back from discolored teeth. He also saw the pattern of raised scar tissue around his eyes.

"Ritual scarring," he murmured.

Mama Minuit gestured with her own machete, gripped tightly in her beringed right hand. "Caste marks. Disgusting! He one o' the baron's own, one o' his beasts. Had me no doubt about it. Now what yo' do? Not too late to leave, y'know."

Falconer turned to face her, responding to the mocking challenge lurking in the woman's question. Mama Minuit's deep black eyes drew his as a magnet draws steel, and they seemed to glimmer with a wisdom peculiar to her alone. Her only garments were wrappings of bright red fabric that left her brown limbs and midriff bare. She was almost as tall as Falconer himself, broadly built and heavy breasted. Her hair was an unkempt explosion of glossy ebony, framing a smoothly contoured, almost regal face. The voodoo priestess had an aspect of the feral about her, but it was in keeping with their surroundings.

Rather than answering the woman's question, Falconer responded with a terse query of his own. "Your people are all in place?"

She nodded. "*Oui.* We must reach the church afore the ceremony is done and he—*it*—has recruited 'nother soldier to his army of the plague."

"Plague?"

"Ocajnik bring disease, he bring plague, he bring the Black Death." She pointed at the pattern of scar tissue wealed around the dead swampie's eyes. "Only those who bear his mark are immune to it. They are his beasts."

"What's he do—inoculate them?" Falconer tried

to conceal the disdain from his tone, but he knew he did a poor job of it.

Mama Minuit regarded him with a level, dispassionate stare. "That he do. An' you will see how…if you have the nerve."

Falconer saw little point in commenting derisively on her superstitious melodrama. He stepped away from the dead swampie, his movements at once lithe and economical. Of medium height, his physique was compact, but he moved with a stealthy ease through the underbrush, despite the weight of the Steyr-Mannlicher SSG rifle slung over a shoulder.

His boots made no noise, and in his black suit he was all but invisible. No sound broke the stillness other than the steady vibration of drums, and if there had been, his ears trained by years in the wild zones would have caught even the faint sigh of a breeze.

The only thing he couldn't hear was a signal from White Sands. The high-frequency receiver implanted in his mastoid bone was designed to relay signals to an organo-metallic synapse in his left ear. But no matter how high or tightly focused the frequency, it couldn't penetrate the miles-wide blanket of debris clogging the sky and choking off sunlight.

It was the time of the endless night, the twentieth year of the nuclear winter. Conditions weren't as horrific as even five years before, but were still bad enough. The sky itself was no longer of a blackish hue—over the past decade it had lightened to the red-brown color of an old bloodstain. The veil of dust and dirt choking the atmosphere was still too thick for radio signals to penetrate more than a few miles from the source of transmission. The satellite uplink on his Road Agent might as well have been a Teflon-coated washbasin for all the good it did him out in the swamps of southern Louisiana.

In all directions, heat lightning flickered luridly, but no boom of thunder came. Falconer wiped away droplets of sweat trickling from the roots of his dark-blond hair, guessing the humidity was close to ninety percent. The combat cosmetics striping his face had become runny. He accepted the discomfort as part and parcel of his duty, but he wished he were back in New Mexico, where the heat might have been fierce but at least it was dry.

The swamp's tangled lianas and creepers made a more impenetrable barrier than any obstacle course he had run during his Special Forces training. A dangling vine snared the barrel of the Steyr and he stopped, trying to disentangle it. Mama Minuit did it for him, murmuring, "You think this will do you any good 'gainst Ocajnik?"

"It's done me a lot of good—and against worse than a madman trying to build a mutie army in the bayou."

Mama Minuit's full lips twitched in a smile, both pitying and scornful. "You can't kill one o' the old ones. We can mebbe contain him, but not kill him."

Falconer retorted with scorn of his own. "He's a scumbag with delusions of grandeur. More and more of his kind have been popping up since the war, calling themselves barons. You may want to think he's some kind of demon, but he came from a bomb shelter, not from hell.''

The voodoo priestess's eyes flashed with anger. ''There are worse places than hell, soldier-man. De *loa* done tol' me what Ocajnik really is.''

Falconer shook his head in disgust and said nothing more. The six days he had spent in Mama Minuit's small settlement, some thirty miles inland from the drowned city of Lafayette, had shown him the futility of overcoming superstition with tales of bioengineering run amok.

In the minds of Mama Minuit and her people, a faith in science was far more insidious than their belief in the paranormal. After all, their ancient beliefs in spirits, bocars, zombies and otherworldly deities hadn't destroyed the world. To them, science was far more monstrous than the blackest voodoo rites. They had never heard of the Totality Concept or Genesis Project or Eternity Enterprise. Therefore, in their view, the swampies were demon-spawned monsters, not mutated human beings.

Falconer wasn't sure if there was much difference any longer between the womb of an artificial fertilization tank and the womb of hell, even though alterations had been performed on his own body. Without the application of bionic science, he would have long ago succumbed to the toxic wastelands of America following a nuclear holocaust.

The former United States had splintered into villes, frontier settlements with only remnants of the old ways. The concept of law and order had vanished in a mere matter of years after skydark. The universals were suffering and death. Baronial rule depended on greed and terror, but the Deathlands beyond the villes harbored beasts and outlaws whose cruelty was unrivaled.

In any event, if Mama Minuit found comfort in the belief that Baron Ocajnik was an inhuman old one, Falconer wasn't going to argue with her. He'd be able to prove to her how wrong she was soon enough. As it was, he was grateful she and her people had agreed to help him fulfill the mission.

The farther they walked through the morass, the more Falconer became aware of people moving furtively around and ahead of them, gliding noisily among the ugly cypress roots and beneath the hanging nooses of Spanish moss. Not even with his augmented vision could he see them clearly. They were of a new breed, born into a raw, wild world, accustomed to living on the edge of death. Grim necessity had taught them the skills to survive, even thrive in the postnuke environment. They might have been the progeny of civilized men and women, but they had no choice but to embrace lives of semibarbarism.

"We ver' close now," the voodoo priestess whispered. "Go careful. My people may not have taken out all de guards."

Falconer obeyed her, wading carefully through the

brownish, vegetation-sticky waters between buttress-rooted cypress knobs. The rotten-egg odor of swamp gas made him want to hold his nose. He saw several moccasins coiled around the roots, but they did not so much as hiss when he passed by. He heard no sound of night birds, crickets or frogs, only the steady rhythm of the drums increasing in volume. After a few minutes, the heavy foliage began to thin out and they reached comparatively high ground.

The man and woman approached a widely cleared area surrounded by brush-clogged thickets. In the center of the clearing rose a building made of blocks of dark stone.

It was a church, or at least it had been. The shape of a steeple could still be identified through a covering of intertwined vines. Although most of the stained-glass windows were broken, a flickering, lurid radiance glowed from within.

"Jean Lafitte built it for his Cajuns, long time ago," Mama Minuit said lowly. "Hauled all de stones from a quarry in Lowellton, floated dem downriver." She shook her head sadly and added, "Place long ago desanctified. It an unholy place."

Falconer was less interested in the history of the building than the noises wafting from the arched, open doorway. Overlaid by the throbbing drumbeats were orgiastic shouts and cries. Knowing there had to be sentries, he closed his left eye and reconnoitered the zone with infrared. After a few moments of his silent surveillance, a hazy human outline stepped from around the corner of the church. He wore a long robe with the cowl tossed back on his shoulders.

Falconer began to unsling the rifle, but Mama Minuit laid a hand on his arm. "*Non*. He one o' mine."

Falconer looked hard at the structure and repressed a shudder. He stepped away from the sheltering tree boughs, paused and glanced back at the woman. "You coming?"

Mama Minuit shook her head. "Time not nigh for me."

"When will it be?"

Her lips creased in a mirthless smile. From a leather pouch hanging around her neck, she pinched a handful of powder and sprinkled it over her head. "After you start it. Then I finish it."

She reached into her robes and drew forth a small object that sparkled dully in the dim light. "Take it. It will keep you safe from the evil and the children of the night that stalk here. Beyond reckoning of man, it is holy."

Falconer took the small crucifix of hammered silver, set with tiny beads. At the ends of the traverse arms, small feathers fluttered. The workmanship was crude, but not primitive.

"This was handed down from my great-great-great-grandfather," Mama Minuit said. "Daddy Lefevre was a *houngan*, like me. Now I give it to you. It is a sword and shield against the ancient evil that stirs in this place."

Falconer only stared at it.

She slapped his arm and said brusquely. "*Tu vas—* you go. Obey the rules."

In a raspy whisper, Falconer responded, "Your rules are really beginning to annoy me."

Pocketing the little crucifix, he moved out into the clearing, noting how the robed guard strolled deliberately around the corner of the church. He followed him.

When he made it to the exterior of the building, the sentry was nowhere in sight, but he saw a tall oak tree, the moss-bearded branches reaching out toward the peaked roof. A limb climbed the wall past a second floor window that had no glass, only an empty frame.

Falconer scaled the tree like a cat. Reaching a point above the window, he gripped the limb with both hands, swung back and forth until he had gained momentum and then let go. He catapulted through the air and landed in a dark room that reeked of mold and mildew.

He had no source of light, but his augmented eye picked up a heat signature in the murk. A rat crouched in a corner, gazing toward him fearlessly, almost defiantly. It rose to its hind legs and lifted its pointed, bewhiskered snout to sniff the air.

Falconer repressed the impulse to use his knife on it, despite the fact that the rodent seemed unusually large, nearly two feet tall. Baring its incisor teeth, the rat chittered, but not in fear. He received the distinct impression of a challenge. Spittle leaked from the creature's wedge-shaped mouth, and its long hairless tail whipped back and forth across the floorboards, sending up scraping echoes.

Flesh crawling in revulsion, Falconer stepped away from the rodent. Placing his feet carefully on the litter-strewed floor, he reached the single door and pushed it open on rust-stiff hinges.

He found himself high on a small balustraded gallery, overlooking the central chapel some twenty feet below. What he saw caused his breath to seize in his lungs, adrenaline to flood his system and to raise the short hairs on the nape of his neck.

All of the church's pews had been cast carelessly aside on either side of the chapel to make an open central chamber. On the podium, where ministers once preached the Scripture and promised unending hellfire for the unbeliever, there now stood a tall, shrouded figure.

He was as still as a carved idol, his features hidden by a red cowl. Around the base of the podium knelt thirteen people, each in an identical hooded robe. They pounded hide-covered drums with their fists, setting a hypnotic rhythm. They shouted words in a singsong chant, but Falconer did not understand them. They didn't sound like Creole or any language he had ever heard.

From a brass censer atop the lectern, yellow cloying smoke poured. The opiated stench filled the chapel, collecting in a cloud beneath the arched ceiling. Falconer inhaled a bit of it and nearly succumbed to a coughing fit.

Torches sputtered at equidistant points around the chapel, the wooden columns thrust into buckets of sand. The red flaring light they cast did not seem to touch the ring of black shadow hugging the chapel wall behind the raised dais.

The figure on the podium made a sharp imperious gesture with both arms, causing the sleeves of his robe to bell and flap like crimson wings. He moved so suddenly, Falconer instinctively recoiled. The drums fell silent, but the chant continued, now in whispering monotone.

Raising his hands, the figure thrust back his cowl and Falconer knew he was the man called Baron Ocajnik. He felt a shock of surprise at the baron's appearance. He'd expected a seamed, malevolent face, but instead saw the epitome of sculpted male beauty. It looked as if all the standards of masculinity had been shaken together in a bag then applied to Ocajnik.

His thick, jet-black hair had just a suggestion of wave, and a comma of it fell over his high, unlined forehead. His nose was exceedingly well-defined, as were his lips and cleft chin. Only his eyes spoiled the effect of perfection. Inhumanly piercing, of a yellowish green, they blazed with more than intelligence and purpose. Falconer sensed the exceedingly charismatic force that radiated from them.

Ocajnik spoke a single word, a harsh metallic syllable. Then the drumming began anew, but with a slower rhythm. One of the people rose from the floor, and the robe dropped. A naked girl, her brown body gleaming with either a coating of oil or perspiration, danced toward the dais. Her hips jerked in a lascivious rhythm to the drumbeats. Her eyes were dull, her mouth slack, but she twisted and gyrated in wild abandon, whipping her coarse black hair to and fro. Falconer saw the half-healed cuts around her eyes.

Ocajnik watched her approach with a welcoming smile on his lips. He shrugged his broad shoulders and the robe slid down over his torso, to his feet. He stretched out his arms, beckoning to her. As Falconer watched, he caught the briefest ripple of motion around his body. The effect lasted only a microsecond, but he wondered if his infrared implant was malfunctioning or if the fumes from the censer were making him light-headed.

He closed his left eye and continued to stare with his augmented right. A dizzy wave of vertigo swept over him, and he experienced the bizarre sensation of seeing two Ocajniks at the same time, occupying the same place, both completely different, one superimposed over the other.

Ocajnik's body rippled, strobed, and for an instant Falconer saw a skeletal figure with every bone of his emaciated frame visible beneath tight-stretched skin. The flesh was yellowed, the color of old parchment. The human features seemed to fade like a watery paint in a horrific transmutation.

Instead of a high-planed, handsome face, he glimpsed a hairless head with malformed ears that seemed far too long, reaching toward the temples and terminating in blunt points, with strands of lank, white hair tufted behind each one. The face was heavily lined, gaunt to the point of emaciation. The nose, cheeks and chin were protuberant.

The sharp turtle's beak of a mouth stretched in gaping grin from which oversize, discolored teeth gleamed. Falconer was nauseatingly reminded of the bared teeth of the rat. Behind the teeth stirred a black tongue, damp with saliva and slithering restlessly in the half-open mouth.

The fingers of the outstretched hands were frighteningly long and bony, like the gnarled twigs of a long-dead tree. They were tipped with curving, dirt-encrusted nails at least three inches long. Only Ocajnik's eyes remained the same.

Falconer fought off the disorientation that threatened to engulf him. The naked girl reached the podium and took Ocajnik's hands. He lifted her effortlessly into his arms. He caressed her slender limbs, shoulders and flanks to the insistent beat of the drums. Falconer's augmented aural receptors heard him whisper, in accented English, "Kiss me and live forever."

Cupping the girl's face between his hands, Ocajnik gently tilted her head back. Her trembling lips opened. From Ocajnik's mouth snaked his tongue, and he plunged it deep into her mouth, down her throat. She convulsed in his arms, not struggling to free herself but rather spasming in reaction to the choking penetration.

As if the entry of his tongue were a signal, the worshipers at the podium voiced a blood-freezing howl in unison. Tossing aside their drums, they ripped out of their robes and flung themselves on each other in shrieking ecstasy. There seemed to be an even number of men and women, though it was hard to differentiate between them when they became a single writhing mass. They howled and bayed in hoarse voices. All of their swarthy faces bore the caste marks.

Falconer watched in mindless revulsion and closed his right eye. Below, on the raised platform he saw a handsome naked man passionately kissing an equally naked and equally ardent young woman. Her knees buckled and her arms dangled limply while Ocajnik kept his mouth pressed against hers.

Then, from the entrance arch came shrieks of pain and confusion. Mama Minuit and at least a dozen machete-wielding men burst into the chapel. They hacked and chopped a path through the naked cultists. The voodoo priestess shouted commands in Creole, and then began the slaughter.

Screaming insanely, the people rushed about the chapel, slamming into one another, stumbling and falling. Mama Minuit's men dashed among them, their razor-keen blades sinking into skulls with grisly crunches. Within an instant, the church was a mob of howling, terrified figures. Bodies dropped like cords of wood about the podium.

At the priestess's appearance, Ocajnik released the girl. She lay in a shuddering, twitching heap at his feet, vomiting blood. Ocajnik's lips were scarlet coated and he roared a few words that sent crimson droplets flying from them in a spray.

Mama Minuit responded with a stream of shrieked invective as she fought her way toward the platform, her own machete slashing out and down. One of the naked cultists rushed at her in desperation, lifting a dagger. A backhand stroke almost severed the man's head.

A half dozen of Mama Minuit's blade-brandishing men surged toward the dais, leaping up to surround Ocajnik. The man-thing voiced a sobbing laugh and snatched them up as if they were dolls, grabbing them by arms, necks and even their stomachs. They screamed as his hands crushed their bones, as talon-tipped fingers punctured their organs, the long, sharp nails flaying the flesh from their bodies as if husking ears of corn.

They fell and flopped and jounced and screamed as Ocajnik flung them away amid crimson sprays. Blood fountained from slashed arteries, splashing the floor with looping artless patterns. In a handful of seconds, Ocajnik cleared the podium of attackers.

Swiftly, Falconer brought the Steyr-Mannlicher SSG to his shoulder, seating the stock firmly and squinting through the telescopic sight with his left eye. Although the range was short, he wasn't about to take chances. He centered the crosshairs on Ocajnik's forehead.

Even as his finger contracted on the trigger, he saw Ocajnik startle almost imperceptibly. His head swung up and around. His flaming green eyes focused and something struck Falconer.

He felt it like a terrible blow at the base of his spine, and Falconer's hand froze. He felt a terrible pressure squeezing his mind, and his nerves seemed to misfire. The tendons and bones in his hand locked. Through the scope, he saw a triumphant smile cross Ocajnik's handsome face.

Falconer didn't waste any time trying to reason out the cause of the sudden paralysis. Without hesitation, but awkwardly, he planted his right eye against the rim of the scope. Once again he glimpsed the strange rippling phenomenon around Ocajnik.

Whatever force had seized Falconer and insinuated itself into his mind ebbed away and he squeezed the rifle's trigger. Switching eyes cost him the head shot, but with the sharp explosive report, Ocajnik staggered across the podium, driven by the devastating punch of the 7.62 mm round high in his chest. As he toppled from the platform, one of his flailing hands caught the smoldering censor and pulled it with him to the littered floor. Embers scattered and ignited a half-dozen small fires.

Apparently inspired by the flames, Mama Minuit wrenched a torch from a bucket of sand and shouted at her followers to do the same. They snatched the burning sticks of wood and pitch, using them first as bludgeons to drive the last of the panicked cultists out of the chapel and then to ignite the splintered pews.

Mama Minuit cried happily, "A fine fuel for the fires of purification!"

The firelight illuminated the deep shadows behind the podium and they suddenly seethed. Hundreds of tiny eyes reflected the flames in crimson pinpoints. At first Falconer saw only a billowing mass of darkness, then it flowed into a chittering, nail-scratching stampede of rats. There were thousands of them and he bit back a curse of horror. Mama Minuit and her people used the torches to drive the rodent horde back, forcing them to scamper through cracks and splits in the stone walls.

When the last of the vermin had fled, Falconer swung himself over the railing, ignoring how the ancient wood creaked beneath his weight. He dropped down into the chapel, beside a skull-split cultist.

"Over here!" called Mama Minuit, gesturing with her torch. Her tone was full of victorious gloating.

Falconer joined her by the podium. She stood over Ocajnik, grinning down into his blood-spattered face. He grinned back up at her, but in pain, his red-filmed teeth bared. He was the handsome man again, his well-formed hands pressed over the bullet wound in his chest. Falconer was shocked that he was not only alive, but still conscious.

Mama Minuit spit at him. "Your faux flesh does not fool me, old man!"

"I am ageless, I transcend all the ages of man. You cannot end me," Ocajnik grated.

With a contemptuous smile, Mama Minuit removed the leather pouch from around her neck and upended its contents over Ocajnik's face. He howled like a dying dog, his tongue uncoiling from his mouth like a blue-black serpent. Wherever the dust settled, huge pustules erupted from the flesh and burst with a thick, white ichor. The stench of putrefaction arose, and Falconer covered his nose and mouth with his free hand. For the first time he felt fear.

He didn't fear Ocajnik as a man feared a human enemy—it was the terror of an ancient evil spawned from an age at the dawn of mankind. He suddenly had the sense of unseen forces swirling all around him, and that he was but a pawn in a game he could never comprehend.

"*Oui,*" spit Mama Minuit. "An old one cannot be ended, but you can be contained."

She lifted a foot as if to stamp on his face, but she checked the movement. "Your army has deserted you, parasite. You are alone again, trapped in the dark, dark sepulchre of the Earth."

The flames from the pews began to spread, but neither Mama Minuit nor Ocajnik appeared to notice—or if they did, they didn't care.

"This is *my* time now," Ocajnik said in a labored

wheeze. "A world of eternal twilight, of skies and seas the color of blood…of shadows masking the sun."

His face, then his body convulsed. In a rasping gargle, he hissed, "There is wisdom in the shadows—the old ones have returned, they who drank the blood of thy kind and feasted on thy flesh and owned thy souls. The spawn of the old ones covered the Earth, and their children endure throughout the ages. Thy race became foolish and spurned them, but their voices still whisper to you in the night."

Mama Minuit threw back her head and laughed, and scorn and fury were in it. "The *loas* whisper to me and safeguard our spirits. They piss on you, Ocajnik. They promise the long night will soon end and the sun will shun you once more. Your reign of blood and plague will be over."

As she spoke, the powder sprinkled over Ocajnik's face thickened, spreading over his body like a corrosive fungus, shriveling his flesh and turning it brown and dry.

Ocajnik's lips twisted into a caricature of a mocking grin. He exhaled and hoarse words rode his breath. "Not so long as thy race of beasts lives. One day thy race will set me free again."

Mama Minuit turned to Falconer. "The cross."

For a moment, Falconer didn't understand what she meant, then he fumbled in a pocket and brought forth the small relic. He started to hand it to her, but the priestess gestured to Ocajnik. "Drop it."

Falconer hesitated, then opened his fingers and the crucifix fell onto Ocajnik's chest. From it, but only for a sliver of a second, burst an aurora of unbearably bright, unbearably pure white radiance. When it faded, only a distorted carcass lay on the floor, a shriveled, monstrous imitation of man, with malformed ears and ratlike fangs. The yellowish-green eyes had lost their mad gleam and become dull and lusterless, as if the light behind them had been snuffed out like a candle's flame. The tiny crucifix sizzled its way through Ocajnik's chest, as if it had been heated and dropped on wax.

The creature's mouth opened wide, far wider than was possible for human jaws. A thick fluid, a greenish mucus-like bile bubbled up over his lips. A fetid stench arose from his body, the vile, loathsome stink of decay. Falconer's belly roiled with nausea. He managed to repress the gag reflex, and as if from a great distance he heard his voice demanding faintly, "What *is* that thing?"

Somberly, Mama Minuit replied, "He be not a living man. He had only a false aspect of life that deceived his followers, mebbe even himself. I never saw him as other than that...*thing*."

"And the rats?"

She shrugged as if the matter were of little importance. "They be his...or he be theirs. They carry his disease."

Falconer suddenly came to himself as if he were waking from a trance. The fierce heat from the burning pews beat at his body, and flickering flames alternately lit and shadowed the dark face of the woman beside him.

Softly she quoted, "'That is not dead which can eternal lie, and with strange aeons even death may die.'"

Then, taking him by the arm, Mama Minuit led Falconer out of the church to where her people stood waiting. All of them silently watched as smoke and flame poured from the broken windows.

"Now what?" asked Falconer, his words sounding strained even in his own ears.

Matter-of-factly, Mama Minuit stated, "Once de fire burns down, we will collapse the walls and inscribe a seal upon the stone. That will trap him in the sepulchre."

He gazed at the licking flames in silence. Then at length he declared, "He's dead." The tone of his voice made it sound more like a question.

The woman sighed sadly. "How can one kill a creature who never truly lived? He be right, you know. This *is* his time. We paved the way for his return. We lost respect for life and returned to the path of savagery, acting like the beasts he claims we be. We forgot the ancient wars against the old ones and fought among ourselves, and his kind returned in crafty guises.

"The ancient terrors of our ancestors have burst free again, overwhelming the world with madness and chaos, plunging it back into darkness. Nature is out of balance, an' if the balance is not soon restored, he an' those like him will rule the Earth again.''

Mama Minuit made a helpless gesture with the machete. ''*C'est fini*. It is finished.''

Falconer struggled to comprehend the meaning of her words. He was a soldier, devoted to wresting a semblance of prewar order out of postnuke anarchy. Little of what the voodoo priestess said made sense to him—or, he realized bleakly, he preferred it did not make sense.

A fearful suspicion arose in him, the grim realization that World War III was more than a struggle between Russia and America for control of the world. It was a dim reflection of a war that had been fought long ago, the eternal battle of order against chaos, of shapes birthed in darkness reaching out to destroy the bodies and souls of humanity.

Turning his face away from the roaring pyre of the church, he looked toward the lurid red sky, desperately seeking an unshadowed sun.

Chapter 1

The Amazon Basin, 175 years after skydark

Kane looked toward the sky, desperately wishing shadows would cover the bright face of the full moon. Then he ducked the cast-net, dodged behind a tree, put his head back and his chest out and ran as he had run few times in his life.

From behind him he heard a savage cry of anger erupt from four throats. Copper-skinned men of short stature rushed after him. Their jet-black hair was twisted in intricate topknots at the back at their heads, and their near-naked bodies were tattooed with ornate spiral designs. They wore short mantles over their shoulders, layers of snakeskin glued to leather. Their fingers were colored a brilliant red, as if the entire lengths had been dipped in scarlet dye. All of them carried short-shafted clubs that sported razor-edged flakes of obsidian, like the teeth of saw blades.

They also wielded long hollow tubes, all of them decorated with bits of gold and gems. As far as Kane was concerned, a blowgun was a blowgun, regardless of the ornamentation. Two of the Indians had stone-weighted nets made of tough, woven grasses slung over their shoulders. The grass braids were coated with an extremely adhesive glue.

Kane knew they'd prefer to capture him as they had Domi and Grant, but their desire to take him alive didn't spring from a respect for human life. His heart pumped hard, and he felt his familiar angry repugnance at being forced into the role of prey. His many years as a Magistrate had accustomed him to being the hunter, not the hunted.

He plunged through the canopied rain forest, realizing it was futile to hope he could continue to evade his pursuers as he had for the past few hours. This was their land, and they had lifetimes of experience in tracking quarry through the tangled green depths. But even standing his ground and shooting it out with the Indians would not free his companions.

The most reasonable option was simply to surrender. That way he would be placed with Grant and Domi, and among the three of them they might find a way to escape—hopefully long before they were stretched out on a sacrificial altar and their hearts ripped out.

But Kane was obeying instincts that had little to do with tactics—to survive long enough to find a place to turn and sell his life at a bloody price.

He sprinted through the jungle, slapping leaves and vines out of his path. Each breath he took of the humid air was a labored gulp. He had been running, hiding and running again since late afternoon, trying to creep back into the city.

The moist heat of Amazonia was more debilitating than the desert wastelands of Utah he had recently visited. There at least it was possible to cool down in the shade. Night brought no relief from the humidity here. Beneath the emerald-tinted roof formed by the intertwining boughs of giant parana and evergreen trees, the heat of the day was captured, making him feel as if he were taking a never-ending sauna bath.

Kane's dark hair was soaked through with sweat, turning its sun-touched highlights completely black. His khaki shirt clung to his perspiration-filmed torso. The weight of the Sin Eater holstered to his right forearm was like having a child hanging on to his hand, and he struggled to keep from reeling to that side as he ran.

Not too long before he had been chased—stalked, actually—through a Louisiana bayou by swampies who wanted his head for the reward it would bring. But his pursuers had been in as much danger from the mutated, lethal flora and fauna as he had been.

The Amazonian Indians who pursued him were perfectly in tune with their environment, and wouldn't be tricked by the same gambits that had worked on the dull-witted swampies.

There was comparatively little underbrush, only the great tree trunks looming in the green-filtered moonlight. Growths of creeper stems carpeted the jungle floor, but none of them snagged his pounding feet and they muffled his footfalls to dull thuds as he dodged and zigzagged among the giant boles.

Abruptly he burst from the dense rain forest and saw the city below him, nestled in a shallow, egg-shaped valley. Three days before, the unexpected discovery of such a place in the jungle had surprised him, Domi and Grant.

The records in the Cerberus database, as well as the brief reference in *The Wyeth Codex* had prepared them for something, but not for a little picture-book civilization with its neat collection of stone houses and tilled fields, all laid out as precisely as an estate garden.

From the center of the city towered a pyramid. The sides rose in a staggered series of steplike ledges, and they looked as smooth as glass from top to bottom. Two smaller wings were on either side of its huge base. A flight of stairs climbed up the sleek center of the ziggurat to the flat top. There stood a sort of temple, a flat stone roof supported by square, intricately carved pillars around which serpents coiled.

The little structure was open on all sides, allowing a view not only of the grotesque stone idols set within it, but of the huge brass bowl occupying its center. Elevated by a pedestal, it looked to be nearly four feet in height and perhaps six in diameter. Not having been permitted to climb the pyramid during his stay, Kane had assumed an altar of some type rested there. The bowl presented a mystery, but one he wasn't particularly inclined to solve.

The silvery moonlight struck iridescent sparkles from the minerals embedded within the pyramid's exterior. Kane guessed it had been constructed of quartz shot through with bits of mica and gold ore. The entire structure loomed over a hundred feet into the sky. Faintly, from the direction of the ziggurat, he heard the rumble of drums and what sounded like a ceremonial chant.

He didn't devote much time to admiring the city's beauty but set off down the gently rolling slope in long-legged bounds. He heard faint, spitting whispers, then the buzz of darts zipping past his ears like angry hornets.

Although Kane knew the projectiles were tipped with a nonfatal neurotoxin, he still didn't want to be stung by one. He had already seen the narcotic effects of the darts on Grant and Domi. Only enormous good fortune and the fact he had stumbled at the critical moment over a tree root had kept him from being captured like them. Since then, he had tried and failed to return to the city without being seen. But he had crossed the path of a search party a couple of hours ago, and they had tracked him ever since.

As yet, he hadn't chilled any of the Amazonians, although he had been sorely tempted. Only the memory of the hospitality shown to them by King Chaac stayed his hand—and the sense that he was only reluctantly going along with the wishes of the chief shaman, Cloud Minder. He had seen him engaged in an earnest, whispered conference with Chaac right before they said their goodbyes.

Kane loped down the hillside, heading toward the city at an oblique angle, ignoring the darts hissing past his head. The warriors were losing the range, and he contemplated briefly turning and driving them back with a burst from his Sin Eater, but he didn't want to alert the entire native settlement.

He dived through a narrow opening in a wall of shrubbery and swiftly surveyed the area. A dense thicket arose in a solid clump of greenery on the opposite side of the clearing. A massive boulder deeply embedded in the grassy earth paralleled the edges of the growth. A patina of moss covered most of the stone's gray, fissured surface.

Kane glimpsed a deep depression where the end of the boulder overhung the hillside and he made for that. With a deliberately heavy foot, he ran toward the boulder, crushing the grass beneath his boots. Springing onto the rock, he ran along its length. When he reached the far end, he jumped down and doubled back, creeping along the far side of the boulder, hugging its base.

When he reached the cavity, he crawled into it feet first, cramming his six-foot-one inch frame into a space that would barely fit a small child. With his knees doubled, he lay still and tried to soften the harshness of his breathing. His heart hammered in his chest and blood thundered in his ears. He was terribly thirsty, but he had been forced to drop the survival kit that contained his bottle of water. He had also lost his transcomm, so he couldn't even attempt to call Grant or Domi, although he knew their own comm gear had probably been confiscated.

As he lay there in the shadow created by the jutting rock overhang, he performed a quick inventory. The three spare clips of ammo were still attached to his web belt, so counting the full clip in his blaster, he had eighty rounds to bring into play. He reached down to the Nylex handle of the combat knife in its boot scabbard. Pressing the positive-release button, he drew the fourteen-inch-long, double-edged blued blade. Absently he thumbed the razor-keen, tungsten-steel point.

Kane swore silently at himself for being caught so flat-footed out on the forest trail. During the three days he, Domi and Grant spent among the Amazonians, they had done nothing to arouse his suspicions—which in retrospect was suspicious. His only consolation, and a very small one, was that Brigid Baptiste was safe in the Cerberus redoubt in the Darks of Montana, busy with another project.

But even that small comfort turned cold when he recollected Brigid's warning to avoid the Indians who at last report lived in the area. Of course the last report was at least a hundred years old, and so hadn't seemed particularly pertinent when Kane first proposed the mission.

The reasons for the trip to South America seemed simple and straightforward. The Cerberus database contained a record of a huge American military munitions depot hidden in the rain forest. There was also a nearby installation equipped with a gateway unit, and although it was computer indexed, it wasn't part of the official Cerberus network.

"Gateway" was the colloquial term for a quantum interphase transducer, otherwise known as a mat-trans unit. The gateways functioned by tapping into the quantum stream, the invisible, linear pathways that ran outside of physical space and back again at distant points.

In the latter years of the twentieth century, the Cerberus redoubt, which was concealed within a mountain peak in Montana, had been devoted to manufacturing the gateway units in modular form. The gateways were then shipped to various Totality Concept–related redoubts. As Kane had reason to know, some of the devices went elsewhere, to places that had no connection to the Totality Concept. The tiny installation in Amazonia appeared to be one of those.

Brigid had conducted a deeper investigation and found a reference to both the installation and the military base in *The Wyeth Codex*. The memoirs of one Dr. Mildred Winona Wyeth. A specialist in cryogenics, Wyeth had entered a hospital in late 2000 for minor surgery, but an idiosyncratic reaction to the anesthetic left her in a coma, with her vital signs sinking fast. To save her life, the predark whitecoats had cryonically frozen her.

After her revival nearly a century later, she joined Ryan Cawdor and his band of warrior survivalists. At one point during her wanderings, she found a working computer and recorded her thoughts, observations and speculations regarding the postnukecaust world, the redoubts and the terrors they contained.

Despite her exceptional intelligence and education, Wyeth had no inkling of the true nature of the redoubts or the Totality Concept that had conceived them. That truth would not be revealed for nearly another century, and it was one Kane still had difficulty accepting.

The Wyeth Codex mentioned a large group of indigenous Indians, apparently descended from the Mayans, who had reverted to the ancient traditions of their ancestors. The journal indicated that one of Wyeth's party had narrowly avoided being sacrificed to the tribe's deity.

Kane and Grant decided that since Wyeth's experience was more than a hundred years in the past, and both the depot and the gateway installation several miles away from the Indian settlement, the risk factor was acceptable. Domi volunteered to accompany them.

After hours of hacking their way through the jungle, Kane, Grant and Domi had found the old base— or the overgrown ruins of it. Most of the Quonset huts had collapsed, and the only ordnance that was halfway recognizable were the rusted carcasses of two helicopters and a few armored vehicles. They found nothing of any value.

On the return trip from the base, they made their first contact with the Indians. They were extremely friendly, even though they reacted strongly to Domi's albino appearance. Their reaction was not fear—it was more like awe.

To Kane's astonishment, most of the Indians spoke fairly good English, and with bitter hindsight, he realized his pointman's sixth sense should have been stimulated not only by that but by their apparent fascination with Domi. King Chaac explained his tribe spoke English because their forebears had learned it from the soldiers posted at the base. It had been passed down over the succeeding generations as a second tongue. He did not address why his people seemed so mesmerized by Domi's bone-white skin and ruby-red eyes.

Kane couldn't help but be impressed by the Indians' city, their gracious manners, their gentle, good-humored demeanor and their apparently high level of culture, despite their isolation. He wanted to leave them with a good impression in hopes of establishing an alliance, like the one he had struck with the tribe of Amerindians living near the Cerberus redoubt. He had been so busy playing diplomat he had overlooked the two cardinal rules by which he had always lived—nothing was as it seemed, and trust no one.

Kane tensed when a rustle of foliage reached his

ears. Within a few seconds, three men materialized out of the underbrush, moving in single file. They scanned the hillside, the red-fingered man in the lead bending down to inspect the ground. They moved slowly, taking short steps. One of them stiffened, grunted and pointed with his blowgun at the crushed grass leading to the boulder.

Kane held his breath as they moved out of his field of vision. He heard the faint scuff of their sandaled feet on the surface of the big rock, then a minute later the faint rattling of leaves as they pushed through the thicket.

Still he didn't move, continuing to lie with his legs doubled and fisting his knife. He had counted four Indians earlier and he knew one had hung back in order to see if his companions flushed out their quarry.

A squat, broad figure stepped silently into view. Kane recognized him as Morning Breeze, the warrior who had offered to escort them back to the gateway installation. Kane had watched him personally fell Domi with a dart spit from his blowgun.

Kane waited patiently until the man moved past his hiding place, then as carefully and as stealthily as he could, he crept from the cavity beneath the boulder. Because of Morning Breeze's treachery, Kane felt no twinge of remorse when he glided up behind him and struck.

He had meant to disable the man with a knee to the kidneys, but the Indian whirled with steel-trap quickness, lifting his blowgun to his lips. Kane knocked it aside with a swipe of his knife blade. At the same time, his knee pounded between the man's breechclouted thighs with a sound like an ax chopping into wet wood.

Morning Breeze lurched over at the waist, and Kane clubbed him on the back of the head with his gun-weighted forearm. The Indian fell to his hands and knees, lips writhing in agony, trying to drag in enough air to voice an alarm. Kane stomped him between the shoulder blades, driving him facefirst against the grass, and then knelt astride his back.

He clamped the Indian's mouth shut and pinched his nostrils closed with his left hand. Pricking the underside of Morning Breeze's chin with the point of the knife, Kane whispered, "No noise. I know you can understand me. When I let you breathe again, you'll answer my questions. Where are my friends being held?"

Kane allowed Morning Breeze to gasp and grunt behind his suffocating hand for a few seconds until he clutched desperately at his wrist. Kane removed his hand from the man's mouth, and the Indian half gasped, "No *habla*."

Digging the tip of his blade deeper into the soft flesh of Morning Breeze's chin, Kane growled, "You *habla* as well as I do, pissant. Where are my friends?"

Morning Breeze grimaced and whimpered in halting, accented English, "They belong to the Feathered

Serpent now. The cloud girl was selected for him, since she is the color of the clouds on which the god resides. The black man is the color of the Feathered Serpent's wisdom and so—''

Kane drew the edge of the blade lightly across the man's chin, the razored steel slicing into the flesh and drawing a trickle of blood. "I didn't ask for a lesson on your religion. Where are they?''

Voice tight with pain, Morning Breeze murmured, ''They await the god in his temple.''

''The pyramid?''

The Indian couldn't nod without risking a slit throat, so he blurted, ''Yes. They are being well cared for. No harm will come to them.''

''Until you stretch them over your altar and cut their hearts out.''

''That will not happen, I swear to you. It is not that kind of ceremony. They will be honored, not tortured.''

''When will the ceremony take place?''

''At midnight,'' Morning Breeze husked out.

Kane hazarded a quick glance at his wrist chron. The time was just shy of eleven o'clock, and he uttered a snarl. Removing the knife from the man's throat, Kane jerked him to his feet by his topknot.

The Indian's dark eyes swam with fear when he took in the imposing sight of Kane. He was nearly a head taller than Morning Breeze, long limbed and rangy, built with the stripped-down economy of a wolf. A wolf's merciless stare glittered in his pale blue-gray eyes.

Twisting the Indian's right arm, Kane pushed it up to the point where the slightest added pressure would pop it from its socket. Picking up the blowgun, he slid it into his web belt. "Take me to them."

Biting back groans of pain, Morning Breeze blurted, "You don't understand! It is a great honor for your friends to be chosen by the god—"

Kane increased the pressure on the man's captured arm. "He didn't ask their consent, so I'm *un*choosing them. And if your Feathered Serpent objects, he'll be permanently plucked."

Kane paused, then added in a low, menacing whisper, "And so will everyone in your city."

Chapter 2

Grant did his best to remember how and why he'd come to be luxuriating on a cloud, but after a moment of concentration he would forget what he was trying to remember.

Memories came to him in scraps and fragments. He vaguely recalled the exquisitely sharp sting on the side of his neck and then a confusing commotion of shouting and much running among the tree trunks. With a distant twinge of remorse, he remembered fighting the Amazonians, trying to kick their guts out and punch their jawbones loose from their heads. He heard Domi shrieking in rage. Then something flexible but choking fell over him and his body was seized in an immobilizing grip. His throat constricted against the roar of fury that never passed his lips. He recalled falling, every muscle and nerve tingling with a pins-and-needles sensation. He tried to fight back to his feet.

The more Grant struggled, the tighter the noose around his throat cinched until his lungs screamed for air. Only when he grew limp did the suffocating pressure ease up. He couldn't feel, much less move his limbs, and he was only dimly aware of the Sin

Eater's holster being ripped from his arm. By the time that happened, his first surge of anger and fear was replaced by a feeling of bemused detachment.

A friendly voice whispered in his ear, "It is a safe drug. You will be alive and conscious to appreciate the Feathered Serpent's wisdom."

There seemed to be little point in trying to fight free of either the net enwrapping his body or the fog shrouding his mind. He recalled being dragged along the green-shadowed tunnel under the trees, wrapped like a bundle of laundry.

At the time, Grant felt mild surprise at how effortlessly he was borne back to the city. He was a big man, four inches over six feet tall and tipping the scales at somewhere around 230. He chuckled when he recollected how uneasy the Indians had looked when they first beheld him. They evidently found his unusually broad shoulders, deep chest and fierce, down-sweeping mustache, coal-black against his coffee-brown skin, a little disconcerting. Few of the Indian men topped five and a half feet tall, so his stature was more than unusual; it was intimidating.

Domi, of course, hadn't presented the Indians with much of a strenuous effort. Barely five feet tall, she weighed only a shade over a hundred pounds. He caught glimpses of her from time to time, as securely netted and as limp as himself. She was albino, her skin beautifully white. She wore her bone-white hair cropped close to her head. Her eyes were crimson, the color of fresh spilled blood. Those eyes were only half-open, and a dreamy smile creased her porcelain lips.

The return path to the city was broad and mostly downhill. Grant couldn't see much but the boughs of trees, even if his vision wasn't blurred. At one point he saw the vastness of the pyramid, looming high overhead, bathed in the variegated colors cast by the setting sun. He vaguely understood he and Domi were being borne into the base of the gigantic zig-gurat. He had a faint recollection of King Chaac mentioning the pyramid had many wings and rooms.

Flickering torchlight replaced the fading sunlight, the flames dancing from sconces bolted to the walls. Grant and Domi were taken into a stone chamber where lanterns made of hollowed-out gourds burned.

A figure waited for them there, and at first Grant was uncertain if it was human. Slowly he realized it was a man clothed in the mottled hide of an enor-mous anaconda. The skull of the giant reptile had been removed and stretched out over a curving framework to form a hood. Atop the snake's head bloomed a spray of multicolored feathers.

The man's arms and legs were painted in alter-nating blue and white spots. By squinting, Grant saw a silver-shot mane peeping out from beneath the shadows of the hood and he guessed King Chaac himself wore the serpent masquerade.

Other people moved in the chamber, murmuring quietly. They were young women and men, wearing feathered headdresses, putting Grant in mind of the warbonnets he had seen on some of the Lakota back in Montana. But other than the feathers, the men and women were completely naked, their bodies coated in blue-and-white paint. The men's artistry even extended to their genitals. For some reason, Grant found that amusing and he laughed like a lion growling in its sleep.

One of the girls knelt beside him, crooning to him in soothing tones. He felt several faraway pinches on his left arm. He noticed she held a clay bowl filled with a pale liquid, and she dipped tiny, sharp splinters of wood into it. She carefully drove the slivers beneath the skin. By craning his neck up and around, he saw a young man performing the same operation on Domi.

At a whispered word from the snakeskinned man, the nets were unwrapped from both of them. The paralysis ebbed slowly away, and euphoria filled Grant. He and Domi sat up and exchanged smiles, but it required too much effort to speak. A wispy worry about Kane ghosted through Grant's mind, but it was too ephemeral to grasp. Nothing seemed to matter but the stone room, the man in the snakeskin and the cooing women who undressed him.

When he and Domi were as naked as the others, they were led, as uncomplaining as lambs, into an antechamber. Nude, Domi looked childlike and innocent, even with her small perky breasts, gently flaring hips and pearly white body, unflawed except by scattered scarring from the hard life she'd lived.

Grant had seen her unclothed many times, since she viewed garments as only occasional necessities. She had never seen him naked before, despite her many attempts to seduce him, and now she displayed little interest in looking at him.

In the next room, both of them were bathed in a great sunken stone tub, the sides beautifully carved. Some of the images depicted in the carvings were a little disturbing, having to do with snakes coiling around humans and swallowing them whole.

Grant let himself be washed by the women. Everything was comfortably blurred, all hard edges smoothed and softened. He gave himself to the moment, smiling agreeably when the sponges caressed his upper thighs and then slightly higher and to the center.

A great deal of ceremony went into the bathing, with small buckets of warm, scented water poured over Grant and Domi at regular intervals. The man in the snakeskin presided over it all, chanting in a singsong falsetto.

Before the procedure became tedious, Domi and Grant were raised from the tub and dried with silken towels. Their bodies were wrapped in robes of blue and white, and they were escorted from the bathing chamber into a large walled compound that adjoined the base of the pyramid. There was no roof, only perfectly cut blocks of white stone rising half again as tall as Grant. The enclosure was lit by many torches. A smooth stone altar, about three feet tall, sprouted from the center of the compound, adorned with colorful blossoms, chains of flowers, feathers and spotted jaguar pelts.

Grant and Domi were directed to seat themselves on wonderfully soft cushions behind a long, low table. It held a wide variety of dishes, smoked pork diced to bite-size chunks, roasted yams and sliced fruit.

They were not allowed to touch the food themselves. The men fed Domi, and the women lifted the delicacies to Grant's lips. As they ate, drums began to rumble, but the steady clamor sounded to Grant's ears like a dull and faraway thunder.

The women danced to the drumming, their lithe bodies gleaming like polished mahogany in the torchlight. They capered in a wide circle around the compound, and after the first circuit the men joined them. They thrust their loins at each other in suggestive motions.

In some dim, remote corner of Grant's mind, he realized he should not have been enjoying the revelry. He glanced toward Domi, and she smiled at him sweetly, the characteristic crimson glint in her eyes dulled to only a spark. He knew her lusterless eyes should have alarmed him, but all of his emotions seemed dammed, flowing flatly along a shallow channel.

The thick cushions on which he sat had the consistency of clouds, molding themselves perfectly beneath his body, making him extremely reluctant to move. Still, his mind stirred, although sluggishly. He reviewed his, Kane's and Domi's arrival at the small gateway installation and the verdant green color of the armaglass walls enclosing the jump chamber. He experienced no strong emotions associated with his recollections. He felt removed from his memories, even though he remembered his profound disappointment when they discovered the arms depot held absolutely nothing of value.

He found it very difficult to sift through his memory for the actual reasons behind their journey from Cerberus, why they had felt it necessary to leave there in the first place.

The man in the snakeskin made a sweeping gesture with one arm, and the naked painted men attending to Domi carefully lifted her from the table and led her to the throng capering about the altar. Grant lost sight of her for a moment, and when she reappeared, she was only a flitting white shape among the ruddy bodies of the dancers. She had dropped her robe and danced shamelessly with the Indians.

The crowd closed in on her again and when it parted, Grant saw Domi being lifted onto the altar. She was placed facedown, eyes half-veiled by her long, sweeping lashes, lips slightly parted. The men surrounded her and dipped their fingers into pots of blue paint. Methodically, they applied the paint in dabs to her white body.

In the dark recesses of Grant's mind, an inner voice shouted an alarm.

DOMI'S THOUGHTS MOVED at random. She floated on a sea of shadowed clouds and she took a childish pleasure in the unreality. It never occurred to her to flee or even to struggle.

Raised in the brutal hardship of the Outlands, accustomed to the cruelty of men, she appreciated the loving attention bestowed on her by the beautiful brown people. If they wanted her to crouch like a white statue of marble while they painted her, she saw no reason to object. She enjoyed the sensual, teasing touch of their wet, blue fingers dabbing at her breasts and belly.

The Indians glided around the altar, their legs and feet moving in a slow, deliberate measure. A low chant arose among them, with the word *Kukulkan* repeated over and over.

Domi lay on the soft animal pelts, enjoying the way the fur tickled her bare skin. She did not expend any effort on reasoning or analyzing why the nice brown people wanted her blue. It simply *was*, and the touch of their fingers simply *was*.

Casting a shy glance toward Grant, she wondered aloofly why he sat there and gazed at her beneath a furrowed brow. Although he still smiled blandly, the expression in his eyes was troubled and confused, and for an instant, she experienced a nudge of unease. Then she felt a delicate, delicious fondling touch at the juncture of her thighs and with a low moan, she ceased to care about the look in Grant's eyes.

Just when the prayers, chanting, dancing and touching began to lose their novelty, the man in the snakeskin stepped up to the altar and gazed into her face. Domi felt a coldness creep through her veins as she looked into the shadows beneath the overhang formed by the serpent's snout. She saw his eyes, but they did not appear to be human eyes. They were luminous, radiant in the moonlight.

He took her by the hands and tugged her off the altar stone and enfolded her in his arms. His lips pressed hers in a long kiss. His tongue carefully inserted itself into her mouth, and on the tip of it was a tiny, fibrous button, like a flake shaved from a root. When her own tongue touched it, she sensed rather than saw a blinding flash of white light. It flared within the walls of her skull with the incandescence of the sun. After it faded, she felt herself slumping in the snake man's arms, incapable of speech or independent movement.

When the kiss ended, two men took Domi by the arms, holding her up. Her head lolled loosely on her neck. High above her, the face of the full moon seemed to acquire a black dot, like a pupil in a vast eyeball. It grew and expanded, and all about her the chant rose higher, a soft, unceasing paean of joy.

The man in the snakeskin gestured sharply and turned away, marching purposefully toward an arch in the wall of the enclosure. The Indians followed him, and Domi glimpsed Grant trudging along. He was not smiling now; the corners of his mouth were turned down beneath his mustache in a slight scowl, as if he were disturbed but uncertain of why.

The procession filed beneath the arch to the foot of the stairs built into the face of the pyramid. Arrayed on both sides of the steps stood men and women, torches blazing in their hands.

A huge deep drum boomed from the top of the pyramid, like thunder from the pinnacle of a mountain. Brass cymbals clashed. The people lining the stairs voiced groaning shouts. "Kukulkan, Kukulkan."

Domi tilted her head back and looked up the stairs rising wide and white to the temple. She almost fell over backward, but with the supporting hands of the men holding her she managed to place a foot on the first step. They urged her on and up. Fear shot through her, a small spasm that briefly unsettled the haze of content clouding her mind. But she could not remember what she feared.

A dew of perspiration formed on her face beneath the spots of blue paint, but the warm breeze wafting from the lush jungle dried it. Domi concentrated only on climbing the pyramid. Her legs felt as if they were filled with molten lead, and only the men on either side of her kept her on her feet. She walked to the measured cadence of chant, drumbeat and cymbal clash. Her body was lost to all feeling, numb to every sensation except putting one foot in front of the other. She had no idea how much time passed before the climb ended.

She stood panting and swaying in the temple, knees trembling from the exertion. The square pillars supporting the flat roof showed bas-reliefs writhing around them. The primary motif was the profile of a man with an aquiline nose and a paternal smile on his lips. On the back of his head, a serpent bared its fangs and a forked tongue coiled. The little stone statues placed at all four corners were similar.

Twisting her head around, she saw Grant, towering head and shoulders above the Indians around him. Pebbles of sweat glistened on his forehead, and he blinked repeatedly, as if trying to rouse himself from a dream. She smiled at him inanely, but he didn't return it.

Six figures in blue robes, each one wearing a wooden mask bearing the stylized likeness of a snake's head, stood around the huge bowl occupying most of the temple floor. Plumes of feathers nodded above the masks. They crashed cymbals in unison. The chanting voices of the people on the stairs held one long, yearning note, then the painful clash of the cymbals broke it.

In the sudden, startling silence, Domi thought she heard a dry rustling sound from within the bowl. The man in the snakeskin stood before it and spoke patiently to Domi as if explaining a complicated problem to her. He spoke in his own tongue, and she didn't understand a word.

He gestured to the massive bowl, and again came the slithering noise, as of leather scraping against metal. Her body grew chill, and she knew that within it lay the entire reason for the bathing, the painting, all of the prayers and ceremony.

Four of the six masked men lowered their cymbals and took up positions around the bowl. They fitted their hands into small notches set into the rim and strained to lift it. Metal grated, followed by a faint but prolonged hiss, as sibilant as steam escaping from a valve. Something bumped against the inside of the lid.

One of the robed men gestured for Domi's escort to step back. With questioning murmurs, they obeyed. The masked man stood behind her, hands possessively on her shoulders. She noted absently that he seemed at least a head taller than the men identically garbed.

Lowering his head, he whispered into her ear in a language she knew and a voice she recognized.

"When I give the signal," Kane said urgently, "move."

Chapter 3

The descent down the hillside into the city wasn't difficult, but it required more time than Kane initially estimated. Forcing Morning Breeze ahead of him while trying to evade the Indian's companions added minutes he didn't want to spare. He heard the piercing whistles of night birds several times but he didn't need Morning Breeze to tell him they were signals from the other warriors.

A couple of times, Morning Breeze protested Kane's rough treatment, assuring him that Grant and Domi would not have their hearts cut out. However, he refrained from describing what his people actually had in mind for them.

As a general rule, Kane sympathized more with primitives than with the ville bred. Usually he found them far more honest, mannerly and ethical than the so-called civilized people raised in and around the baronies.

He went out of his way to respect aboriginal beliefs and taboos, regardless of how irrational they might seem to him. But he drew the line when those superstitions put him or his friends in jeopardy.

Morning Breeze led him at an elliptical angle toward the tilled fields. Kane concentrated so much on keeping to the shadows and watching for the other three Indians that the chant rising from the vicinity of the pyramid hardly penetrated his consciousness.

"The ceremony has begun," Morning Breeze murmured. "Soon your friends will be taken to the temple of the Feathered Serpent and will bask in his love and wisdom."

"The temple on top of the pyramid?"

Morning Breeze nodded.

"That's where we'll go."

The Indian stiffened, digging his heels into the ground. In a scandalized whisper, he declared, "It is forbidden—it is blasphemy. You have not been purified! You will insult the Feathered Serpent—"

Morning Breeze struggled against Kane's grip and reverted to his own language, babbling shrilly about Kukulkan. Kane tried to restrain him, then muttered, "Fuck it."

Reversing the grip on his knife, grasping it by the shank, he struck Morning Breeze sharply with the pommel across the base of his skull. He had to hit him twice before the man sagged unconscious to the grassy sward.

Swiftly, Kane used the variety of straps and rawhide thongs about his clothing to hog-tie and gag him. As an added measure, he took one of the drugged darts from the Indian's pouch and drove the point into the side of his neck.

He started to drag him beneath the drooping fronds

of a plantain tree when he heard the keening cry of the night bird again, this time much closer.

Crouching over Morning Breeze's body, Kane scanned his surroundings, trying to penetrate the pattern of moonlight and shadow with his eyes. He saw nothing but brush, but he knew the three Indians were backtracking. Not having come across either Morning Breeze or Kane, they moved toward the outskirts of the city. Under similar circumstances, it was what Kane would have done.

Reflexively, he stiffened his wrist tendons, preparing his hand to receive his Sin Eater. With a conscious effort, he relaxed and the blaster remained in its holster. The Sin Eater was more than a Magistrate's assigned weapon; it was as much of a badge of office as the black body armor worn by Mags into the field.

The Sin Eater was a big-bore automatic handblaster less than fourteen inches in length. The magazine carried twenty 9 mm rounds, and the stock folded down when it was holstered along his right arm. Actuators attached to the weapon popped the Sin Eater into Kane's waiting hand when he flexed his tendons in the right sequence, putting it there in an eyeblink. There was no trigger guard, and when the firing stud came in contact with Kane's finger, it would fire immediately. Since the handblaster did not come equipped with a noise suppressor, firing it in the valley would be like the roar of a howitzer, alerting every Indian, monkey and dog for miles around.

Kane withdrew the blowgun from his belt. Carrying the pouch of darts, he crept away from Morning Breeze, taking up a position beneath the plantain tree where it backed onto a wall of shrubbery. If Morning Breeze had led him on a standard route to the city, then his fellow Indians would follow the same path—he hoped.

He examined the blowgun, cursing softly when he couldn't distinguish between the spitting end and the shooting end. Carefully he removed the darts from the pouch. They were a little more than six inches long, with a brown, tarry substance smeared on the needle-sharp, tapered points. Inserting one of the projectiles point first into the tube, he raised it to his lips. Then he waited.

The minutes dragged by. The drumming from the city continued unabated with a lulling rhythm. Then, with a suddenness that nearly made him swear aloud, three men stood warily on the hillside. There had been no sound preceding their almost magical materialization, and Kane felt a grudging admiration for their stealthy art.

The Indians scowled around, then stalked forward, studying the ground. The man in the lead placed his fingers in his mouth, preparing to whistle, but instead he stiffened, grunted and gestured with his stone-bladed club toward Morning Breeze's crumpled body.

The three Amazonians clustered around him, nudging him with their feet, talking in faint but excited whispers. One of the Indians stooped over Morning Breeze to untie his wrists. He presented Kane with an unobstructed view of his nearly-naked backside.

Filling his lungs with air, then holding it, Kane took advantage of the target of opportunity. He placed his mouth on the hollow bore of the blowgun and expelled all of his breath in a single, powerful gust.

The Indian howled, leaping straight up, slapping frantically at his buttocks. By the time his fingers found the dart and plucked it away, Kane had loaded a second wooden needle and spit it on its way.

Another warrior cried out, clawing at his back, dropping his weapons while he reached for the spot between his shoulder blades where the dart had embedded itself.

The third Amazonian instantly realized what was happening and assessed the trajectory and direction of the darts. He came savagely to the attack, plunging toward Kane's position with his war club held over his head in a double-fisted grip.

Kane managed to spit a dart at him, but he had no idea if it struck home or not. The Indian tore away the fronds of the tree and bowled into him, chopping at his head with his bladed bludgeon.

Throwing himself backward, Kane instinctively raised the blowgun to ward off the blow and the club easily sheared through it. He tried to entangle the warrior's legs with his own and knock him down, but the tough stems and roots of the bushes tangled up his own legs.

The Indian dropped onto him, sitting down heavily on his chest, flailing wildly with his club, but the plantain tree impeded his movements. With a click and the whir of a tiny electric motor, the Sin Eater sprang into Kane's hand, but he kept his index finger well away from the firing stud. He used the blaster to parry a bludgeon blow, the crack of stone striking metal sounding almost as loud as the Sin Eater's report.

The Amazonian squeezed Kane's chest between his powerful thighs, compressing his upper rib cage, pushing the bones against his lungs. Then, with a protracted sigh, the man leaned forward, his body shaken by a shudder. He went completely limp, his black eyes still open but seeing nothing. The club fell from his slack fingers.

Kane pushed against his chest with the barrel of his blaster, and the Indian bent backward at the waist as if his spine had turned to rubber. Only then did Kane see the little pinpoint of blood shining on his left pectoral where the dart had penetrated but fallen away.

Climbing to his feet, Kane swept his gaze over the four motionless bodies, tamping down the impulse to surrender to his training and deliver killing head shots to each one of them. But he was no longer a Magistrate, and regardless of the Indians' treachery, he and his friends were still interlopers in their world.

He didn't bother tying up the three men as he had done with Morning Breeze. They were still conscious, but paralyzed, and he was running out of time. A glance at his wrist chron showed how the precious seconds ticked away, like water from a leaky faucet.

Kane crossed a field then entered the city, his dark clothing blending with the night. He could hear every rustle of whipcord and creak of his leather boots. The dim passageways between the houses seemed to hold danger in every shadow. He tensed with anticipation, his teeth clenched, waiting for an Indian to glance out a window and then raise an alarm.

He couldn't help but be reminded of his penetration into Mesa Verde canyon almost a year ago to the day. That hard-contact Magistrate mission had set into motion a sequence of events that resulted in his exile from Cobaltville. He smiled bitterly at the irony. If he hadn't gone into that Colorado canyon, he would not now be skulking through alleys in South America.

He saw no one in the side lanes or even on the main thoroughfare. The houses were deserted, but Kane refused to relax. He kept his eyes on the towering edifice of the pyramid, noting how a fire flickered near it, staining the sky with orange shadows. The drumming went on, now overlaid with a singsong chant.

Peering around the corner of a house, he saw a procession of Indians scaling the long stairway that stretched to the top of the pyramid. They took up stiff-backed positions on either side of the steps, each holding an unlit torch. A man carrying a sparking firepot moved to each in turn, and they thrust the pitch-coated ends of their torches into the pot to set them aflame.

Kane had no idea what the people were doing or why, but their presence on the steps explained the absence of activity in the city streets. Moving in fits and starts, he circled around to the rear of the immense structure, belly-crawling into the mouth of another alley. He reached a wall encircling the grounds of the pyramid and straightened up for a quick look on the other side.

From an arch in the base of the pyramid emerged six figures wearing long blue mantles that draped their bodies from throat to ankle. Their faces and heads were concealed by monstrous serpentine masks. From their crests floated colorful plumes of feathers. The man in the lead carried a staff that supported a grinning human skull.

Kane watched as the shamans began to climb a small series of stairs set into the pyramid, moving at a measured, ritualistic pace. His next move was the most obvious one suggested by tactics and opportunity. He slid between the double gates in the wall and rushed toward the last man in line. Kane counted on the drums and the headpiece to mute the sound of his rapid approach.

The man's peripheral vision was impaired by the

mask, so he had no idea of who belonged to the arm that cinched tight around his throat and yanked him backward.

The man struggled and tried to shout. Thrusting out a leg, Kane swept the Indian's legs out from under him and slammed him painfully to the paving stones surrounding the base of the pyramid. Air exploded from the man's lungs in a muffled whoosh. Kane deprived him of further oxygen by knee-dropping his entire weight onto his diaphragm.

As the Indian convulsed, Kane snatched off the headpiece, revealing the swarthy face of a man in middle age. He was almost unconscious, lips writhing over discolored teeth. Kane recognized him as the shaman Cloud Minder, as he leaned close to jab the last of the drugged darts into his jugular vein.

Whipping off the blue cloak, he drew it around his shoulders and quickly tied the thongs around his neck. He placed the mask over his head, wrinkling his nose at the odor of stale sweat and the ripe scent of breadfruit. He had difficulty seeing out of the eye-holes, but managed to reach the steps without stumbling. The figure ahead of him turned his head awkwardly toward him as if asking a silent question. Not to do what was expected would arouse instant suspicion, so he lengthened his stride, falling in three steps behind the man.

As they ascended the stairs, Kane heard them muttering one word over and over: "Kukulkan, Kukulkan."

By the time they reached the top of the pyramid, Kane's lungs labored for air inside the stuffy headpiece, and the tendons at the back of his knees ached. Without being too obvious about it, he stared with interest at the pillar carvings, the little idols and in particular at the huge metal bowl. A monotonous chant from many throats wafted up from below, climbing in volume.

The shaman with the skull staff made a gesture, and Kane's companions took from stone shelves small discs of metal. They passed them around, a pair to a man.

Kane held them uncertainly, watching the others. When they began to strike them together, setting up a nerve-stinging racket, he followed suit, trying to match their rhythm. He was far too apprehensive to feel foolish.

He remained beside the bowl, his left arm occasionally brushing it. He felt movement in the metal and at first he attributed it to sympathetic vibrations caused by the clashing of the cymbals. But as the minutes wore on, the movement inside the bowl became more frequent, completely out of sync with the noise. With a sinking sensation in the pit of his belly, Kane realized there was something alive within it, something big and anxious to get out. He took a surreptitious, sideways step away from it.

At that moment, an incongruous shape appeared on the opposite side of the temple, rising from the stairway. For a split second, Kane's heart thudded in instinctive fear, then he recognized King Chaac decked out in an elaborate costume made of cured snakeskin and feathers.

A group of people followed King Chaac to the top. Young men, their naked bodies decorated with spots and whorls of blue paint, half carried a diminutive girl between them. Domi's nude body was covered in blue paint, and if not for her white hair and half-closed crimson eyes, Kane would not have been able to identify her.

Her head wobbled drunkenly, and she breathed in great gasps, gazing around with unfocused eyes. Kane clenched his teeth but did nothing except to crash his cymbals together.

A few seconds later, Grant stepped beneath the roof of the pyramid, surrounded by a bevy of Indian maidens. He wasn't naked, although his female escorts were, but he didn't look particularly happy about it. In fact, his eyes were narrowed to slits and he gnawed at his lower lip. Sweat glistened on his dark face, as if he struggled to break invisible chains.

Both people were obviously under the influence of some drug, but the extent of its effects was determined by their individual physiques and metabolisms. Domi, small and childlike, appeared to be only semiconscious while Grant reminded Kane of a man just roused from slumber—still groggy and disoriented, requiring only the proper stimulus to come to full wakefulness.

The chant reached a high note, then ended. At the

same moment, the masked men stopped clashing their cymbals together.

King Chaac faced Domi and spoke to her gently, in a pleasant, soothing voice, gesturing to the massive bowl behind him. Eardrums still recovering from the racket of the cymbals, Kane thought he heard a rasping, scraping sound from within it.

Four of the six masked men put their cymbals on the floor and grasped the lid of the bowl by small, almost invisible niches. Kane heard the rustling sound again, then a bump and a sibilant hiss. On impulse, he handed his cymbals to the man next to him and moved toward Domi, waving back the young men around her. Though they murmured questioningly, they obeyed his gesture and Kane stepped behind her, grasping her bare shoulders. The wet paint on her body slid beneath his fingertips. King Chaac said something in a demanding, suspicious tone.

Lowering his head, Kane whispered into her ear, not knowing if she could hear him through the headpiece or if she was alert enough to understand him.

"When I give the signal," he said, "move."

"Huh?" she responded in a faint, querulous voice, as if she resented being shaken awake from a pleasant nap.

Before he could repeat himself, the masked priests heaved up the lid of the bowl and lifted it away. With a mounting fear, Kane noticed how everyone in the temple seemed frozen by the soft, dry rustling from within its concave interior. An icy hand touched the buttons of Kane's spine. The sound was the unmistakable whisper of pliant scales slithering over metal.

Even through the mask, he smelled a fetid, dank odor. Cold sweat beaded his face and trickled into his eyes as a vague form reared upright from the bowl, swaying slightly. Yellow eyes flamed in the indirect torchlight, and Kane caught only an impression of the huge, wedge-shaped head. From it flowed a crest of fluttering feathers.

Kane did not need King Chaac's awed whisper of "Kukulkan" to tell him what it was.

Chapter 4

Kane had seen only a few mutie animals in his life. Most recently he had encountered—and nearly been killed by—the legendary Ourboros obscura, the huge sand worm of the desert wastes. The mutie animals spawned by the aftermath of the nukecaust that tended toward gigantism had very short life spans and were virtually extinct by the time Kane was born.

The serpent rearing up from the bowl exceeded all of his notions about reptilian development, mutated or not. He had no idea of the creature's true length, but at least twelve feet of it was visible. The diameter of the scaled, barrel-shaped body was twice that of his torso. Its triangular head was as large as that of a horse. A forked tongue flickered in and out of its mouth. In the torchlight, Kukulkan's mottled scales glistened like a coating of molten metal.

Kane knew that snakes were essentially deaf but they were exceptionally sensitive to vibrations. The crashing of the cymbals reverberated through the metal of the bowl and roused the giant serpent—and probably aroused its temper, as well.

Kukulkan's gleaming eyes fixed upon Domi. Although Kane told himself the snake was just an animal, he couldn't help but detect an ancient and certain evil in those unblinking eyes.

The monstrous snake arched its neck and swayed back and forth in almost hypnotic motion. As it did, Kane saw that the feathered plumes upon its spade-shaped head were artificial adornments fastened by thin straps. The fakery did not make him feel better. His belly still turned cold flip-flops of revulsion and denial.

All of the people in the temple fell to their knees except for King Chaac, Domi, Kane and Grant. They bowed their heads, murmuring in aspirated whispers, "Kukulkan."

Chaac reached for Domi, grasping her by the hands and tugging her forward.

Kane tightened his grip on Domi's shoulders and half shouted, "Now!" He pulled her backward.

Chaac stumbled, crying out in angry confusion as Domi's paint-slick hands slid through his fingers. Pivoting at the waist, Kane lifted Domi completely from the floor and pushed her into Grant's arms. He spun back around and back-fisted Chaac across the chin. The king staggered and fell almost directly beneath the elevated bowl.

The snake's eyes fixed on Kane, its attention attracted by the fact he was the nearest human still standing erect. Beneath the folds of the mantle, he unholstered his Sin Eater just as the serpent's massive head darted out and down toward him. Its jaws opened with a loud pop—actually dislocated—so as to be able to fit Kane's head and shoulders into its mouth.

He caught a glimpse of the double rows of slanting fangs lining the creature's upper and lower jaws as he bounded to the right, struggling to fling back the cloak and bring his blaster to bear.

Kukulkan's blunt snout drove like an arrow into his flapping mantle, the cloth snagging on the needle-tipped teeth. The snake instantly whipped its head back, snapping its jaws shut. Kane tried to resist the drag, but he was jerked forward, the knotted leather thongs biting cruelly into his throat. He struggled to untie the knots, but with the strain on the mantle he couldn't secure a grip. The headpiece wobbled and slid askew, obstructing his vision.

Boots sliding across the stone floor, blind and gagging, Kane raised his Sin Eater and depressed the trigger in the general vicinity of the snake's head. The stuttering triburst sounded obscenely loud, as did the keening wails of the rounds ricocheting from the temple's ceiling.

Kukulkan flailed its head back and forth, trying to free its teeth of the unappetizing mantle. Kane was tossed to and fro, feeling like a rat caught in the jaws of a terrier. His toes scrabbled on the stone floor, his breath coming in hoarse, pained gasps. He clawed at the rawhide thongs sinking into his windpipe, but he couldn't fit his fingers between the knots and his neck.

Desperately, he groped for his combat knife in its

boot sheath. After two tries, he touched the release button and drew it from the scabbard. Attempting to slice through the leather tie-thongs would more than likely result in a severed artery, so he awkwardly slashed behind his head. The blade's razored edge cut through the mantle. The pressure on his larynx and windpipe decreased.

With a loud ripping of fabric, the gargantuan serpent tore its fangs free of the cloak, and Kane caromed headlong against a stone pillar, colliding with a carved snake head. The wooden mask splintered upon impact, but it saved him from a fractured skull.

Falling to the floor, Kane rolled frantically, dropping his knife as he tried to pull off the ruined headpiece and disentangle himself from the ragged mantle at the same time. He managed to toss off the mask with furious shrugs and shaking his head.

Neck arched, Kukulkan towered above him, shreds of cloak snagged on its fangs. Kane scooted backward on the seat of his pants until he was at the very edge of the temple. Raising his Sin Eater, he tried to center the snake's bobbing head with the blaster's front blade sight.

Shouting half in fear and half in outrage, King Chaac rose from the floor and dived toward him, reaching for the pistol. At that instant, Kukulkan's feathered head shot down and struck Chaac between the shoulders with an echoing thud. The blow knocked the king from his feet, flattening him with piledriver force to the floor. The serpent's massive jaws closed on the back of his hooded head. The snap and splinter of bones were clearly audible. Kukulkan's gigantic, sinuous shape slithered out of the bowl, glistening coil after coil looping around Chaac's body. Kane made a swift, half-inchoate estimate of the monster's length, figuring it was at least fifty feet.

As the creature oozed out of the bowl, pandemonium exploded atop the temple. Screaming incoherently, the Indians came to their feet, some charging pell-mell out of the temple and down the steps, trampling their fellows. A few others rushing toward where their feathered god squeezed their king to death, voicing mingled cries of terror as if trying to convince Kukulkan that he was crushing the wrong sacrifice. A couple of the masked, mantled shamans apparently held Kane responsible for the disruption of the religious service and dashed toward him, obsidian knife blades in their fists.

The thick, muscled trunk of the snake looped out in a side arc and slammed into one of the priests, pitching him over the side of the pyramid with a wild cry of terror. The other grappled with Kane as he was in the process of raising his fist, slashing at him in a frenzy with his knife.

Kane blocked the thrusts with his Sin Eater. The blade snapped off near the hilt with a dull chime, and he crashed the metal frame of the blaster against the man's mask, crushing the fragile wood and breaking the skull beneath it.

As the man sagged, Kane cast a quick glance over his shoulder. Grant, with Domi enfolded in his arms, stared dazed and uncomprehending at the huge snake sliding its body around King Chaac.

"What the hell are you waiting for?" Kane bellowed at the top of his lungs so as to be heard over the shrieks of the Indians. "Your turn?"

Grant had watched all the proceedings from a safe remove, as emotionally distant as if he were observing a faintly ridiculous play staged for his amusement. Even when the masked priest revealed himself to be Kane, he still didn't get the point. He was particularly baffled when the feathered serpent god appeared to devour the feathered serpent man. He knew there was some deep, symbolic meaning at hand, but it required too much effort to reason it out. Even the profane question Kane shouted at him seemed utterly irrelevant.

He stood motionless as the floodtide of Indians screamed and swirled around him. He didn't move until one of the blue-robed, masked figures latched on to Domi and tried to wrest her from his arms. Grant refused to relinquish his grasp, and for a long moment Domi was the object of a determined game of a tug-of-war.

A black-bladed knife appeared in the shaman's fist and bit into the meat of Grant's left shoulder just above the armpit. It blazed with a searing pain like an animal sinking fangs into his flesh.

Galvanized by the burst of hot agony, Grant roared

and pistoned his right fist directly into the wooden snake head. The mask caved in at the point of impact, and the man catapulted backward. The thrashing tail of the serpent slapped his ankles, and he fell right into its coils. Grant tore the knife from his shoulder with his right hand and glared around, breathing deeply through his nostrils.

In a high-pitched, little girl's voice Domi quavered, "What's going on?"

Grant swiped a hand over his eyes, blinked and watched Kane pistol-whipping one of the blue-mantled shamans. Ignoring the burning throb in his shoulder and the trickle of blood sliding down his left arm, Grant shouted, "Kane!"

Keeping his eyes on the snake only a few feet away, Kane tore at the fastenings of the cloak and bellowed fiercely, "*Fight,* goddammit!"

Grant did so, shoving the obsidian knife into Domi's hands and bulling ahead, punching at the bodies hemming him in, striking with fists and feet, clearing a path to Kane. As he shouldered a man off the edge of the pyramid, he saw Kane's combat knife lying on the floor. He reached down and scooped it up.

Kukulkan lifted its head from Chaac and curved toward Kane again, jaws snapping open. Kane triggered another triburst, but the giant serpent's head weaved with lightning swiftness, and only one round came close to finding a target, shearing off the tip of a feather.

The hard, horny snout of Kukulkan battered deep into Kane's midsection, ramming him off his feet and driving him against a stone column. All the breath left his lungs in an agonized bleat between his teeth. Sour bile climbed up his throat in an acidic column. He was only dimly aware of collapsing to the floor in a heap, but he knew Kukulkan's open jaws hovered above him.

Through the haze of pain swimming across his eyes, he caught a blurry impression of Grant bounding forward, combat knife raised. Gasping, he forced himself to his knees, wadding up the torn remnants of the cloak and shoving them into the creature's gaping maw.

Kukulkan arched backward, head shaking furiously, trying to dislodge the choking mass of fabric in its throat. At that instant, Grant locked both arms around the snake's neck, just behind the thick knots of jaw muscles.

The snake reared up, lifting him clear of the floor, rising to smash him against the ceiling. The crest of feathers flattened. Grant felt the crown of his head slam against the roof, and little multicolored stars flared behind his eyes. He strained and wrestled, stabbing with the knife, feeling the blade sink to the hilt through the tough scales. In a volcanic convulsion of contraction and expansion, the serpent thrashed, hissing in fury and pain. Its tail whiplashed against the base of a pillar with sledgehammer force, chips of stone flying from it, cracks running halfway up its length.

Legs kicking empty air, Grant hung on to the knife handle, goring, ripping, working the blade through the shuddering, rippling bulk. He secured a tight grip on the leather straps holding the snake's feathered crest in place. Kukulkan stretched up again, and once more he was slammed into the ceiling. The impact sent shivers of pain from the crown of his head to the middle of his back, and his brain reeled with the punishment he was taking.

Kneading his midsection, desperately dragging air into his lungs, Kane used the pillar at his back as a brace and pushed himself to his feet. When he saw the pattern of cracks Kukulkan's blow had riven into a support column, inspiration flashed into his mind.

Before he could leap into action, Domi bounded nimbly over the lashing tip of the monster's tail, face stark with terror. With a black-bladed knife in her hands, she slashed at Kukulkan's mottled hide, the glassy point scoring a bloody gash in the trunk. A muscled coil looped outward in an instantaneous reaction, bowling her backward. Arms windmilling, she would have fallen from the pyramid if Kane hadn't grabbed her. Her ruby eyes were glazed, but wide and wild with frightened confusion.

"Help him!" she shrilled.

Shooting at the serpent's body would have little effect, Kane knew. He could waste an entire clip trying to hit a vital organ or break its flexible vertebrae.

Only a head shot would kill the creature, and with Grant still clinging tenaciously to the creature's whip-sawing neck, he would be at as much risk of being shot as Kukulkan.

Domi started to lunge forward again, but Kane restrained her with his left arm. He aimed the Sin Eater at the cracked pillar, flicked the selector to full auto and depressed the trigger. The high-velocity 248-grain rounds tore across the temple and ripped savagely into the support post. The air filled with the jackhammering thunder and the sharp, sweet smell of cordite. Spent shell casings arced up and tinkled down. A section of the post dissolved in sprays of dust and rock fragments.

He shifted the barrel of the Sin Eater to the pillar at the far corner and emptied the remainder of the magazine at its base. When the firing pin clicked against the empty chamber, he ejected the spent clip and slapped home another one.

Grant yelled, "What are you doing?" He still clung to the creature's neck, hanging on like a bulldog to the hilt of the knife, which he could not withdraw.

"Let go of that damn thing!" Kane shouted back.

Grant instantly obeyed, releasing his chokehold and falling to one knee, leaving the knife buried in Kukulkan's neck. The feathered headdress came with him, clenched in one fist. At the same microsecond, Kane let loose with another full-auto fusillade at the pillar. He played the bullet stream over the pillar as if he were washing it down with a hose.

Grant rolled frantically toward him, beneath the barrage, barely avoiding a vicious snap of the serpent's fangs. He flung the feathered crest into the creature's face, and it recoiled, curving up and back. A couple of bullets tore into Kukulkan's body, destroying fistfuls of flesh and muscle amid sprays of dark blood. It tumbled backward, away from the barrage, hurling King Chaac's crushed corpse from its coils. The monster's sibilant hiss took on a high-pitched, keening note.

With a grate and crack of stone, the rear portion of the temple's roof tilted, then crashed down. The entire pyramid seemed to tremble with the violence of the impact.

The huge, multiton rock slab bisected Kukulkan's body, pinning it to the floor. The creature's trunk knotted, looped, unlooped and whiplashed in crazed efforts to free itself. It turned to bite at the temple roof, its teeth breaking against the stone.

Resting the barrel of his Sin Eater on his forearm, Kane held his breath and squeezed off one more round. Kukulkan's right eye broke apart in a gelid spray. It tossed its head back and forth, jaws opening and closing with a castanetlike clacking, forked tongue flailing as if it were trying to dislodge a bone stuck in its throat. By degrees, the huge head drooped and fell to the temple floor. Postmortem spasms still rippled along the serpent's body.

Domi, Grant and Kane backed away to the lip of the temple, watching with stupefied eyes and listening to the agonized hisses and the thud and rasp of the snake's trunk against the floor as it convulsed in its death throes. For a long moment, no one moved or spoke. Far in the distance, a night bird screeched in outrage over the disturbance.

Then, from the Indians assembled below on the steps burst hysterical shrieks of horror and grief. They made no move to ascend the stairs but only wailed and howled. As quickly as he could, Kane thumbed out the spent clip and inserted his last magazine.

"Where are your blasters?" he asked in a tight, breathless voice.

Grant shook his head, winced and gingerly touched the stab wound in his shoulder. "Not sure." He nodded toward a wing of the pyramid below. "Mebbe in one of the rooms down there."

Domi trembled violently, crossing her arms over her breasts, further smearing the paint, already running due to the cold sweat that had sprung from her pores.

"What we do now?" she whispered. Under stress, she reverted to her abbreviated mode of outlander speech.

"No choice but to brazen it out," Kane replied tersely. "Their king and god are dead, but they think you're something special, Domi. You'll have to go first. Don't show fear—act like you own the place."

She hesitated, lower lip quivering. Then she drew in a deep, steadying breath and lifted her head at a defiant angle. With a regal, deliberate stride, Domi descended the pyramid. Grant and Kane followed, Kane keeping the Sin Eater at his side.

Eyes fixed on the foot of the steps far below, paying no heed to the babbling Amazonians, Domi led the two men to the base of the structure. The Indians parted at her approach, although some of them were openly weeping, others blank-faced with shock.

The skin at the back of his neck crawled, but Kane resisted the impulse to look behind him. Despite all that had happened, he still did not want to chill any of the Indians unless they gave him no choice.

At the foot of the steps, Domi paused, looking back and forth uncertainly for a few seconds before walking beneath an arched doorway. Inside the chamber where she and Grant had been bathed and further drugged, they found their clothes and weapons.

While Kane watched the doorway, his two friends quickly dressed. Domi didn't bother to wash the paint from her body with the water still in the tubs. Neither she nor Grant thanked Kane for coming back for them. There was no need. The two men in particular had spent most of their adult lives watching each other's back until it was an ingrained reflex, almost as automatic as breathing.

Grant grunted as he examined his stab wound. "Where's our medical kit?"

"Lost it on the trail," Kane answered, coming to his side. He grabbed Grant's left elbow and, ignoring the man's wordless growl of protest, pulled the arm up. "Does it hurt?"

"Goddammit!" Grant felt a blaze of agony scorch a path through his arm down into his hand.

"No muscles are cut," Kane observed. "It'll mend."

"Kiss my ass," Grant snapped, pulling away.

Domi slid into the shoulder rig for her .45-caliber Detonics Combat Master, unleathered it and checked the action. In a subdued tone, she asked, "How could those nice people believe that mutie snake was a god?"

Kane shook his head, replying distractedly, "Nice people can believe in as many crazy things as bad people. Gods come in all shapes, I guess. And so do monsters."

As Grant strapped his Sin Eater to his right forearm, he said grimly, "We've got no choice but to try to make it back to the gateway tonight."

Kane nodded. "It's a three-hour walk—probably longer because it's dark."

"Why can't we stay here until sunrise?" Domi demanded, cycling a round into the chamber of her blaster. "Hold 'em off here."

"The longer we give the Indians to think about what happened," Kane stated, "the more pissed off they'll get. They're in shock right now. That'll wear off."

Grant nodded. "Let's do it."

The three of them marched out of the room. The crowd that had assembled on the pyramid's steps was gone, and they met no one as they walked to the main thoroughfare. Torches flared smokily at wide intervals.

The few Amazonians on the street stood unspeaking, watching them pass with black eyes seething with a combination of hatred and fear. The numbers of the people decreased as Grant, Kane and Domi neared the outskirts of the city. The moon was beginning to wane, and its fading, silvery light gave the entire scene an unreal and oppressive atmosphere.

They reached the fields unmolested, but none of the three relaxed. They crossed a small bridge over an irrigation ditch, and the solid forest wall of the jungle loomed before them. The trees were colossal, the spaces between them dark and quiet. Rather than seeming majestic, the vast rain forest looked haunted. Kane's imagination easily populated it with all manner of loathsome creatures, far worse than giant mutie snakes.

They stuck to the path as it entered the jungle. At first it seemed pitch-dark beneath the towering trees, but their eyes adjusted to the gloom and they were able to stay on the well-worn trail. Up ahead came the faint rushing of a stream.

Then they heard spitting sounds, and darts whizzed about them from all sides. Indians emerged from the shadowed foliage, giving voice to shrill, maddened cries. Kane, Domi and Grant immediately broke into a sprint, hearing the patter of bare feet on the ground behind them.

The jungle resounded to the vengeful yells of the Amazonians. Kane didn't remind anyone—least of all himself—that if they were recaptured, being crushed and devoured by a snake-god would seem like a pleasant pastime. The Indians would probably torture them for days, keeping them alive in unceasing pain.

Grant fired an indiscriminate burst over his shoulder, the barrel of the Sin Eater smearing the murk with flickering flame. He heard a howl of pain as at least one bullet found a flesh-and-blood target.

"Keep going!" Kane shouted tensely, voice tight with the exertion of running. "If anybody gets hit, sing out!"

Gusting out a sigh, Grant muttered to no one in particular, "I can tell this is going to be a *long* night."

Chapter 5

Whenever Brigid Baptiste reviewed the events of the past year, she didn't know whether she was still alive through luck, divine intervention or simply the proper application of skills to circumstances.

She knew some of her survival skills were underdeveloped, so she walked forth from the sec door with a blaster in her hand. Behind her, the mountain peak lifted gray stone crags and broken turrets to the blue midmorning Montana sky.

In front of her, on the far side of the plateau, the broad tarmac tumbled down into an abyss. The precipice dropped a thousand feet. In a streambed at the bottom rested a pile of rusted vehicles.

The ragged remnants of a chain-link fence ran around the plateau. A single road curled down to the flatlands, along the forested slopes of the Bitterroot Range. At one time, steel guardrails had bordered the rim of the plateau, but only a few rusted metal stanchions remained. Before he had made the jump to South America, Kane had erected a man-shaped and -sized target between two of the stanchions and urged her to get in some practice with the gun he had chosen for her. She paced off thirty yards from the edge of the abyss.

Brigid examined the Iver Johnson TP9 in her hands. The autoblaster was fairly small and light-weight, less than twenty-six ounces. Carefully, she clicked the ambidextrous safety switch to the off position. Her lack of true skill with firearms had been a point of contention between her and Kane for months. For a while, she had carried an H&K VP-70, then a Beretta, but she found the weight and recoil of both guns a little uncomfortable. She had opted for a .32-caliber Mauser at one point, but its range was limited and its accuracy unreliable. She'd carried an Uzi a time or two, but other than firing a few practice magazines, she never had used it in the field. Recently, Kane had recommended the Iver Johnson.

She assumed a combat stance, arms stretched out, pistol nestled snugly between both hands, legs planted wide and firmly. Impatiently, she tossed a windblown strand of sunset-colored hair from her face. For an instant, she thought about the incongruous picture she made. With her unruly mane of red-gold hair clubbed back, and wearing a white body-suit, the duty uniform of the Cerberus personnel, she presented an unlikely image of a gun enthusiast. She squinted through wire-framed, rectangular-lensed eyeglasses. They were the only memento of the many years she had spent as an archivist in Cobaltville's Historical Division.

After the mission in the Western Isles, Brigid had devoted more thought than usual to her looks, about the effect her tall, willowy body had on men. She remembered how more than one male colleague in Cobaltville had made it obvious that he thought far more than she ever did about her full breasts, her feline-slanted eyes of deepest, clearest emerald, her smoothly contoured cheekbones, lightly dusted with freckles.

Apparently, Ambika, their most recent adversary, had devoted a considerable amount of thought to the effect her physical appearance might have on men, or one man in particular.

Brigid brought the white outline of the human head into target acquisition. Kane had cautioned her repeatedly about the difficulty of scoring with head shots, pointing out that the body was bigger and even a nonlethal wound would be incapacitating. But she had her reasons for centering the TP9's sights on the head.

Holding her breath, she mentally superimposed the smirking face of Ambika over the featureless target and squeezed the trigger. She maintained her finger's pressure, firing off all the rounds in the magazine, one shot following another so fast the twig-cracking reports tripped over each other. She held the pistol steady, instantly correcting for recoil and elevation.

As she fired, she was only dimly aware of chanting, "*Die,* you bitch queen. *Die,* you whore goddess."

The firing pin clicked on the empty chamber, and Brigid lowered the blaster, the mountain peak beating back the echoes of the shots like a frantic tattoo rapped out on a snare drum by a madman. Fanning away the planes of cordite smoke, she peered toward the target and saw a number of ragged holes neatly grouped in the center of the face.

She whispered hoarsely, ''Regenerate that, you mutie slut.''

She felt a flush of pride, then almost immediately a twinge of shame. As far as she knew, Ambika was truly dead, her mutagenic regenerative abilities notwithstanding. If the wounds she had incurred during the final bloody battle aboard her flagship hadn't been fatal, then the warrior queen had drowned when she pitched over the side.

Regardless, Brigid wasn't convinced of Ambika's death, and although he hadn't spoken of it, Brigid was sure Kane wasn't, either. Nor was she at all certain that the possibility Ambika had survived didn't intrigue him more than just a bit.

Brigid swallowed a sigh, trying to drive the memory of that beautiful, merciless face from her mind. Due to her eidetic memory, Brigid knew she would never forget it, nor how Ambika had humiliated her—by binding, gagging and caging her, forcing her to watch as she and Kane made love. Or least, that had been Ambika's plan before Kane improvised one of his own.

"La Belle Dame sans Merci," she murmured to the mountain air.

Hearing the scuff of footsteps on the asphalt behind her, she turned to see Banks and Auerbach climbing down from the slope on the opposite side of the plateau. Banks was a youthful black man with trimly blocked hair and bright, alert eyes. Auerbach was considerably larger, a burly, freckled man with a red buzz cut.

When Banks saw Brigid, he gave her a nod, but Auerbach paid her no attention, keeping his gaze fixed on the ground, studiously ignoring her. Brigid knew why and reciprocated with the same lack of notice. He was returning from the grave of Beth-Li Rouch and was in no mood to speak even if she felt like engaging him in conversation—which she didn't.

Dealing with Ambika's crazed jealousy was one thing, Brigid reflected. At least the bioengineered queen of the Western Isles had been straightforward about her designs on Kane. And though Ambika might still be alive, there was no doubt at all about Beth-Li's fate. She was most thoroughly dead, killed by Domi and buried in an unmarked grave. It was decorated by bouquets of wildflowers picked by her dupe, Auerbach. Only in the past week had the man been released from a detention cell. He was free on a form of parole, permitted to venture outside the redoubt only with an escort. Every day, he visited Beth-Li's grave.

Brigid wasn't sure why he did so. He had been the woman's pawn, seduced into participating in a conspiracy to kill Kane and Grant, foolishly believing Beth-Li's promise that Brigid would be spared. Apparently, Beth-Li had manipulated him by vowing that once Grant and Kane were out of the way, Cerberus would be his personal stud farm, where he would be serviced on demand by all of the female personnel.

But that was only speculation, derived primarily from the scornful reasoning provided by Wegmann, the redoubt's engineer, who had never liked Auerbach from the outset.

Auerbach himself had offered up very little in the way of a motive. He had ably served DeFore, the installation's medic, for quite some time. He had never displayed any aberrant behavior until Lakesh brought Beth-Li Rouch into Cerberus as part of his ill-conceived plan to turn the redoubt from a sanctuary into a colony.

Brigid removed the empty magazine from the butt of the Iver Johnson and slapped in a full one. She aimed the pistol at the target again, this time with a fierce, conscious effort to see only a paper outline, not Ambika's blue-eyed, triumphant sneer.

Squeezing the trigger, she fired only four rounds before relaxing her finger. She gazed toward the target and made a wordless utterance of disgust. She saw no new bullet holes. Every one of the four shots had missed completely.

She contemplated substituting Beth-Li's delicate, exotic face for Ambika's, but gave up the whole endeavor as a wasted effort—not to mention a bit on the unhealthy side. On a psychological level, Brigid felt no unfinished business existed between her and Beth-Li, and therefore imagining her as a target wouldn't make much difference. With Ambika, as much as she detested the emotion, she felt the thirst for revenge.

Brigid policed the area, picking up the shell casings and taking down the target. She crossed the plateau to the peak. Recessed into the base was the massive vanadium-alloy sec door. It opened like an accordion, one section folding over another.

When Cerberus was built in the late twentieth century, the plateau had been protected by a force field powered by atomic generators. Sometime over the past century, the energy screen had been permanently deactivated, so new defenses had to be created. Although they couldn't be noticed from the road, an elaborate system of heat-sensing warning devices, night-vision vid cameras and motion-trigger alarms surrounded the mountain peak.

Planted within rocky clefts of the mountain peak and concealed by camouflage netting were the uplinks with an orbiting Vela-class reconnaissance satellite, and a Comsat. It could be safely assumed that no one or nothing could approach Cerberus undetected by land or by air—not that there was any reason to do so.

The few people who lived in the region held the Bitterroot Mountain Range, colloquially known as the Darks, in superstitious regard. Due to their mysteriously shadowed forests and deep, dangerous ravines, sinister body of myths had grown up around the Darks. Enduring myths about evil spirits lurking in the mountain passes to devour body and soul was a form of protective coloration that every exile in the redoubt went to great pains to maintain.

Cerberus redoubt contained a frightfully well-equipped armory and two dozen self-contained apartments, a cafeteria, a decontamination center, a medical dispensary, a swimming pool and even detention cells on the bottom level. Constructed primarily of vanadium alloy, with design and construction specs aimed at making the seat of the Totality Concept's Project Cerberus an impenetrable community of at least a hundred people, Cerberus redoubt had weathered the nukecaust and skydark. Its radiation shielding was still intact, and its nuclear generators still provided an almost eternal source of power. The trilevel thirty-acre facility also had a limestone filtration system that continually recycled the complex's water supply.

Entering the dimly lit main corridor, Brigid punched in the code on the keypad to close the sec door. Painted on the wall beneath the pad was a large, luridly colored illustration of a three-headed black hound. Fire and blood gushed between yellow fangs, and the crimson eyes glared bright and baleful.

Underneath it, in ornate Gothic script, was written Cerberus.

Once when Brigid asked about the artist, Lakesh opined that one of the original military personnel assigned to the redoubt had rendered the painting sometime prior to the nukecaust. Although he couldn't be positive, he figured Corporal Mooney was the artist, since its exaggerated exuberance seemed right out of the comic books he was obsessed with collecting.

Lakesh had never considered having it removed. For one thing, the paints were indelible, and for another, it was Corporal Mooney's form of immortality. Besides, the image of Cerberus, the guardian of the gates of Hell, represented a visual symbol of the work to which Lakesh had devoted his life. The three-headed hound was an appropriate totem for the installation that, for a handful of years, housed the primary subdivision of the Totality Concept's Overproject Whisper, Project Cerberus.

Project Cerberus was devoted to locating and traveling hyperdimensional pathways through the quantum stream. Once the gateways had been developed, the redoubt became, from the end of one millennium to the beginning of another, a manufacturing facility. The gateways were built in modular form and shipped to other redoubts.

On the few existing records, the Cerberus installation was listed as Redoubt Bravo, but the dozen people who made the facility their home never referred to it as such.

Brigid strode along the wide passageway beneath great curving ribs of metal that supported the high rock roof. The vanadium alloy that sheathed the floor muted her footfalls. She walked down the corridor past the vehicle depot and workroom and entered an open doorway. The overhead fluorescent fixtures flooded the armory with a harsh white light.

The big room was stacked nearly to the ceiling with wooden crates and boxes. Many of the crates were stenciled with the legend Property U.S. Army. Glass-fronted gun cases lined the four walls, containing automatic assault rifles, many makes and models of subguns and dozens of semiautomatic blasters. Heavy assault weaponry occupied the north wall—bazookas, tripod-mounted M-249 machine guns, mortars and rocket launchers.

Brigid had been told that all of the ordnance was of predark manufacture. Caches of matériel had been laid down in hermetically sealed Continuity of Government installations before the nukecaust. Protected from the ravages of the outraged environment, nearly every piece of munitions and hardware was as pristine as the day it had rolled off the assembly line.

She placed the Iver Johnson automatic back in its case, glancing quickly at the two black figures standing near the rear wall. Kane's and Grant's Magistrate body armor was mounted on metal frameworks that resembled grim, silent sentries.

Leaving the armory, Brigid continued on down the twenty-foot-wide corridor to the central operations complex, the nerve center of Cerberus redoubt.

The room was long, with high, vaulted ceilings. Consoles of dials, switches, buttons and flickering lights ran the length of the walls. Circuits hummed, needles twitched and monitor screens displayed changing columns of numbers. She gave only a glance to the big Mercator-relief map of the world that spanned nearly one entire wall. Spots of light winked on almost every continent, and thin, glowing lines networked across the countries, like a web spun by a radioactive spider. The map delineated all the geophysical alterations caused by the nukecaust and pinpointed the locations of the functioning gateway units all over the world.

The control complex had five dedicated and eight shared subprocessors, all linked to the mainframe behind the far wall. Two hundred years ago, it had been the most advanced model ever built, carrying experimental, error-correcting microchips of such a tiny size that they even reacted to quantum fluctuations. Biochip technology had been employed when it was built, protein molecules sandwiched between microscopic glass-and-metal circuits.

The information contained in the main database might not have been the sum total of all humankind's knowledge, but not for lack of trying. Any bit, byte or shred of information that had ever been digitized was only a few keystrokes and mouse clicks away.

On the opposite side of the center, an anteroom held the mat-trans unit, its eight-foot-tall, translucent, brown-hued armaglass walls enclosing the jump chamber.

DeFore stood over Lakesh at one of the comp terminals. She was stocky and buxom, and her bronze skin made her ash-blond hair, in intricate braids, stand out starkly. As usual, she wore the white form-fitting bodysuit that was the usual attire of the redoubt inhabitants. Her full-lipped, brown-eyed face was composed and didn't reveal anything that might have been on her mind.

Lakesh looked up at Brigid's approach. He resembled an animated cadaver with astigmatism. Thick glasses covered his rheumy blue eyes. A hearing aid was attached to the right earpiece. His sparse ash-colored hair was disheveled, and despite the appearance of advanced age, he looked better than he should have.

He'd been born in 1952, long before the nukecaust that had wiped out so much of the world. He'd been a scientist then, with degrees in cybernetics and quantum mechanics at age nineteen, and he'd worked for premier institutions afterward. When he'd gone to work at the Overproject Whisper site in Dulce, New Mexico, his life changed forever.

Shortly after the nukecaust, Lakesh had been put into cryogenic stasis. When he'd been awakened nearly 150 years later, medics replaced body parts that had worn out with bionics and organ transplants.

Then he'd been put to work to serve the Program of Unification. Only then had he seen what the Totality Concept had truly wrought. That, Brigid knew, had dropped a burden of guilt on Lakesh the man would never escape.

"What are you reading on the biolinks?" Brigid asked.

"Nothing," Lakesh bit out.

A cold fist of fear closed around her heart, but she kept her voice level and steady. "Explain."

"How do you explain nothing?" Lakesh snapped in his reedy voice. "All of their signals vanished at the same time."

The fist in Brigid's chest relaxed somewhat. "So it's more likely an uplink or transmission failure than a simultaneous cessation of their vital signs?"

DeFore nodded brusquely. "At least that's what we've been telling ourselves. We won't know for sure until the systems diagnostic is done."

Bry raised his copper-curled head from the master ops station. A round-shouldered man of small stature, his white bodysuit bagged on him. Almost defensively, he said, "I'm ninety percent certain that's the reason, maybe caused by weather conditions. Even solar flares are a strong possibility at this time of year."

He paused, as if screwing up his courage before adding, "Or the Comsat has simply relayed its last signal from the subcutaneous transponders. It's been in orbit for over two centuries, you know."

The subcutaneous transponder was a nonharmful radioactive chemical that fit itself into the human body and allowed the monitoring of heart rates, brain-wave patterns and blood counts. Lakesh had ordered all of the Cerberus redoubt personnel to be injected with them. Based on organic nanotechnology developed by the Totality Concept's Overproject Excalibur, the transponder fed information through the Comsat relay satellite when personnel were out in the field. Excalibur was the division of the Totality Concept that dealt with bioengineering and was responsible for many of the mutations in animal and human life that had arisen after the nukecaust cashiered out the world on January 20, 2001.

The signal was relayed to the redoubt by the Comsat, one of the two satellites to which the installation was uplinked. The computer systems recorded every byte of data sent to the Comsat and directed it down to the redoubt's hidden antennae array. Sophisticated scanning filters combed through the telemetry using special human biological encoding.

The digital data was routed to the console before which Lakesh now sat, and then run through the locational program to precisely isolate the team's present position.

Lakesh swung his head around to face Bry. "It isn't necessary to point to age every time we have a minor glitch with the Comsat or the Vela. How will your constant harping on how old the satellites are solve our present problem?"

Two spots of red appeared on Bry's cheeks, and to stave off an argument, Brigid interposed hastily, "I think it's best to assume we've temporarily lost the signals through some kind of outside interference. Kane said to give them three days, and the third day isn't over yet by half."

Lakesh exhaled a weary sigh and knuckled his deeply grooved forehead. Bitterly, he said, "Technology is like a chain. One weak link, and we're all back to the Stone Age."

No one responded to his sour observation. The world from which he came was one where technology had been taken for granted. Malfunctioning or worn-out parts could be replaced, transatlantic telephone lines and computer networks decreased vast distances and television kept people informed of the events shaping their lives.

For all the other exiles in the redoubt, technology remained an arcane and eldritch set of sciences not too far removed from magic. For people raised in the villes, technology was doled out piecemeal, its use reserved for the elite. Brigid easily recollected her shock upon learning about the scientific sorceries conjured by the Totality Concept and its many subdivisions.

Turning toward Bry, DeFore asked, "What about the radio signals we've been intercepting from Samariumville?"

Samariumville was one of the nine baronies across the continent that had come to power after the Program of Unification. Based in what was once known as Louisiana, Somariumville's influence extended to almost all of the deep South.

Bry lifted his down-sloping shoulders in a shrug. "The same. The Samariumville medical division is asking for aid from the other villes to help them fight the epidemic."

"Epidemic?" Lakesh echoed. "The outbreak has gotten worse?"

Bry nodded. "It was confined to the bayou country, around Lafayette. But it appears to be spreading."

"That fast?" demanded Brigid. "We didn't pick up the first reports until two weeks ago."

"That's only when we were able to patch into the comm web and listen in," Bry replied testily. "The outbreak could've been reported long before that."

Only recently, Lakesh and Bry had created a communications scanner with ville radio frequencies and channels that involved using the redoubt's satellite uplinks. So far it had worked smoothly, but now that the Comsat was down, so was Cerberus's ability to eavesdrop.

"Have you picked up anything regarding specific symptoms?" DeFore asked.

Bry gestured to a stack of spreadsheets on a nearby desk. "That's the record of the last communications exchange before we lost the Comsat signals. I ran it through an interpolations program, but I haven't had the chance to look it over."

DeFore sat down at the desk and began thumbing through the sheaf of papers, a line of concentration creasing her forehead. A constant fear in the villes revolved around the outbreak of designer viruses, bioengineered contagions cooked up before the nukecaust and stored in hidden facilities.

Biowarfare had not played a large role in the final war, mainly because the global nuclear conflagration had done its work too well. Bacteria and germs were scorched off the face of the Earth along with the humans they had been created to infect.

"Lafayette," Brigid murmured. "Seems like I read something about that region."

Lakesh's eyes narrowed behind the lenses of his glasses. "I confess it strikes a faint chord of recognition with me, too, but I can't immediately place it."

Brigid seated herself in front of a terminal and switched it on. Despite her photographic memory, she wasn't quite the walking, talking encyclopedia Kane often accused her of being. While possessing a profound knowledge of a great number of subjects, she knew there were some that were unfamiliar to her.

Lakesh swiveled around in his chair to face her. "Access the Overproject Excalibur file—keyword Enterprise Eternity. See what you come up with."

She nodded, fingers flying over the keyboard. Uneasily, she inquired, "Do you think the epidemic in

Louisiana has something to do with Overproject Excalibur experiments?''

Lakesh made a dismissive gesture with one hand. ''I think we can both agree that anything is possible, particularly with all the X factors arising out of the Totality Concept researches. We've certainly contended with their residue enough times.''

The old man's reference wasn't as veiled as it seemed. Many of the missions Brigid and the others had undertaken over the past year had their roots buried in two centuries of tinkering with genetics, quantum mechanics and artificial intelligence. The Totality Concept's many subdivisions had served as the sterile holy grail for three generations of predark scientists, and although the researchers were long dead, the buds of their labors continued to bear poisonous fruit.

DeFore suddenly voiced a half-gasped groan, full of shock and denial. Brigid turned away from the screen to see the woman gazing wide-eyed at the spreadsheets, her finger pressed down on a line of copy.

''Oh my God,'' she muttered. ''Oh my dear God.''

''What is it?'' Lakesh demanded irritably.

DeFore swallowed hard before answering, ''This last communication was between a field team and the Samariumville medical division. It lists the symptoms of the disease.''

''What are they?'' asked Brigid, a little unnerved by DeFore's uncharacteristic break in composure.

She read off the information on the paper. "High fever, swelling of the lymph nodes, massive tissue infection, hemorrhaging of the lungs, complete shutdown of the respiratory system."

"Sounds like some kind of plague," Bry commented tonelessly.

DeFore lifted her face from the paper, her expression stricken. Fear swirled in the dark depths of her eyes. "Not just *a* plague. It's *the* plague. The Black Death."

Chapter 6

As an archivist, Doyle didn't believe in demons or zombies. As a self-proclaimed conjure man, Veley did. Neither man had much choice but to stick to the convictions ingrained in them from a lifetime of conditioning. What the three Magistrates who had accompanied Doyle from Samariumville believed was anybody's guess.

Veley sat on his sagging stoop in front of his clapboard shack and smoked a filthy hand-rolled cigarette. He looked very old, and his dark brown skin resembled a leathery chocolate bar. Doyle eyed the bleached alligator skull nailed above the doorway and waited for Veley to complete his tedious, nonspecific story—about a horror forgotten by men for nearly two hundred years, monstrously resurrected from the black, lost time of skydark.

Doyle's own thoughts were as far from supernatural menaces as the thoughts of a man could be. His ruminations, though dark, were materialistic in nature. He was on a mission from Baron Samarium and he couldn't afford the time to stand and listen to folk tales. But he couldn't afford to alienate the conjure man, either, since he claimed to know the source of the epidemic sweeping through the bayou and creeping into the baronial lands.

Being a midgrade archivist in the Samariumville Historical Division, Doyle knew he should have been interested in the tale creaking out of the old man's wattled throat, but his field of expertise was medical history, not Cajun legends. Archivists were not historians, as generally believed. They were primarily data-entry techs, albeit ones with high security clearances. Midgrade archivists like Doyle were researchers.

A vast amount of predark historical information had survived the nukecaust, particularly documents stored in underground vaults. Tons of it, in fact—everything from novels to encyclopedias to magazines printed on coated stock that survived just about anything. Much more data was digitized, stored on computer diskettes, usually government documents.

The primary duty of archivists was not to simply record predark history, but to revise, rewrite and oftentimes completely disguise it. The political causes leading to the nukecaust were well-known. They were major parts of the dogma, the doctrine, the articles of faith, and they had to be accurately recorded for posterity.

Doyle was engaged in researching the effects of biowarfare in predark days when the first reports of the disease out in the swamplands reached Samariumville. The ville administrators' first course of action was to do nothing. No ville citizen cared about what happened in or to the Outlands. For many decades after the nukecaust, the Gulf Coast had been all but submerged by bomb-triggered tidal waves.

After the drowning seas had finally receded, almost all of Louisiana, Alabama and Georgia had become one vast, steaming lagoon. Therefore, the reports of disease percolating in the tainted, simmering wetlands elicited little surprise and even less sympathy for the people who eked out a marginal existence in them.

The bayous were essentially under a form of permanent quarantine anyway. Technically, the swamps fell under the jurisdiction of Baron Samarium, but they were so difficult to navigate, their citizens were left to their own devices. Very rarely did the Magistrates venture into them.

However, when reliable reports of the disease's symptoms reached Samariumville, the administrators began tracking the epidemic—and discovered that the most recent outbreaks had occurred within seventy miles of the ville proper. The plague was approaching like ripples caused by a pebble dropped into a pond.

After weeks of ignoring the situation and additional weeks of discussing it, the administrators decided to look for the area where the pebble had been dropped.

The first team dispatched into the Outlands made regular reports for the first few days. They described finding settlements full of corpses, bodies lying about in advanced stages of decomposition but untouched by scavenger birds or animals. The settlements and the bodies therein were burned, as per procedure.

The reports made almost casual mentions of seeing rats near the settlements. After a day or two, the rodent reports ceased being casual and became the primary topic. The team saw thousands of rats, hordes of squealing, chittering rodents making bold forays into the team's base camp, even dropping from trees onto them. Amid the sightings of the rats, glimpses of small, dark people with scar tissue around their eyes were mentioned. They were just as furtive as the rats, dodging and flitting among the swamp shadows.

Anyone born in Samariumville had heard of the swampies, a breed apart from the Cajuns, but who coexisted with them in the bayous. Rumor had it they were muties, but since their own enclaves were so deep in the tropical wilderness, no one knew for certain.

What was known for certain was that the reports from the field team stopped, abruptly and with a chilling finality.

Doyle was the man charged with the task of collating all the information in the reports and producing a diagnosis. The answer was so obvious he was surprised none of the ville administrators or the senior archivist reached the same conclusion. The bubonic plague, the Black Death of the Middle Ages, so called from the blackened skin eruptions that broke out on those afflicted. It was transmitted by sick rats, sometimes by bites of the fleas carried by the rodents, sometimes by the bites of the rats themselves.

Doyle also triangulated the spread of the plague and came up with a pretty solid set of coordinates from which it appeared to spring. When he presented his findings, he presumed one of two things would happen—he would receive a small material reward like an expanded food ration card, or more likely, his superiors wouldn't acknowledge his contribution at all.

Not in his wildest imaginings did he picture being assigned to lead another field team into the Outlands. There was no point in lodging a protest, or trying to explain that as a ville-bred academic he was singularly unsuited for such a mission. He had come to the attention of the baron, and that was all that was necessary.

In the company of three hard-contact Magistrates, Doyle had first stopped at the small ville of Brampton, a fairly typical Gulf Coast pesthole. Nestled on the edge of the sprawling wetlands, Brampton was indeed another in a long line of shit villes. Doyle had been told the place was nothing to get excited about, and after they arrived, he'd agreed wholeheartedly, but he hadn't expected an open-air charnel house.

It was a ville populated only by the dead and dying. Young and old, men and women, all felled by the same sweep of the scythe. They lay on porches and on streets, mouths open in silent screams of agony, bodies swollen and covered with pustules. The ground was moist with blood coughed up from hemorrhaging lungs.

They didn't find any rats, or signs of the first recce team, but they found one survivor. The woman lived long enough to helpfully direct them to a conjure man who, according to local lore, knew just about everything. If anyone knew about the fate of the first team, she croaked, he would.

So, after a day of crossing the bayous in a swamp wag, Doyle stood sweating in the hazy, greenish light, one foot propped up on the porch of the weather-beaten shack. A simple structure, the aged construct appeared to be more ruin than secure dwelling—a series of blacked-out windows, a tilted chimney oozing an upward spiral of wood smoke and a curiously flat tarpaper roof. Once, the sickly green house might have stood tall and defiant among the grassy tendrils that passed for ground cover in the back waterways surrounding it, but now it looked as if the walls had grown up whole from the damp earth instead of being built by human hands.

On either side of the conjure man's dwelling rose cypress and mangrove trees, the branches smothered by Spanish moss drooping from every limb like the beards of old men. He stood in front of the wizened Veley and waited for him to wind up his convoluted tale. Veley had ducked all questions about the first team dispatched from Samariumville, only smiling cryptically.

"De old ones are gone, but dey cannot die," said Veley in his strained voice. His accent was so thick, Doyle thought at first he was speaking a foreign language. After an hour, he'd finally reached the point where he could understand every third word out of the old man's mouth. "De first men turned upon dem, and mankind conquered, so long ago dat naught but legends come to us t'rough de ages. Yet even as man drove dem forth into de wastelands of de ancient world, dey only hid…knowing dat when man grew weak and forgot dem, dey could return."

Veley paused to take another drag on his cigarette and coughed rackingly. "One o' dem did return, back in the days when de sky be black."

Doyle waved away the cloud of pungent smoke stinging his eyes. "Do you mean the nuclear winter, the skydark?"

Veley nodded. "My great-gran'mama, a powerful *houngan,* returned him to the sepulchre of de earth. He been layin' dere now—not dead, only asleep. Waitin' for his time to come round again."

"Where is this sepulchre?" Doyle demanded.

"De plague rose from it," Veley replied. "It is no good place. Let hidden t'ings rest. Best not disturb what is hidden in de earth."

"Are you talking about an Indian burial mound?" He knew that Chickasaw and Natchez burial mounds were still found here and there deep in the swamps.

Veley snorted derisively. "Indians? Who spoke of de Indian? Dere been more dan Indians in dis country. In de olden times, strange t'ings happen here. I have heard de tales of my people, handed down from generation to generation. An' my people were here long afore yours.''

Doyle didn't refute that. He couldn't even if he'd wanted to. He palmed away sweat from his forehead and turned his head to glance at the three Mags standing behind him, hot and miserable in their body armor. The diffused sunshine struck dim highlights on the molded chest pieces and shoulder pads. The only color anywhere about the black armor was the red duty-badge disks affixed to the left pectoral. They carried their helmets under their polycarbonate enclosed arms. Flandry, Raeder and Brackett were all of a type—tall, rangy and as tough as whalebone.

By contrast, Doyle was of medium height and build, with the beginnings of a paunch. His brown hair receded from his high forehead. He couldn't properly seat his rectangular-lensed, wire-framed eyeglasses on the bridge of his beaky nose because they always slid out of position on a layer of sweat. He continually had to push them back.

He sensed the Mags' impatience. He knew they silently wondered why he wasted so much time— and probably what seemed to them an inordinate amount of courtesy—on a slagging outlander.

"How far is this so-called sepulchre?" asked Doyle.

"Yo' got no business dere, ville man.''

"I'll be the one to make that assessment.''

The effect of that simple statement on Veley was nothing short of electrifying. He recoiled and his dark face went ashy. His black eyes flared. The cigarette dropped from his lips and lay smoldering between his feet.

"*Sacre, non!*" he cried. "Don't do dat! Dere is a curse—my gran'mama tol' me—"

"Told you what?"

Veley lapsed into sullen silence. At length he muttered, "I cannot speak. I am sworn to silence. But believe me when I say better had you cut your t'roat dan to break into dat fuckin' sepulchre."

"Goddammit," snapped Flandry. "Tell us where it is."

"I cannot tell you dat!" Veley said desperately. "I am sworn to silence on de cross of de *zanges!*"

He fumbled inside of his ragged shirt and withdrew a small crucifix hanging by a leather thong. Doyle glanced at it curiously, at the feathers and beads attached to it.

"What's the *zanges*?"

Veley inhaled a deep breath. "Yo' would call dem angels. Ever' member of my family has sworn an oath on such a cross since de time of Mama Minuit! De sepulchre is a t'ing so dark, it is to risk eternal damnation even for my own people to visit dere."

With a click and a whir, Flandry's Sin Eater sprang from its holster into his hand. He stepped forward, putting the barrel against the side of the old man's head.

"I've had enough of this shit," he grated. "Tell us or die."

Veley gazed into the hollow bore of the blaster and said mildly, "I do not fear death, child."

Doyle's throat constricted. He had seen plenty of corpses—bloated by disease—on the trip to this point in the bayous, but he had never seen a man chilled. He realized he did not want to see it, either. He wasn't accustomed to dealing with Mags, nor were Mags accustomed to dealing with archivists. Although their respective divisions were only a level apart in the Administrative Monolith, they might as well have come from different planets.

The taciturn Flandry in particular scared him, with his pale eyes that seemed to stare right through him, silently judging him and finding him wanting.

Hastily, Doyle interposed, "We ask you this question because of the sickness. We may be able to cure it."

Veley cackled, spittle strings clinging between his toothless gums. "De sickness is no more dan de old ones' dreams. But my oath say nothin' of what is writ' down."

Dubiously, Doyle asked, "You have a written account of what you know?"

"*Oui*. De old priests taught my people dere letters. We may be outcasts, but we be no illiterates."

"You've got this account?"

Veley cackled again and stiffly heaved himself up from the stoop, completely oblivious to the blaster pointed at him. "Long time ago, my great-great-gran'father write it all down, 'bout what happened here in de days o' Lafitte. Wait here."

He shuffled into the shack, and Doyle heard him rummaging and murmuring to himself. Within a minute, he returned with a number of dingy leaves of wood-pulp paper, bound with twine, held between his gnarled fingers.

Without preamble, he shoved them into Doyle's hands. "Here. Read dem. It is my gran'papa's tale of *his* gran'papa's traffic wit' an old one. De story will not save you, but at least yo' will know what snatches yo' souls."

Doyle looked at the papers uncertainly. "What do you want for them?"

"If yo' read dem and not believe what dey say, den yo' will pay a very high price. Everyt'ing has its price."

Sighing with impatience, Doyle asked, "Which way do we go to find this sepulchre?"

Veley made a gesture to the southeast. "Dat way. Follow de stream. You come to sepulchre by and by. Watch for de rats…and dere keepers."

"Keepers?" echoed Doyle.

Veley traced lines around his eyes with a fingertip. "De minions of de old one. Dey still watch over de sepulchre, though they can't break de seal. An' now dey watch for *yo'* an' wait for yo' to do it for dem."

Veley fluttered his hands dismissively. "Now I

gots no mo' to say to yo'. Iffen you break de seal, yo' be back here by an' by.''

Flandry still had his Sin Eater unholstered. He obviously wanted to bid goodbye to the conjure man with a bullet, but when Doyle turned and walked toward the swamp wag, he reluctantly leathered his weapon and fell into step behind him.

The swamp wag resembled a wheeled boat. The six huge tires held it nearly eight feet off the ground, and only by climbing the small metal ladders affixed to the hull could the open control compartment be reached. Its three-inch-thick armor plate bore streaks and flakes of rust.

Doyle had no idea how old the vehicle might be, but he guessed its manufacture dated well before the nukecaust. They had requisitioned it at a border outpost between official Samariumville territory and the Outlands. The wag was a miserable conveyance, but it was preferable to slogging through the mud flats and cypress groves on foot.

Raeder took the controls, firing up the diesel engines. Smoke spouted from the exhausts in dark gray palls, blending in with the heat haze. The massive tires spun, throwing rooster tails of foul water and mud in back-arching sprays.

Since the buggy operated like a land vehicle and a boat, Raeder took the rudder bar to steer it when the wag entered deep water, the inflated tires providing buoyancy.

They had been under way only a few minutes, following Veley's vague directions, splashing and bouncing along the bank of the shallow stream, when blurs of motion overhead caught their eyes. Small shapes appeared, scurrying over the intertwining branches of sycamore and cypress trees.

"Fucking rats," snarled Brackett.

All of them had seen rats before, particularly down in the Tartarus Pits, the cheap-labor quarters of Samariumville. But these were the size of house cats with fiery red eyes and snow-white coats.

"Albinism," Doyle declared, striving for a tone of clinical detachment. "Common down here, I'm told."

Flandry unleathered his Sin Eater, took aim and pressed the trigger. The blaster bucked and roared, gouting flame. The fusillade of 9 mm rounds sheared through the tree limbs, splitting bark and shredding leaves. Two of the rats burst apart in greasy sprays of viscera. Droplets of blood splattered down onto the deck.

"Goddamn you," Doyle shouted angrily. "You want to let every swampie between here and the Missip know we're here?"

"Like that old piece of Outland shit said," sneered Flandry, "they know we're here already. We can take on some piss-poor swamp muties."

"Like the first team did?"

Flandry didn't respond, but he slid his Sin Eater back into its holster.

Chapter 7

Veley remained sitting on the stoop until the engine rumble of the swamp buggy faded to a dull, distant rumble. From the open doorway, a voice spoke to him in Creole. "You did well, old man. All those years of baiting hooks finally paid off. You fulfilled your part of the master's prophecy."

Stiffly, Veley pushed himself up and went inside the dimly lit interior of the house. The strong, wild smell of wood smoke wafted across his nostrils, and he struggled not to sneeze. The only illumination came from the roaring flames in the fireplace on the far back wall. The room was sparsely furnished with crude wooden chairs of different sizes, a faded print sofa, shelves filled with crumbling books and jars and two end tables that looked to be as old as the house itself.

Two swampies stood on either end of the sagging sofa, their eyes glittering in the pits of scar tissue surrounding the sockets. Dark-skinned, stocky and solid of build, well under medium height, they wore curving kaiser knives at their hips. Grimy, callused hands without fingernails held small, crude crossbows pointed at the bound and gagged naked girl seated on the couch.

The quarrels themselves were less than six inches long, but Veley knew the brown, tarry substance on the sharp points was a poison so deadly that even a scratch could bring death.

The girl eyed the crossbows fearlessly, scornfully. She was as darkly complexioned as the swampies, but her skin was much smoother, fine-pored and flawless in texture. Glistening pinpoints of perspiration shone on her forehead, between her firm breasts and on her flat stomach. Her black hair tumbled in thickly braided dreadlocks, draping her body to below her waist. Her full lips were parted to accommodate the dirty bandanna tied around her jaws, and her slender arms were bound at the small of her back. Her indigo eyes seethed with hatred of the two swampies.

"Are you all right, child?" Veley asked her softly.

She jerked her head in a nod full of repressed fury, the veins and tendons standing out on the slim column of her throat.

"Your granddaughter is fine," said LeGrand. "We didn't harm her, just like we promised."

Veley's mouth twisted in a contemptuous smirk. "I've known you all of your life, LeGrand. You, too, Craufux. I knew your fathers' fathers. None of them could keep promises. Why should I expect anything different from you?"

LeGrand didn't seem offended. "We serve different gods, conjure man."

Casually, he reached over and untied the knot in the girl's gag. She spit it from her mouth, shaking her head, the dreadlocks flying. She glared at LeGrand, then at Craufux. In a surprisingly deep, throaty voice, she demanded, "Do you dung beetles have *any* idea of the wrath you've called down upon yourselves, upon your entire misbegotten clan?"

Craufux retorted vehemently, "You haven't been invested yet, slut. The *loa* haven't recognized you."

She drew herself up and stared in regal haughtiness at the swampies. "Mother Midnight lives in me. I carry her blood, I carry her powers. How dare you mud-spawn question me, let alone lay hands upon me and my grandfather."

Veley saw anger flash in the eyes of both swampies, and he interposed, "Enough, Esther. We did what they wanted and sent the ville men to the sepulchre. What will be will be." He turned to LeGrand. "I know you want to be back on your way before the moon rises and darkness falls."

"We can afford to wait a little while," LeGrand replied. "Though the stars are right for the old one to return, we must see what awaits him upon his awakening."

To Esther, he said, "Mama Minuit was a seer. If you have her powers, you will tell us what is to come."

Esther spit toward the fire. "I'll tell you nothing, dung man."

Craufux shifted his crossbow, the sticky point aiming at Veley's heart. "Then you'll watch your grandfather die."

Neither Veley nor Esther spoke or moved. After a stretched-out moment, she nodded slightly, shoulders sagging in resignation. "My hands must be freed."

LeGrand said to Craufux, "Cut her loose." To Veley, he said, "If she plays us false, you will die."

Craufux used his kaiser knife to slice through the rawhide thongs binding Esther's wrists. She rubbed them briefly to restore circulation, then slid from the sofa, crouching very close to the fire, so close to the licking tongues of the flames that perspiration began literally rivering down her naked body.

For long, quiet minutes, Esther stared into the fireplace, the only sounds the popping of the flames. Then, at last, she spoke, "You want to look down the road, yes?"

LeGrand cleared his throat. "That's right. Moving forward."

"Such glimpses may be dangerous. There is always a price exacted by the *loa*."

"All they have to do is ask, and the request will be met."

The woman turned her face away from the dancing flames, angling an eyebrow at the swampies. "That is not what I meant. You are not aware of the one true price...no man can be. But that which you worship is not a man. You need his protection, his guarantees, his good favor.''

Esther closed her eyes, her entire body seeming to relax in a posture of prayer. She made motions with her hands, intricate, peculiar, circular gestures. Breathily, she murmured, ''The flames show me. They speak to me—they reveal the road to me.''

Somewhere outside, a dog began howling dolefully.

She moaned, then she spoke. ''The earth burns, the world turns, the sky is flame, the ground is ash and still, like the parasite, the cockroach, the legend and the myth, the old one endures...the old one survives. But so does man.''

''As he always has, as he always will,'' LeGrand whispered.

Her voice became stronger with each spoken word. ''But so does man. How many times will man destroy himself? Following the road laid out by his maker, exercising what he believes in his heart to be free will, and yet keeping to the pathways chosen aeons ago by the old ones.

''There are always two paths to follow, two choices to be made. The do and the do not. Up or down? In or out? One way or the other. Such is the curse of man.''

''Yet there are those who know otherwise—they see the right direction,'' LeGrand replied. ''Like the old ones.''

The woman's head turned to look at him, yet her

eyes were still closed tight. Her firelight-sculpted face was unreadable, unknowable. "I have seen the future...in all of its terrible, colored glory, I do not like what I see."

"What do you see of the old one?" LeGrand prodded. "What do you see of him?"

Esther moaned again. "They come for him, they come..." she said, her speech slurred. "They come from within."

"Who comes?" Craufux demanded excitedly.

"They come across the sky and back again. Across the world over and over. A patchwork, a joining of lands...thread through a needle, the pathways hidden." The words came out of her mouth in a jumble. "They travel by lightning, by thunder, through the magic of the storm. Harnessed in the caves, the energy electric. Worse, the energy forbidden, explosive, destructive. Yet still they come, they still come."

"Who travels?" LeGrand persisted. "How many?"

"There are two men, brothers in all but blood. Brothers in arms and in souls. They will seek two women who possess healing knowledge. They will come from the pathways hidden and arrive at the forbidden place of dead science."

A stealthy step padded outside the door, but neither swampie looked away from Esther.

"Can they be stopped?" asked LeGrand.

"These things are governed by immutable laws,"

she whispered hoarsely. "The *loa* enforce the laws. I do not altogether understand them myself. No human can. Events must work out to either salvation or damnation."

Esther drew in a breath and leaned back from the flames. She opened her eyes and stared unfocusedly at the fire. "That is all I see. Two women, two men, following the path invisible."

The woman's body slumped, her head bowed, the dreadlocks coiling on the floor like snakes. Esther remained still, and the room was thickly silent. A piece of wood in the heat of the fireplace popped softly, yet still sounded like a gunshot in the stillness.

"What's that noise?" Craufux whispered.

"I hear nothing," Veley replied.

"You can't hear that?" Craufux demanded, no longer whispering, his voice tight and pinched and frightened. "That sound, like footsteps, right after she stopped talking."

"I hear nothing," Veley insisted. "My eyes may be poor, but my ears are clear."

Esther suddenly laughed, a husky sound that didn't warm the blood. "The *loa* have many servants."

Craufux aimed his crossbow at her bare back. "And they're about to lose another one."

With a wordless shriek, Veley flung himself at the swampie. The string of the crossbow twanged, and the quarrel drove into the old man's chest, striking with a sharp slap. He fell half on, half off the sofa, clawing at the shaft sprouting from his body.

From the doorway, a black and sleek shape hurtled toward Craufux, who had just enough time and presence of mind to turn around before 115 pounds of growling animal flesh fell upon him, striking at enough of an angle to send the man staggering sideways onto the dirty floor.

Craufux fell over on his hip, grit pressing into his cheek, the smell of the huge mastiff's breath filling his face and his mind as the dog thrust a long snout up under his bearded chin. Bone white flashed in the flickering firelight as the dog's mouth sought the right spot to strike.

Spittle from the mastiff sprayed Craufux's neck. He screamed shrilly, a loud and long scream that was cut off, sudden and harsh, like a phonograph needle slung up and across the black grooves of an old-time long-playing record. There was a grisly, prolonged crunching, as of bones grinding together. LeGrand could hear the rise and fall of the dog's heavy breathing, along with the distinctive sound of vertebrae splintering between the animal's huge jaws.

The room fell silent once more, save for the small pops and crackling from the wood burning in the fireplace, and the slightly nauseating noises from the vicinity of the feeding animal. Esther spoke a word to the dog, and it stopped chewing. It backed away, great head sunk as it lapped once at the blood forming a pool around Craufux's head.

Quietly, Esther said, "The *loa* have many servants. He is one of them. The price they exacted for my services was the life of one of you."

The swampie nodded once. "I know. Everything has its price. And he was disrespectful."

LeGrand heard the padding of the dog's large paws as it walked to Esther's side and rubbed its giant shoulder against her knee. Blood dripped from its muzzle.

The swampie unconsciously gripped the handle of his kaiser knife and said, "This was not supposed to happen. The old one would have dealt with you and the conjure man if that was necessary."

Esther smiled at him, a savage flash of teeth. "Trust me, dung man. It will be now."

He cleared his throat and said, "I am sorry. I'll go now."

"Sorry?" Esther repeated with withering disdain. "Are you sorry your master's disease spreads through the country, killing indiscriminately?"

"It kills the unbelievers."

"It kills everyone—sometimes only their souls. Like those of your clan."

"Long, long ago, my clan vowed to serve him," LeGrand stated stolidly. "We owed him a debt, and now Ocajnik calls it due."

"There is no Ocajnik!" she said in a fierce hiss. "There hasn't been for centuries. There's only the outer shell, possessed by an entity older than the world, an entity who wants to enslave mankind.

When the first bombs fell, how he must have laughed!

"He uses you. As he uses the rats, as you use the ville men's ignorance to free your master. You are nothing but beasts to him."

"The stars are right," LeGrand said doggedly. "The prophecy must be fulfilled. Do you not work to fulfill the prophecies of your gods?"

"There is one difference," Esther said bitterly. "When you worship your god, you worship pestilence and perversity. My gods offer peace of the soul. Yours offers only evil in this life—and in the next."

LeGrand nodded. "Perhaps that is so. But everything has its price, and that price must be met."

Averting his eyes from the bloody mess of meat that had once been Craufux, he made himself step over the shredded corpse and onto the porch.

Esther arose and went to Veley, cradling the old man's head in her lap. With the swampie gone, tears sprang to her eyes. Veley's face glistened with sweat, but he managed a smile. "Child," he wheezed. "Take the cross. It is the symbol of your investiture."

He touched the crucifix, but his fingers trembled too violently to keep a grip on it. She closed a hand over his gnarled paw. "Without you, without the ceremony, the *loa* will not recognize me."

Painfully, Veley said, "I am but a vessel of the

loa. They will either recognize you or they will not. A ceremony is meaningless.''

His lips writhed back from his gums. ''And if they recognize you, so will others. Allies will be drawn to you—and enemies. Your allies can be found in the beforetime place...I purified it myself, long ago, but the old ones' energy will taint it once more.''

With groaning effort, he managed to half raise his head. Esther removed the crucifix from around his neck and slipped it on. ''The old ones were, the old ones shall be,'' he said. ''Their children endureth throughout the ages. They have only as much power as we grant them. You must remember that.''

He closed his eyes, and his body went slack, as if he were drifting off to sleep. The mastiff whined softly and nuzzled his limp hand. Esther laid Veley down on the sofa and arranged his body carefully, arms crossed over his chest, feet together. Swiping an angry hand over her tear-filled eyes, she stepped to the fireplace. With a pair of rusty tongs, she removed a flaming brand and inserted it beneath the sofa. The ancient fabric and stuffing caught almost immediately, flames bursting and licking from under it.

She repeated the procedure, using burning sticks of wood to set everything in the house on fire. As she did so, a voice whispered in her head, ''A fine fuel for the fires of purification.''

At length, when the interior of the house was a roaring inferno, she left her grandfather's dwelling and stood outside watching it burn, still naked except for the silver cross glinting between her taut breasts.

Absently, she stroked the mastiff's great head as it pressed against her thigh. She whispered half to herself, half to the giant dog, "Everything has its price."

Chapter 8

As it had done for thousands upon thousands of years, the Archuleta Mesa stood a silent vigil over the harsh, dry sands of the New Mexico wastelands. It rose sheer from the sunbaked sands, a monstrous monolith of stone nearly five hundred feet high, scarred by ages of erosion. It looked like an enormous tombstone, marking the grave of dead aeons.

Although nothing beyond thorny scrub-brush stirred around it, life still picked its way through the tunnels and levels constructed within its stony, deeply furrowed walls.

Within those walls, Baron Samarium spoke lowly. "If it is true that men manufacture explanations for things they cannot understand, then what must we concoct to explain this catastrophe?"

Standing beside him on the railed walkway, Baron Sharpe didn't even bother concealing the mockery in his tone when he echoed, "Catastrophe, brother? I'd judge it to be a death blow."

Thirty feet below lay a broad mezzanine. The pylons of the voltage-converter system tilted at twenty-degree angles, the ceramic facades cracked, split and burst. The fusion reactor was silent and dead. Built like a pair of solid black cubes, with a smaller cube balanced atop a larger, it didn't drone or rotate or generate even a tiny spark of power.

Baron Samarium said nothing for a long moment. Then softly, meditatively he commented, "Then unity is dead, too."

Baron Sharpe started to titter, then quickly pressed long, slender fingers over his mouth. "Is that why you asked me to meet you here, outside of the Council of the Nine, to tell me something I've known for months?"

The two men were dressed identically in the ceremonial garb of the baronial oligarchy—flowing, bell-sleeved robes of gold brocade, and tall, conical crested headpieces, ringed by nine rows of tiny pearls. Not only was their mode of dress identical, but they were also so similar in appearance, they might have been twins. In many ways, they were.

Their builds were small, slender and gracile. Both of their faces had sharp planes, with finely textured skin stretched tight over prominent shelves of cheekbones. The craniums were very high and smooth, the ears small and set very low on the head.

They shared the same close-cropped, blond hair, which possessed a wispy, duck-down quality. Baron Samarium's was perhaps a shade darker than Sharpe's. Their back-slanting eyes were very large, shadowed by sweeping, supra-orbital ridges.

Only eye color differentiated the two faces. Baron Samarium's eyes were jet-black, like damp pieces of obsidian. Sharpe's had the milky-blue color of mountain meltwater. They also held some spark, a glint that in a human being might have been interpreted as a sign of dementia.

The two barons made their way along the catwalk to the point where it abruptly became a stairway. They crossed the bare concrete to a square opening in the floor. A dim passageway led below. The air wafting up from below held a mixture of odors—the acrid sting of chemicals, stale smoke, and overlying it all, the sweetish stench of cooked meat.

Baron Sharpe fingered his nose. "A rather eclectic blend of stinks."

Without looking at him, Baron Samarium entered the opening, walking down the short flight of steps to a low-ceilinged anteroom. Splintered fragments of a wooden door hung within a frame, like rotten teeth coming loose from the gums. The barons pushed on through, entering a tile-floored corridor. At the end of the hall, they saw sheet-metal-sheathed double doors, askew on their hinges.

Beyond them lay a wide passageway. Under jury-rigged work lamps, splinters of glass glittered like a vast ice field beneath a noonday sun. Metal frame-works and support posts were twisted and bent, as if they were composed of paraffin exposed to extreme heat. Sections of the ceiling had collapsed, the I-beams projecting downward at forty-five-degree angles.

Slender figures in bodysuits picked their way

through the wreckage, looking to salvage anything that might conceivably be repaired.

"The damage is far more extensive than I was told," Baron Samarium murmured.

Sharpe nodded agreeably. "Indeed, brother. No reports, either verbal or in dispatches, could accurately convey the devastation wrought here."

"It's difficult to believe a handful of insurrectionists did all of this," Baron Samarium commented.

This time, Sharpe didn't even try to stifle a giggle. "As I understand it, they didn't do it directly, and perhaps not even intentionally. They certainly caused it to happen by turning our own deified technology against us."

Baron Samarium bit back a bitter retort. He had received the same information as Sharpe and so couldn't argue with him. According to the intelligence reports, the unbelievably destructive chain reaction had been triggered by the crash of an aircraft.

The aircraft itself hadn't been ordinary. In fact, two hundred years before, it had been the pinnacle of avionic achievement. Before the nukecaust, the Aurora enjoyed the status of the most closely guarded of military secrets. Supremely maneuverable, the aircraft were capable of astonishingly swift ascent and descent, able to take off vertically and hover absolutely motionless.

Powered by pulsating integrated gravity-wave engines and magnetohydrodynamic air spikes, the Aurora was a true marauder of the skies, and as such, the baronial hierarchy relied upon the aircraft to locate a source of raw genetic material, kill the donors, harvest their organs and tissues and return to the Archuleta Mesa for them to be processed.

The Aurora had crashed back into its underground hangar within seconds of its vertical launch. No one really knew how or why, but speculation was put forth that the aircraft was shot down while it hovered, most likely with a rocket launcher.

The crash breached the magnetic-field container of a fusion generator in the hangar. The result had been akin to unleashing the energy of the sun itself in an enclosed area. Although much of the kinetic force and heat was channeled upward and out through the hangar doors, a scorching, smashing wave swept through the installation. If not for the series of vanadium blast bulkheads, the entire mesa could have come tumbling down.

The technology for the Aurora aircraft had derived from the same source as the barons themselves—the so-called Archon Directorate.

If not for the Directorate, the vast installation within the Archuleta Mesa, on the border of New Mexico and Colorado, would not have been built. The facility had served as the headquarters for two overprojects relating to the Totality Concept. The various research projects dated back to World War II, when German scientists were laboring to build what turned out to be purely theoretical secret weapons for the Third Reich. The Allied powers adopted the researches, as well as many of the scientists, and constructed underground bases, primarily in the western United States, to further the experiments.

The Totality Concept was classified Above Top Secret. It was known only to a few very high-ranking military officers and politicians. Few of the Presidents who held office during its existence were ever aware of the full ramifications.

Buried within and beneath the Archuleta Mesa was a six-level research complex, built solely to house two major divisions of the Totality Concept; Overproject Whisper, which spawned the Operation Chronos and Project Cerberus subdivisions. The other division was Overproject Excalibur, which dealt primarily with bioengineering. If not for Excalibur, the barons would not have existed.

"I don't think you grasp the true implications this..." Baron Samarium paused, groping for a proper descriptive term. He realized that no matter what word he chose, it would still be woefully inadequate.

"Event?" Baron Sharpe supplied helpfully. "Incident? Affair? Or perhaps final solution, though less dramatic, would be more appropriate."

Samarium swung his head toward the other man, feeling a rush of anger at his brother's bantering tone. "Final solution to what?"

Sharpe fluttered his unnaturally long fingers through the air. "To who finally wins the contest for survival of the fittest—we of the hybrid dynasty, or the slouching throwbacks, our dispirited serfs and vassals.''

His fingers waggled over the wreckage, as if he were a stage magician about to perform a sleight-of-hand trick. ''In other words, the same oppressed, defeated race who somehow, magically, did all of this.'' He added softly, ''Hey, presto.''

As they made their way along the passageway, skirting heaps of debris, they saw a female hybrid digging through a tangle of coaxial cable and a litter of electronic components. Her compact, tiny-breasted form was encased in a silvery-gray, skintight bodysuit. As the barons approached, her huge, upslanting eyes of a clear crystal blue gave them a silent appraisal. The eyes looked haunted.

Turning to face them, she began swaying back and forth, like a reed in a mild breeze. The precise movements were a form of ritual greeting, an instinctive show of respect, if not submission.

''What is your name?'' Baron Samarium asked.

''I am called Quavell, Lord Baron,'' she replied crisply. A soul-deep weariness lurked at the back of her voice.

Samarium gestured to the wreckage. ''This happened two months ago. Is this all the progress that has been made in restoring the facility?''

''It happened a little less than two months ago,'' Quavell corrected him blandly. ''Fifty-three days and nine hours, to be exact. Our damage-control efforts have been severely hampered due to a lack of personnel. Nearly three-quarters of the installation's permanent staff were obliterated. Those closest to the epicenter of the explosion were vaporized. What little power we have was restored only ten days ago. Fortunately, the gateway unit on Level Four has its own independent nuclear generator, else you would not be on this tour at all.''

Baron Sharpe made a sound in his throat like a repressed chuckle. Samarium detected the gentle admonishment in Quavell's tone but decided to ignore it. Her name touched a chord of recognition within his memory.

"I remember your report," he said. "You actually came face-to-face with Kane, did you not?"

"I did, my lord. He spared my life."

Baron Samarium wagged his head in frustrated confusion. "Why would he do that?"

"I can only speculate. I no longer presented a threat, and therefore he saw no logical reason to kill me."

Baron Sharpe murmured, "Not exactly the behavior of the psychopathic maniac Baron Cobalt has made him out to be. He could have killed me, too. But he allowed me to live."

Samarium ignored the observation. Addressing Quavell, he stated, "This was the gestation ward. How fared the birthing ward?"

Quavell gestured down the debris-clogged passageway. "The survivors were placed in a room down there, Lord Baron.''

Baron Samarium tried to summon up a regal, dismissive nod. "As you were."

Quavell ducked her head. "Yes, Lord Baron."

He and Sharpe continued on down the corridor. Despite the dim light, they saw the rows of corpses lying on almost every inch of the glass-littered floor. They had to walk a circuitous route, stepping carefully between legs and pale faces. Although most of the bodies were hybrids, Samarium noticed a few humans mixed in.

"Why haven't these bodies been disposed of?" he demanded.

"I would imagine," replied Baron Sharpe, "that the corpses outnumber the living by a three-to-one margin. You shouldn't be so disturbed by the sight of death, brother. It can be a liberating experience. I should know."

Samarium knew of Baron Sharpe's bizarre delusion that he had died before and crossed back and was therefore immortal. Of all the oligarchy, Sharpe displayed the most human emotional characteristics—he could be capricious, ridiculous and unpredictable. For his high councilor he had chosen a crippled psi-mutie who, because of his horizontal form of locomotion, was known as Crawler.

He was further distinguished from his brothers by the fact he was the only baron other than Cobalt who had faced off against Kane. The renegade Magistrate had shot him, and if not for the intervention of Crawler, Sharpe would have died for a second time.

Strangely, Sharpe displayed no animosity toward Kane, no desire for vengeance. Baron Samarium didn't know why. He attributed Sharpe's equanimity to his own particular and peculiar psychology.

Still, Samarium scowled at him. "We are all facing extinction, brother. Me, you, the entire oligarchy."

Sharpe threw back his head and laughed. His headpiece fell from his domed cranium, but he made no move to pick it up. "Why should I fear death, brother?"

Samarium swallowed a sigh of annoyance.

"However," Sharpe continued, his high-planed face split by a disturbingly humanlike grin, "I am most curious about why the Archon Directorate has yet to step in. You and our brothers have been sidestepping that question for months, since the assassination of Baron Ragnar. We've been waiting for them to take an active hand in opposing our sea of troubles. And yet we who carry their blood, their agenda, their heritage, stand gaping at the stars, holding our collective underdeveloped pricks in our lilywhite hands and wondering where they are. Has it not occurred to them that if we—the barons—die, so do they?"

The nine barons knew the Archons had interfaced with and influenced human affairs for many thousands of years, and that their manipulation of humanity and religions was nearly all-pervasive. The nukecaust and the subsequent 150 years of barbarism

and anarchy were as much a result of the Directorate's intervention as the Program of Unification that
resulted in the rule of the nine baronies.

The philosophy was elegantly simple. Since irre-
sponsible humanity had allowed its world to be destroyed, humans would no longer be permitted to
have responsibility, even over their own lives. The
barons accepted the responsibility, or rather had it
ceded to them.

Not every human was invited to partake of the
bounty of the barons. Only the best of the best were
allowed full citizenship, with caste distinctions based
primarily on eugenics.

The barons paid a price for their superior abilities.
Physically, they were fragile, at the mercy of infec-
tions and diseases that had little effect on the primitive humans they ruled. Nor could they reproduce
by intercourse. All barons were the product of in vi-
tro fertilization, as were their offspring.

Therefore the barons lived insulated, isolated lives,
cloaked in theatrical trappings that not only added to
their semidivine mystique, but also protected them
from contamination—both psychological and physical.

Once a year, the oligarchy traveled to the installation beneath Archuleta Mesa for medical treat-
ments. They received fresh transfusions of blood and
a regimen of biochemical genetic therapy designed
to strengthen their autoimmune systems, thus grant-
ing them another year of life and power.

Though they were a biological bridge, hybrids of human and Archon DNA, the barons weren't precisely sure of the reasons behind the hybridization program.

They knew the Archons had been a dying race, on the verge of extinction before the nukecaust. They also knew the nukecaust itself to have been a major component of their program. After the masses of humanity had been culled, the herd thinned, then the hybrids would inherit the earth, carrying out the agenda of the Archon Directorate. All of the barons believed that they acted as the plenipotentiaries of the Archons.

But no baron had ever seen an Archon, although one had allegedly lived within the vast labyrinth of the mesa. Regardless, the barons weren't so blinded by arrogance that the irony was lost on them—in order to rule humans, they were dependent on the biological material the Archons provided.

Barons Sharpe and Samarium awkwardly climbed over a pile of rubble, lifting the hems of their robes. A jagged piece of rebar snagged Sharpe's robe and, muttering peevishly, he shrugged out of it. Samarium kept his face blank and composed when he saw what the baron wore under it. A violet jumpsuit with huge belled legs, flame-colored satin facings and a bat-winged collar encased his slender frame. Long fringe streamed from both sleeves. Worked in glittering rhinestones on the back were three letters: TCB.

Baron Samarium had seen him in this ridiculous

ensemble before. He knew his brother had found it in his ville's archive of vintage clothing and adopted it as his personal uniform. He also knew that Sharpe interpreted the TCB to mean To Cross Back. He had no idea of what it really meant.

The corridor opened into a huge room nearly a hundred yards across. It was filled with cribs. Actually, the cribs were more like little plastic boxes, transparent cages with no tops to them. In the cages were hybrid children, ranging in age from newborns to four month olds. All were naked and lying listlessly on excrement-stained foam pads. The room was illuminated by naked, red light bulbs jury-rigged to extension cords drooping from the ceiling.

As the two barons entered, some of the children raised huge eyes to them, but most cringed back into the pools of crimson-hued murk.

Baron Samarium moved from infant to infant, touching their overlarge craniums, whispering softly to them. "Most of them are already suffering from malnutrition and vitamin deficiencies," he said quietly.

He lifted one of the hybrid infants who seemed all ribs and distended belly, laying its bald and scabrous head against his shoulder. In a hoarse whisper, he said, "This is how our world ends...not with a snarl of defiance, but with the whimper of helpless babes."

Baron Sharpe said nothing.

Samarium returned the child to its cage, ignoring the thin arms straining toward him, a silent plea to be lifted again. "We must make plans, brother, if any of our kind is to survive. If not, what we see here is the last generation of the new human."

Sharpe shrugged. "We know that Kane and his group of terrorists are responsible for this. We just don't know where they can be found."

Baron Samarium shook his head. "A virulent disease is sweeping through my territories. If it spreads outward, with our diminished autoimmune systems and this treatment facility in ruins, the nine barons will perish. Survival is the key here, not seeking out and avenging ourselves on terrorists."

A thin, mirthless smile creased Sharpe's lips, but his tone was surprisingly grave when he said, "I concur. I suspect few of our fraternity will be in agreement with us, however. Particularly brother Cobalt. He among all of us is most obsessed with revenge upon Kane—and consolidating his own power, in flagrant disregard for the terms of unity."

Thoughtfully, Baron Samarium muttered, "Yes, I am aware of his efforts to monopolize the ore trade in Utah. Perhaps we should turn our minds and energies to unifying against him."

Baron Sharpe did not react with shock or horror at the implications of the suggestion. "It will be difficult to convince the others to see the situation as we do."

Face mottled with sudden spots of fury, Samarium swept the room and the cages with a wild wave of his arm. "They have not seen *this!* We of the hybrid dynasty are doomed if we do not seek outside aid. And it doesn't appear as if any will be forthcoming from the Archon Directorate.'' The last two words fairly dripped with scorn. ''If necessary, we must circumvent the oligarchy altogether and find other allies.''

Sharpe's thin smile broadened. ''Allies who have shown themselves to be extraordinarily resourceful?''

''Just so, brother.''

''Has it occurred to you that if brother Cobalt cannot locate Kane and his company of insurrectionists, the task you and I set for ourselves will be very formidable. Not just to find him, but to recruit him.''

Baron Samarium gazed sadly at the mewling infant in the cage. ''If we do not craft a new form of unification, then only annihilation awaits us. To prevent a biological armageddon, genocide, we must accept any task, no matter how insurmountable it may seem. The humans who caused this tragedy are now the only ones who can save us from it.''

Chapter 9

The swamp wag continued rolling on its rumbling, splashing path. Doyle sat down in a camp chair on the deck and untied the dirty twine from the packet of papers given to him by Veley. Trying to read while the vehicle jounced and bounced was laborious. It also gave him a headache when he tried to decipher the vile handwriting, but he persevered.

As he read the crude cursive script, he realized that Veley's great-great-grandfather had indeed written a genuine folktale, a tale of superstition handed down from generation to generation, a story from hundreds of years before.

They who ruled the night are gone—Atlach-Nacha, Cthuga, even great Cthulhu. It was a grim and secret war at the dim time of Man. Among the men of the Earth stole the frightful old ones, safeguarded by their horrid wisdom. No man knew who was true man and who false. No man could trust any man. Yet by means of their own craft, they formed ways by which the false might be known from the true.

Yet again the fiends came after the years of

forgetfulness had gone by—for man is still an ape in that he forgets what is not ever before his eyes. As holy men they returned, and for that men in their luxury had by then lost faith in religions and embraced them.

Such is the old ones' power that people bow again to them in new forms, and blind fools that they are, the great hosts of men see no connection between this new power and the power men overthrew aeons ago.

After the baffling, melodramatic preamble, Veley's ancestor launched into a narrative of the early nineteenth century.

Jean Lafitte, the notorious pirate, smuggler and black marketeer of the Gulf Coast, found willing allies in a colony of Cajun swamp dwellers. They were more than helpful to his illegal operations, from storing stolen merchandise to leading trains of slaves to the largest plantation in that part of Louisiana, owned by Ashley Cornelius.

Acceding to their wishes, Lafitte saw to the construction of a church deep in the bayous, because they were shunned by the citizens of the nearest settlement, the village of Lafayette. The colony lived in squalor, they were an admixture of many races, and were believed to retain the worst qualities of each, with none of the good points. So the Cajuns had no choice but to marry without the sanction of the church, and their children went unbaptized. Criminals they might be, but still they sought redemption.

Lafitte not only built them a place of worship but provided a priest, as well. The latter seemed a far more difficult undertaking than the construction of the church, but Lafitte found a priest who agreed to go into the swamps and redeem the heathen. The circumstances under which the buccaneer found a willing holy man were unusual, but nobody questioned them.

Father Ocajnik had been rescued from a foundering ship in the Gulf of Mexico. The crew and passengers had all died of plague. Ocajnik claimed to be a Serbian nobleman by birth who had relinquished his title and lands to serve the Catholic Church. In gratitude for his rescue, Ocajnik joined Lafitte's expedition deep into the interior of Louisiana.

Doyle read of their wanderings, told in a surprisingly florid style, as the old Cajun's ancestors had handed down the tale for more than three hundred years before he inscribed it to paper. The bare written words hinted at all the hardships, the deprivations, the attacks by Indians, the outbreaks of malaria.

But it was another peril the manuscript described—of men dying of disease, coughing up blood. By the time the little expedition reached the Cajun colony, only Father Ocajnik had survived. He immediately took up housekeeping in the newly constructed church and prayed for the souls of all the men who had died bringing him there. He ended each service by kissing the parishioners and telling them they would live forever.

But the strange plague continued. People began deserting the settlement, staggering through the wilderness, lost, dazed and helpless. They reeled through the swamps, calling on the saints or blaspheming them in their terror.

First they sought help from Ashley Cornelius, but the plantation owner drove them off. It was whispered that Cornelius benefited from Ocajnik's arrival, since the father provided him with slaves for his fields in return for his protection. Further rumors had it that Cornelius had been kissed by Ocajnik and was now one of his flock.

The people then sought aid from the *houngan* of the local voodoo cult, Daddy Lefevre. They spoke to him of fighting frenziedly against sleep, of their brothers, children and wives falling from exhaustion and dying in their sleep.

But then they awoke as revenants, arising from their deathbeds and taking orders only from Father Ocajnik.

The *houngan's* suspicion centered on the priest. Doyle read:

And now it was evident to the *houngan* that the priest was actually a creature who subsisted on the blood of the living, and infected them with a plague that made them choose between life and death. He did not seek to save souls, but to claim them.

Daddy Lefevre and the few colonists who still lived went searching for Ocajnik and found him stretched out in sleep beneath the great paving stone of the chapel. The *houngan,* with his arcane knowledge of herbs and spells, called on the entire assemblage of *loa* to help him contain the evil. He invoked the names Papa Legba, Maitre Carrefour, Amelia, Bazo, Danger Mina, Gangan, Ogoun, Wangol and Erzilie.

"With their help," wrote Veley's great-great-grandfather, "the *houngan* placed the spell of the not-dead on Ocajnik and buried him beneath the site of the church—God grant until Judgment Day."

There the manuscript ended. Doyle lifted his eyes from the papers, his heart pounding. For all intents and purposes, Judgment Day had arrived, nearly two hundred years before.

The vehicle gave a great, shuddering lurch, nearly throwing Doyle to the deck. He cursed, trying to keep the papers from scattering. Over the throb of the engines, Raeder announced, "I think we're here."

Steadying himself, Doyle walked to the driver's seat. He saw that "here" was only a comparatively high, fairly open piece of ground surrounded by underbrush. The buggy's blunt prow tore through it, uprooting shrubs and snapping off saplings. Every-

one was forced to slap aside the dangling strands of
Spanish moss.

In the center of the clearing rose a peculiar grassy
hump, overgrown with weeds and kudzu vines. Only
by peering closely could Doyle make out the outline
of a structure. Patches of dark gray stone were visible
beneath the covering of plant growth.

"*This* is the place that old fart talked about?"
Flandry demanded skeptically.

Doyle didn't answer. To Raeder he said, "Stop us
here. We'll go the rest of the way on foot."

Raeder pressed down on the brake, shifting the
gears with a nerve-stinging clashing, and keyed off
the engine. The four men alighted onto the marshy
ground surrounding the glade.

Brackett pointed down. "Look here."

They saw the prints of small bare feet impressed
into the moist earth. They were sunk far deeper than
their size indicated they should.

"Whoever made them were little but solid,"
grunted Raeder. He swept the surroundings with a
fierce, penetrating gaze.

Doyle wasn't interested in footprints, regardless of
their size. He strode deliberately across the thirty-odd
yards to the mound, heedless of the briars and creepers snagging his clothing.

He crossed the clearing and stopped at the sloping
edge of the hillock, examining it closely. Chunks of
black, burned wood that had turned to charcoal jutted

up between the weeds. Flandry, Raeder and Brackett joined him.

"Now what?" Flandry asked impatiently.

"Let's clear away some of this shit," Doyle replied.

Flandry didn't move. "What the hell for? That's grunt work."

A sudden flash of anger sublimated Doyle's fear of the man. He whirled on him, snapping, "You *are* grunts! And we do it because there's something I want to check out. Because it may have bearing on the outcome of this mission. And most importantly—" he slapped his chest "—because *I* fucking say so!"

Mags, although reeking of arrogant self-confidence, were conditioned to always obey orders. Doyle's surprising display of angry assertiveness reminded them he had been chosen by Baron Samarium himself to lead the mission. After a silent moment, Flandry, Raeder and Brackett fell in and began uprooting weeds.

They cleared a path to the summit of the mound, their labor punctuated by panting curses. They shed parts of their armor, working in their Kevlar undersheathings. Doyle sent Raeder back to the swamp wag to fetch tools, and he returned with spades, pry bars and a heavy-duty flashlight.

The sun had not yet set, and Doyle believed he could open the mound deeply enough to determine its nature before dark. If not, he decided to work by flashlights, He set to work with the frenetic energy characteristic of an academic dedicated to solving a historical mystery. The task was no light one; the soil baked by generations of sun was iron hard and mixed with rocks and pebbles and splintered timbers.

Doyle sweated profusely and grunted with his efforts, but the fire of the discovery was on him. He shook the sweat out of his eyes and drove in the short-handled pick with deep strokes that ripped and crumbled the packed dirt.

The sun began its slow descent, and in the long purple twilight he and the three Mags worked on. Doyle was almost oblivious to time or space and certainly to the breathless complaints of the other men. In the gathering dusk, he felt his pick strike heavily against something stonelike and unyielding.

Examination by feel, as well as by sight showed him a solid block of stone, roughly hewed, five feet wide and three feet thick. Doubtless it had formed one of the old structure's walls. Knowing it was useless to try to shatter it, Doyle chipped and pecked about it, scraping away the dirt and pebbles. Raeder turned on the flashlight, directing the beam onto the block of stone. Silver glimmered beneath a film of soil.

It was in the shape of a crucifix, as if the ore had been melted and, while still molten, poured over the stone in a design similar to the token Veley wore around his neck.

Doyle dug around the corners of the block until

he felt that wrenching it out would be but a matter of sinking the pick point and pry bar underneath and levering it out.

"Let's get this stone up," he grunted.

"Are you fused out?" Flandry demanded. "You don't think the source of the plague is down there, do you?"

Doyle groped for a response, unable to find a reasonable-sounding answer. All of a sudden, he realized he had been caught in the grip of a compulsion and he had no inkling why.

While he stood there, blinking the sweat out of his eyes, Brackett raised his spade and brought its edge down against the silver seal. One arm of the cross broke away entirely from the vertical main body.

Doyle swung on him, raging. "What the fuck do you think you're doing?"

Brackett regarded him dispassionately. "Why the fuck not?"

He bent down and picked up the flat ribbon of gleaming metal, turning it over in his hands as if he were trying to gauge its weight. "This looks like solid silver. Probably worth some jack."

Flandry all of a sudden looked interested. "There may be more of it under all this shit. Be nice to go back to the ville with something other than bug bites."

"Yeah, it'll be something other than scrip to barter with," Raeder said.

Hard currency, or "jack," didn't exist in and around the villes. Each baron printed up his own scrip, and since all ville citizens had their needs met in terms of lodging, food and medical attention, anything other than the scrip was considered superfluous.

But down in the Tartarus Pits, it was a different story. All sorts of unique contraband forbidden to the citizens who lived in the Residential Enclaves could be found and traded for there.

Raeder knelt down and shoved the end of his pry bar beneath the stone, heaving on it with gasps of exertion. Doyle watched him silently.

A bird called hauntingly from the dark shadows of the tree line. Doyle became aware of a faint, foul odor exuding from the cracks in the stone. It had a charnel house reek about it.

Raeder swore and straightened up reluctantly, covering his nose. Then he stiffened. All of them heard a faint rustling from beneath the block of stone. Doyle's first thought was snakes. There might be a dozen rattlers or cottonmouths coiled up beneath the square of finished rock. He shivered at the thought and backed away.

"Don't do anything more," he ordered. "Let's leave it alone until morning."

The three Magistrates didn't acknowledge his command. Doyle caught the brief eye exchange between them and cringed inwardly.

"Why don't you go back to the wag and get some sleep?" suggested Brackett helpfully.

"Yeah," drawled Flandry, tone heavy with sarcasm. "Leave the grunt work to the grunts."

Doyle opened his mouth to voice a profane protest, then he flinched beneath the steady, unblinking pressure of Flandry's gaze. He realized he could do nothing. The Mags had cooperated with him earlier because they saw no sound reason not to do so. Now they couldn't give a shit about what he said. They would do what they wanted, and if Doyle interfered, the least he could expect would be the spade laid upside his head.

Without another word, trembling with frustration and fatigue, Doyle turned on his heel and left the mound. He hadn't even reached the swamp wag when the heard the clinking sounds of their renewed excavations.

He climbed the ladder to the vehicle's deck, not about to sleep on the ground where snakes and rats could bed down with him. He threw a tarpaulin on the floor and lay down, noting how the clouds piling over the starscape were blue-black in color. He heard the rumble of distant thunder and briefly considered crawling beneath the tarp, but while he was still thinking about it, he fell asleep.

His slumber was deep but fitful. The mystic unfathomed reaches opened in the recesses of his unconscious, and his mind's eye gazed back through the vast gulfs that spanned life and death. Through the vague and ghostly fogs, he saw dim shapes reliving the dead aeons—men in combat with hideous creatures, vanquishing a planet overrun with frightful terrors.

Doyle jerked awake, gasping, snorting water from his nose. Without a preliminary drizzle or patter of raindrops, the storm had swept in with full fury. Gale-force gusts of wind rattled the leaves and branches of trees. The sky was crowded with thunderclaps and lightning strokes.

Wind-driven sheets of cold rain poured down, mixed with tiny fragments of hail. Within seconds of awakening, Doyle was soaked to the skin. Thumbing away beads of moisture from the LED of his wrist chron, he saw it was almost one o'clock in the morning. With a start, he realized he'd been asleep for nearly six hours.

Using his hands to shield his eyes from the downpour, he peered around the deck of the buggy and saw nothing but widening pools of water. Neither Raeder, Flandry nor Brackett was aboard. He sat for a few seconds, blinking through the shroud of rain, wondering what to do. Calling to the Mags would be a pointless exercise. Even if they had been aboard, they could not have heard him over the constant pounding of the rain, the overlapping thunderclaps and the thrash of wind-whipped foliage.

Doyle heaved himself to his feet, took a flashlight and Browning Hi-Power handblaster from the supply case. He climbed over the side of the swamp buggy, sinking nearly ankle deep in the water-saturated ground. He slogged through the mud, in the direction of the mound.

He passed into the shadows of the trees and dense

underbrush, noting that he didn't see the glow of the flashlight Raeder had fetched from the wag. He sensed an expectant tension in the night. The shadows suddenly seemed too thick, too breathless.

By the time he reached the mound, the worst of the downpour had eased to a steady drizzle and the thunderclaps were no longer as frequent. He lifted his flashlight and swore bewilderedly. Not only were the three Mags nowhere in sight, but the beam revealed the great block of stone thrust carelessly to one side. Warily, he climbed the hillock and shone the flashlight into the niche made by the stone. At first he saw nothing but wet earth, then the beam touched a silver glint in the mud.

Doyle bit back a cry of surprise. He picked up the object and held it close to his water-beaded eyeglasses. It was caked and corroded with rust, worn almost paper thin, but he knew it for what it was— a duplicate of the crucifix worn by Veley.

With a sudden revulsion, he dropped the tiny cross back onto the ground and shouted, "Flandry! Raeder! Brackett!"

Doyle heard nothing, not even the trill of a night bird. He stared across the shallow mud flats and saw a shadow move. The stars were still obscured by thunderheads, and the shadows made vision uncertain. But he knew he saw a man-shaped figure.

Doyle swallowed, wondering why a peculiar trembling had suddenly taken hold of him. He tried to drown the feeling that there was something odd about the gait of the dim shadow-shape, which had seemed to move with a sort of slinking, silent lope.

Doyle climbed off the mound, standing silent and uncertain. Then he yelled again, at the top of his lungs, *"Flandry!"*

He didn't expect to hear anything, so when the frightful scream knifed through the stillness, he staggered as from a blow. He wanted to clap his hands over his ears to shut out the soul-freezing horror of the sound that rose unbearably, and then broke in gurgles and gasps.

He ran through the foliage in the direction of the scream as fast as his legs could carry him. He struck a sapling and rebounded from it. He shouted for Flandry, for Raeder and Brackett, but again received no answer. He readied himself for what he might see, but no amount of preparation could have prepared him what he saw under the boughs of a sycamore.

All three of the Magistrates lay on the dirt, arms spread wide, eyes staring, mouths gaping open in slack-lipped idiocy. Reluctantly, he knelt beside the corpses of the Mags. Whatever sort of death had come to them, it had been been swift but unpleasant. The waxy faces of Flandry, Raeder and Brackett were frozen in twisted masks of horror and agony.

Doyle examined them and realized they weren't dead as he had first feared, but in some sort of coma, their respiration so shallow and labored it was almost undetectable. By shining the beam of the flashlight upon them, he found no wounds, no marks of knives or bludgeons. All he saw was a thin smear of blood on each of their lips, as if they had internally hemorrhaged. But there didn't seem to be enough blood to have caused them to lose consciousness.

A grisly speculation rose up in the dark corners of Doyle's mind. He remembered what the account written by Veley's ancestor had said: "The *houngan* placed the spell of the not-dead on Ocajnik and buried him beneath the site of the church—God grant until Judgment Day."

Doyle shrank from the black visions crowding into his mind. An undead monster stirring in the fetid gloom of the sepulchre, thrusting from within to push aside the stones loosened by human tools—a shadowy shape loping through the swamp.

He started to curse, but the words froze in his throat. He glimpsed a hint of stealthy movement among the stunted shadows beneath the Spanish moss. In the gloom beyond, tiny points of red fire seemed to dance and shift in weird rhythm. Faintly, at the edges of his hearing, he heard the soft pattering rustle of many feet on loose leaves.

Doyle sprang to his feet, feeling the hairs on the nape of his neck tingle and lift at the prospect of the horde of rats encircling him. He whirled and ran in the opposite direction, fleeing as a panicked rabbit might run, heedless of direction or obstacles. He blundered through brush, stumbled and fell in the mud, rose to run again. He felt his heart pounding so violently, he wondered if it might burst in his chest.

Lightning occasionally flashed in the sky, but didn't provide enough illumination for him to see by.

He stumbled on a cypress knee and staggered against the trunk of a tree. Hugging it, his breath rasping in and out of his throat in ragged sobs, he knew he could run no longer. He had either evaded the rats or he hadn't. He turned around, putting his back to the trunk, and squinted into the darkness.

A flash of lightning showed him nothing but murk-clotted foliage, and he sagged in relief. Then a dozen figures appeared out of the shadows, suddenly and silently. One second there was nothing but darkness; the next second the creatures were there. They stood in a motionless cluster, staring at him silently. They were stocky of build, not one of them taller than five feet and not one of them looked to weigh less than 220. Most of them had negroid features and dark complexions, but their hair was varied in color and texture.

What did not vary about them was the pattern of raised scar tissue around their eyes.

The swampies stared at Doyle and he stared back, very slowly lifting the Browning in a trembling hand. They didn't react to it, either as a weapon or an object of interest. They merely stood and stared. Doyle smelled, borne on the wind, the foul scent that had hung about the mound.

The swampies moved in a slow, shuffling sidestep, the group parting. Out of the darkness behind them, two icy eyes glared. Doyle backed up, his gun shaking in his hand. The eyes grew larger, but he didn't scream. He could not. His tongue was frozen to the roof of his mouth, his throat constricted.

Framed in the blackness stood a vulpine shape, seeming to radiate a savage cold and the stink of foul mud and charnel house decay.

Doyle stared at the yellow-green eyes, the pale starlight making them luminous, inhuman pools. He took in the long black fingernails, the hairless head with malformed ears. The lipless mouth curved back in a grin, exposing oversize, discolored teeth. The body was naked, the pallid flesh streaked with wet dirt and mud. He could just make out a small livid red scar in the center of the creature's chest, in the shape of a cross. The thing took a long, deliberate step toward him.

Doyle fired point-blank and saw a shred of flesh fly from the creature's breast. It reeled beneath the impact of the high-velocity slug, then righted itself. Its eyes flamed, and for an instant there was an impression of blurring movement over the creature's body, such as ripples made in water when a fish swims close to the surface.

The bony, ridged face melted away, and a warm, comforting smile sat upon handsome, chiseled features. Doyle focused on the yellow-green eyes, and something like an electric shock struck his mind.

The tendons and bones in his hand suddenly spasmed, and the Browning dropped from his nerveless fingers to the dirt. Doyle staggered blindly back against the trunk of a tree.

The swampies silently surrounded him, grasping his arms, spread-eagling him against the tree, transfixing him like a butterfly pinned to a board. The handsome, smiling man approached him, the smile widening to a grin. A dark and mottled, glistening thing uncoiled from his mouth, like the questing head of a serpent.

At its tip, Doyle saw a tiny, black barb, like the stinger of a bee. From the open mouth, the stench of rotting flesh rolled, wafting over Doyle's face, filling his nostrils until his belly lurched.

"Kiss me and live forever," Ocajnik croaked.

Chapter 10

DeFore slapped the stack of spreadsheets and declared, "If the symptoms weren't enough to convince me, then the rat reports are the clinchers."

Puzzled, Bry inquired, "Rats?"

"The bubonic plague was transmitted from sick rats to humans by fleabites."

"Yech," Bry muttered.

Lakesh grunted disinterestedly. "Outbreaks of the plague still happened in the twentieth century, particularly in Third World countries, even in poverty-stricken areas of India. The disease there was largely eliminated by the mass extermination of rats."

"You don't seem particularly perturbed about this," Brigid commented dryly.

Lakesh grunted again. "There are remedies available in the ville medical sections."

DeFore gave him a scowl. "Yes, antibiotics like oxytetracycline, streptomycin and chloramphenicol, but they're not always effective, partly because the disease is so communicable. As far as we know, this is a mutated strain resistant to antibiotics. If it continues to spread unchecked, we're looking at a very real possibility of a repeat of medieval history."

Lakesh said nothing, folding his arms over his chest. Studying his expressionless face, Brigid suddenly understood his uncharacteristic apathy.

"The barons," she stated. "If the plague is fatal to humans, you're hoping it will be fatal to the hybrids as well. They're already susceptible to an entire range of congenital immune-deficiency diseases, and now, without the Dulce installation to provide them with medical treatment, you *want* the plague to spread."

Lakesh finally showed some emotion. Eyes flashing in annoyance, he countered, "If the barons contract it, wouldn't it be a faster and more bloodless way to end their reign than our guerrilla war against them?"

DeFore snorted in derision. "In my medical opinion, using the Black Death as a weapon certainly qualifies as a case of the cure being worse than the disease. Like I said, what if it's mutated and there's no effective cure? I'd expect that kind of callous, overkill attitude from Kane, but not from you."

Lakesh only shrugged, and Brigid felt a chill at the base of her spine. Up until a couple of months ago, Lakesh had made all the decisions in Cerberus, from policy to diet. Now decisions were no longer within his exclusive purview. The mini coup d'état staged by Kane, Brigid and Grant a short time before had seen to that.

Lakesh hadn't been unseated from his position of authority, but he was now answerable to a more democratic process. At first he bitterly resented what he construed as the usurping of his power, but recently he seemed to have come to terms with it. He really had no choice, because Kane, Grant and Brigid were privy to his secret recruitment program.

Almost every exile in the redoubt had arrived as a convicted criminal—after Lakesh had framed them for crimes against their respective villes. He had admitted it was a cruel, heartless plan with a barely acceptable risk factor, but it was the only way to spirit them out of their villes, turn them against the barons, make them feel indebted to him.

This bit of explosive and potentially fatal knowledge had not been shared with the other exiles in the redoubt. Now Brigid wondered if Lakesh's acceptance of the new democratic order was a facade, and his bitterness all-consuming.

"Friend Kane's extreme confrontational methods have accomplished far more than my cautiously planned approach," Lakesh said. "I don't think anybody here can debate that."

"We're not debating strategy," Brigid shot back. "We're—"

The computer beeped, signaling the completion of the search process. On the monitor screen glowed a symbol resembling a thick-walled pyramid, enclosing and partially bisected by three elongated but reversed triangles. Small disks topped each one, lending them a resemblance to round-hilted daggers. It was the unifying insignia of the Archon Directorate, one adopted by Overproject Excalibur. Brigid knew the symbol represented a pseudomystical triad functioning within a greater, all-embracing body.

But to her, all it represented was the co-optation and deliberately planned extinction of the human race.

She directed the cursor to the menu and made her selection. "Enterprise Eternity," she read aloud.

She swiftly skimmed the words, glowing amber against black. "It was less an actual subdivision of Excalibur than a kind of general melting pot for bioengineering concepts. There are links here to privately funded researches like Project Calypso, which was evidently connected to the SCOU."

"SCOU?" echoed DeFore.

"The Special Cybernetics Operations Unit headquartered in White Sands," Lakesh said. "A sort of last-ditch attempt at a police force. It ceased any and all functions over 150 years ago."

"What connection does it have to this Enterprise Eternity thing?" Brigid asked.

Lakesh swiveled his chair, peering over the rims of his spectacles. He read a few lines and made a "hmm" sound of realization. "Now I remember. Enterprise Eternity dealt with life extension, with retarding the aging process."

Impatiently, DeFore demanded, "Well, don't keep us in suspense. Tell us about it."

Brigid read far faster than Lakesh, faster than anyone in the redoubt—in fact, faster than anyone she had ever met. "Essentially," she said, "the enterprise based its initial experiments on Donner Denckla's proposal, that as we get older, the pituitary gland, the master gland that controls the activity of our other glands, produces a hormone that causes us to age and die."

DeFore chuckled sardonically. "It would be nice to believe the whole matter of aging is caused by a hormone or a particular gene. But that's bullshit."

Absently, eyes skimming the file, Brigid replied, "According to this, Denckla's proposal was never fully discredited. It led to the discovery of genes that regulate the production of two enzymes that serve as antioxidants. Disabling those genes in lab rats increased the production of these enzymes and lengthened their life spans by seventy percent."

"How long does a rat live anyway?" DeFore challenged. "A couple of years? If aging is genetic in nature, then you'd expect to find the occasional humans who, because of a hormonal mutation in the relevant gene, would be basically immortal. I don't recall reading of any records of immortal mutants."

Brigid suddenly straightened in her chair, her spine stiffening. "Apparently, Enterprise Eternity was trying to make a few. But they approached the problem from a unique angle…by trying to control a form of nutritional deficiencies, through the processing of chemicals like squalamine and AKG."

"AKG?" DeFore repeated. "Alkyglycerol?"

Brigid nodded.

"Those are compounds that help produce and stimulate white blood cells, a natural booster to the immune system."

"Yes," replied Brigid. "According to this file, AKG is an extraordinarily potent antioxidant that can retard, even reverse the aging process."

"You're talking blood therapy?" DeFore asked.

"Again, in a way. The human test subjects were screened for the genetic component of pernicious anemia."

DeFore threw up her hands in frustrated bewilderment. "What the hell does a blood disease have to do with immortality?"

Brigid didn't answer for such a long time that an exasperated DeFore almost repeated her question. Brigid finally said, in a low, hoarse voice, "It has a lot to do with it...when you're trying to manufacture vampires."

THE OBJECTIVE of Enterprise Eternity was, on the face of it, insane. But by reading further, Brigid gradually admitted the methodology it employed was firmly rooted in the genetic sciences.

The undertaking began in 1999, utilizing hybrid cells. The report was unclear, perhaps deliberately so, on how the cells were obtained or why they were unidentifiable, though a footnote in the body of the copy indicated a link to the SCOU file.

Redoubt 47 was a biolab, its location in the bayous chosen because of its proximity to an extended family group who, for generations, had lived in the area. The Cornelius family was chosen because of a hereditary form of pernicious anemia they passed on. Their disease was instrumental to the effects the enzymes produced by the transgenic cells.

Apparently, the Cornelius family was convinced to cooperate by being promised a cure. In reality, they were being transformed.

Over a period of sixteen months, two siblings in the family developed an adaptation in their digestive tract that allowed them to absorb blood and extract the genes that produced hemoglobin in the human body. Hemoglobin was, of course, the oxygen-carrying component in the blood.

Furthermore, the two subjects were able to internally process the blood into its constituent parts, which distributed the RNA for maximum reconstruction of their immune systems and minimized the cellular deterioration caused by aging.

However, Enterprise Eternity didn't foresee the host of side effects that began to afflict the two most responsive members of the Cornelius family. One of the symptoms was diagnosed as porphyria, a blood disease that could only be treated by massive transfusions of hemoglobin—or in the case of the two siblings, an almost obsessive thirst for human blood that they began to ingest orally.

The Enterprise Eternity report didn't state with any certainty what befell the unfortunate Cornelius family. It simply ended with the words: Observations: Ongoing.

The link to the SCOU file was even more maddeningly incomplete, added at least twenty years after the final entry on the Cornelius test subjects. With an almost mocking dearth of details, it told of a mission undertaken by a SCOU soldier code-named Falconer to the bayous in and around Lafayette. He had been dispatched to nip in the bud the organizing force behind a rising army of swamp muties. The organizing force was referred to as "Ocajnik," but the report did not state if Ocajnik was a man, woman, animal or vegetable, or bigger than a breadbox.

Lakesh nodded frequently throughout Brigid's verbal encapsulation of the file.

"Redoubt 47," he said when she was done. "I remember mentions of it now."

Brigid frowned slightly. She had been told that all the official designations of the Totality Concept–related redoubts were based on the radio call signs for letters. She said, "A number doesn't fit in with the coding of the rest of the installations. Bravo, Zulu, Papa—"

Lakesh held up a hand before she recited the entire list of redoubts. "That's because Redoubt 47 wasn't intended to be a permanent facility. As I recall, the installation of a quantum interphase inducer was a very late addition."

Brigid looked toward the Mercator map stretching across the far wall. "Are the jump lines still active?"

"Let's find out. Mr. Bry…?"

"On it," the man responded. After a few moments of key-tapping, a yellow light glowed in the lower portion of the southeastern United States.

"It is," Lakesh announced.

"If Redoubt 47 was a bioengineering facility," DeFore ventured uneasily, "roughly in the same region as the outbreak of bubonic plague, the conclusion is fairly obvious. Somebody opened a door and let the bacillus out. And it's probably mutated."

"Not necessarily," replied Lakesh. "I'm sure the sanitary conditions down in the bayous are probably worse than they are in the Tartarus Pits. Hygiene doesn't play a large role in day-to-day lives there."

DeFore heaved a weary sigh. "None of this makes much sense, even taking into account the fused-out brains of most of the whitecoats working for the Totality Concept back then."

She noticed Lakesh's lips twitching in a moue of distaste and she put in hastily. "Present company excluded, of course. Anyway, we've got scientific attempts to make the myths of vampires a reality, all springing from unidentifiable chimeric cells. Where did those genes come from? Surely not Balam."

Over the past few months, they had learned that the source of genetic material that created the barons and the hybrids had derived solely from Balam, by his own admission, the last Archon on Earth. Archon DNA was infinitely adaptable, its segments achieving a near seamless sequencing pattern with whatever biological material was spliced to it. It could be tinkered with to create endless variations.

"That's a possibility," said Lakesh, tugging at his nose distractedly. "But in the instance of Enterprise Eternity, it doesn't seem very likely. Creating human mutations cast in the mold of fanged creatures of folklore who have to ingest human blood in order to survive doesn't seem very efficient, regardless of their longevity."

"I recollect an entry in *The Wyeth Codex* pertaining to an encounter with a family of Southern aristocrats down there," Brigid declared. "Dr. Wyeth called them the Cornelius family. She claimed they were vampires—or rather she said they *thought* they were vampires and so behaved accordingly. Her opinion was they got some sick thrill out of playing vampire, saying they'd overdosed on Anne Rice... whoever she was."

"A twentieth-century novelist," said Lakesh flatly. "In a series of books, she popularized the concept that becoming bloodsucking cadavers was an attractive aspiration."

DeFore squinted toward him suspiciously. "Attractive to whom?"

"Nobody you'd want marrying your daughter," he answered.

"At any rate," Brigid went on, "if the Cornelius family contracted porphyria, their relentless drive for human blood wasn't just psychological—it was biological."

"I still don't understand what any of this has to do with an outbreak of bubonic plague," DeFore said doggedly.

Slowly, Lakesh declared, "In ancient times, particularly in Europe, the plague and vampirism were believed to be aspects of the same phenomenon. Vampires were considered plague bringers, and it was thought necessary to find and destroy the original vampire, not his every victim, to end the epidemic. The historical correlation between outbreaks of plague and reports of vampirism is strange."

Brigid inhaled a long breath through her nostrils. Quietly, she said, "Does anybody else want to say it or shall I?"

Lakesh angled a quizzical eyebrow at her. "Say what?"

"There's only one sure way to find out."

DeFore's brown eyes widened, then narrowed to slits. "You're proposing to jump to Redoubt 47?"

"Why not?"

"Off the top of my head," she answered icily, "I can think of a dozen reasons why not. But I'll just point out the major one." She paused, then declared very loudly, with a great deal of vehemence, "It's probably the epicenter of a goddamn epidemic!"

Brigid smiled wryly. "An epidemic that is spreading outward, maybe mutated, maybe treatable. Until we find out its cause, all we can do is sit here and compile a body count."

Lakesh shook his head. "We're not even sure of

the actual symptomology. All we have to go by are those disjointed reports from Samariumville.''

''All the more reason to do a hands-on investigation,'' Brigid replied.

Bry peered over the big VGA monitor screen that dominated the master ops console. ''And maybe become infected yourself and bring the bug back here.''

''We can wear the environmental suits, the ones we used when we jumped to the *Parallax Red* space station.'' Brigid turned her level gaze to Lakesh. ''You told us they were designed to be used in toxic environments, that they were completely airtight.''

Lakesh nodded reluctantly. ''That's right.''

Brigid swung around to face DeFore. ''How about it, Doctor? Ready for an excursion into the field?''

The woman wet her lips nervously. ''When?''

''As soon as possible.''

Shocked, DeFore demanded, ''You mean just you and me?''

''Me and you.''

''Without Grant or Kane?''

Brigid swallowed an angry retort that leaped unbidden to her tongue. ''They aren't our nursemaids. They don't always have to tag along when we conduct recces. You're more important to this one than Kane—I mean, than both of them are.''

Uncertainly, DeFore inquired, ''We're just jumping to the redoubt?''

''To collect some samples and bring them back

here for analysis. I'm not interested in taking a tour of the swamps.''

Lakesh had not offered any word of encouragement or discouragement, but Brigid felt his appraising stare and she knew what he was thinking. Over the past couple of months, Brigid's resentment over a perceived reliance on Kane had become more difficult to conceal.

Ever since Lakesh had relinquished his position of final authority, most of the Cerberus personnel looked to Kane as the decision maker and arbiter of policy and actions. Brigid understood why, but she sometimes felt she had been forced into the role of Kane's sidekick, incapable of deciding courses of action of her own.

She supposed she knew Kane better than anyone else in the redoubt except for Grant, but in many ways she knew more about him than Grant. It was true he was decisive, but his choices weren't always right. Not only had she suffered, but she had watched people die due to his swift decisions.

DeFore pushed out an anxious breath, half groan, half sigh of resignation. ''Shouldn't we at least wait until they come back? They may need medical attention. They usually do, you know.''

Brigid didn't need the reminder. ''That could be days from now. Besides, Auerbach is free from confinement, and you've been training Banks in medicine.''

Lakesh bristled. "Auerbach may be free, but—" He bit off the rest of his words.

"Let him start earning his keep again," Brigid said coldly.

Sounding a little intimidated by Brigid's tone and demeanor, Bry said hesitantly, "There's another consideration…with the glitch in the Comsat, we won't get any telemetry from the transponder."

"All I'm proposing," Brigid declared in a measured, deliberate tone, "is a look-see at Redoubt 47 and some sample collection. Whether the biolink transponders are off-line won't make much of a difference. I don't recall anybody sending in the cavalry when the transponders transmitted stress signals before."

Bry muttered something in concession and sank back behind the monitor screen. Brigid rose from the chair and faced DeFore. "I'd prefer it if you went with me, but I'm going regardless of your company."

DeFore nodded. "I'll go with you."

Brigid sympathized with her reluctance and appreciated her decision. During her nearly four years as an exile, DeFore had only once ventured from the redoubt, and then as part of a rescue party to retrieve the imprisoned Lakesh from Cobaltville. Most of the time, she didn't even like to walk outside on the plateau.

"I'll inventory the antibiotics I have in storage,"

DeFore continued, ''and bring along what may be of use.''

''Thanks. Let's meet in the ready room in say—'' Brigid glanced at the wall chron ''—two hours.''

Noticing the tense glance DeFore cast toward the chron, she added, ''Maybe Domi, Grant and Kane will be back by then.''

Even that prospect didn't seem to relax her. She nodded and murmured dubiously, ''Maybe.''

Chapter 11

In the privacy of her own quarters, Brigid had no problem admitting to herself that the prospect of embarking on a mat-trans journey without Kane made her extremely nervous.

She had made jumps without him in the past, but never had she experienced this degree of trepidation. She wondered if her relationship hadn't turned into one of codependence. That possibility only increased her anxiety and awakened anger—not so much at him, but at herself.

In the living room, she took a seat at the comp-equipped desk against one wall. She had been forced to leave behind her few personal items when she escaped Cobaltville, but she'd found some big reference books in a storage room to take up space on the shelves. Once known as "coffee table" books, they were full of photographs of predark cities, and she enjoyed leafing through them. Their pictures allowed her a tantalizing, poignant glimpse into a world that had ended nearly two centuries before her birth.

She switched the comp on, trying to force her mind away from speculation about Kane's present situation. He had proved time and again his almost supernatural resourcefulness, his ability to turn the tables on death and snatch not just survival but victory from the Grim Reaper's skeletal, strangling fingers.

Once the comp had warmed up, she accessed the linguistics bank and input the word "Ocajnik." Within seconds a definition appeared on the screen. It was not a proper name at all, but an old Serbian word that originally meant "he who walks in darkness" and later came to mean "undead." Derivations included Orlok and Nygotha and Rakshasha. A footnote on the entry allowed her to open a link to the folklore database.

A line of consternation appeared on her forehead as she read:

In the apocrypha of the Greek Orthodox Church, the Hindu epic *The Mahabharata,* and the eighth-century Arabic treatise *Kitab al-Azif,* the Orlok is an old one, a race of immensely powerful entities who dwelt on Earth in the distant past, long before the rise of mankind. Orlok lusted after something in man and other normal life.

According to legend, the Nygotha was a loathsome creature with a scorpionlike stinger in its mouth with which it enslaved the human soul. The Nygotha reportedly lived in the most lonely, inhospitable spots in the world. The Nygotha was later incorporated into classical Greek mythology as a chimera.

Brigid felt gooseflesh pimpling her arms, and her shoulders quaked with an involuntary shudder. She knew the chimera of myth were monsters that combined aspects of different creatures. She made a mental note to ask Lakesh if he knew anything about the Rakshasha. The entry ended with a quote from the *Kitab al-Azif*:

The old ones were, the old ones are and the old ones shall be. From the dark stars they came ere Man was born, unseen and loathsome they descended to primal Earth. And the spawn of the old ones covered the Earth and their children endureth throughout the ages.

Almost too quickly, she closed the file and tapped in "SCOU."

When the Special Cybernetics Operations Unit file appeared, she scanned the personnel records until she came to the entry marked "Falconer," and she stopped the cursor there.

S. D. Falconer had served as a sergeant in a Special Forces division commanded by one Major Drake Burroughs, headquartered in White Sands, New Mexico. The entire division had participated in Project Calypso, yet another life-prolongation experiment tied in with Enterprise Eternity. As a volunteer for the SCOU, Falconer had undergone a process of cyborganization.

This was not an unusual procedure among survivors of the nukecaust. It had been implemented on a vast scale at the primary Continuity of Government installation, the Anthill complex. Even Lakesh had taken part in it.

Apparently, Falconer functioned as something of a roving police officer during the latter years of skydark, when people were just beginning to straggle out of their shelters and refuges. His assignment was to bring some degree of predark law and order to a country totally ruled by postdark chaos and savagery. The personnel record made no mention of Falconer's ultimate fate, and she wasn't surprised.

Brigid remembered a short, terse paragraph in *The Wyeth Codex* pertaining to Major Drake Burroughs, but like the Enterprise Eternity report, it didn't go into great detail.

Sighing, Brigid pushed back from the terminal and turned it off. The data the machine had provided didn't seem useful. She spent a few minutes braiding her hair and tying it into a knot at the back of her head, then she left her quarters.

She met DeFore just as she was entering the armory from the opposite direction. She carried a medical kit slung over her shoulder and announced, ''I'm bringing broad-spectrum antibiotics, on the off chance we run into anyone who may be infected. I've got Aureomycin, Terramycin and a few tetracylines. They may not help, but they couldn't hurt."

Brigid nodded. "Good idea."

DeFore followed her to a row of lockers standing against the back wall. From one, Brigid removed a pair of gunmetal-gray, one-piece garments. The overhead lights glinted from the many zippers and metal apertures on the sleeves and legs.

The suits were composed of Suprotect3 and neoprene weave and, according to Lakesh, they were nearly indestructible. Their multilayer design afforded internal atmospheric integrity, as well as thermal control. Lined with a layer of lead foil to prevent radiation contamination, and with all the openings sealed and the helmets and breathing apparatus attached, they were airtight. Pouches on the legs held small compressed air tanks.

The helmets were of dark gray color like the suits, and made of a lightweight ceramic-alloy compound. The treated Plexiglas faceplates polarized when exposed to light levels above a certain candlepower.

The Suprotect3 lining hung down from inside the helmet to be attached to the suit's collar by an arrangement of tiny snaps and zippers.

The two women struggled into the tight-fitting environmental suits, and DeFore had a little difficulty zipping up all the seals. Although the fabric hugged the contours of their bodies, it was stiff and a little unwieldy.

They slipped on their helmets, helping each other

to zip the collar attachments securely. Compressed air hissed into the headpieces, and it required a few moments to regulate the flow and adjust their respiration patterns. They heard not only their own, but each other's breathing over the voice-activated UTEL comms built into the helmets.

The two women performed a final check on all the seals, then Brigid went over to the gun case and took the Iver Johnson automatic, slipping it into the looped, slide draw holster of the web belt around her waist.

"Do you want a blaster?" she asked DeFore.

The woman tried to shake her head, realized it wasn't easy and answered, "No, thanks." She patted the medical kit. "All the weapons I need are in here."

They left the armory and walked to the ops center, both of them a little annoyed by the constant sound of respiration echoing within their helmets. Bry and Lakesh were still there, and Lakesh said loudly, in order to be heard through the helmets, "The destination lock coordinates have already been entered into the interphase computer program."

Brigid nodded in acknowledgment and beckoned for him to come closer. When Lakesh did so, she asked, nearly in a shout, "Have you ever heard of the Rakshasha?"

He squinted. "Say again?"

She made a dismissive hand wave. "Never mind. It'll keep."

On the table in the ready room lay two trans-comm units, Nighthawk microlights and a pair of rad counters. Brigid and DeFore attached the counters to the fronts of their suits and slipped the comm devices into zippered pockets. They affixed the microlights around their wrists by Velcro straps.

The translucent armaglass walls of the Cerberus gateway bore a rich, brown tint. Right above the keypad encoding panel hung an imprinted notice, dating back to predark days. In faded maroon lettering, it read Entry Absolutely Forbidden To All But B12 Cleared Personnel.

Since the destination coordinates had already been set, the automatic jump initiator circuits would be engaged by simply closing the heavy, counterbalanced door.

DeFore and Brigid took their places on the hexagonal floor plates, and Bry pushed the door shut, the heavy solenoids catching with such a loud click it could be heard through the helmets. Brigid heard DeFore's rate of breathing increase and she didn't blame her. Traveling the quantum stream always induced apprehension.

The familiar, yet still slightly unnerving hum arose, muted due to the helmets. The hum climbed in pitch to a whine, then to a cyclonic howl. The hexagonal floor and ceiling plates shimmered silver. A fine, faint mist gathered at their feet and drifted down from the ceiling. Thready static discharges, like tiny lightning strokes, arced through the vapor.

The mist thickened, blotting out everything.

STANDING OUTSIDE the jump chamber, Lakesh listened to the sound of the mat-trans unit cycling through its dematerialization program. The hurricane howl descended in scale, then faded away altogether. It would be another few moments before the Cerberus sensor link registered a successful transit on the Mercator map.

The Cerberus gateway unit was the first fully operable and completely debugged quantum interface mat-trans inducer constructed after the success of the prototype in 1989. The quantum energies released by the gateways transformed organic and inorganic matter to digital information, transmitted it along a hyperdimensional pathway and reassembled it in a receiver unit.

To accomplish this, the mat-trans units required an inestimable number of maddeningly intricate electronic procedures, all occurring within milliseconds of one another, to minimize the margins for error. The actual matter-to-energy conversion process was sequenced by an array of computers and microprocessors, with a number of separate but overlapping operational cycles.

Since Lakesh had been the overseer of Project Cerberus and had been instrumental in developing the inducers from prototype to final model, he had witnessed firsthand every permutation of its operation. It was the only thing in his life in which he took much pride. Matter transmission worked on the principle that everything organic and inorganic could be reduced to encoded information. The primary stumbling block to actually moving the principle from the theoretical to the practical was the sheer quantity of information that had to be transmitted, received and reconstituted without making any errors in the decoding.

The string of information required to program a computer with every bit and byte of data pertaining to the transmitted subject, particularly the reconstruction of a complex biochemical organism out of a digitized carrier wave, ran to the trillions of binary digits.

Matter transmission had been found to be absolutely impossible to achieve by the employment of Einsteinian physics. Only quantum physics, coupled with quantum mechanics, had made it work. As the physicist who had made the final breakthrough in reconciling relativistic and quantum mechanics, he knew he should have been as famous and as admired as Einstein. Instead, he had labored not just in obscurity, but in anonymity. Although the gateway units had been put to uses he had never envisioned, he still felt proud that he had accomplished what two previous generations of scientists had failed to do.

Lakesh started to turn away, then whirled back around at the sound of a fierce, rushing wind erupting from the emitter array concealed within the raised platform. It swelled in volume, climbing in pitch.

"Incoming jumpers!" Bry shouted from the ops center.

Lakesh squinted away from the flashes of light bursting on the other side of the heavy translucent portal. He stepped back as the unit cycled through the materialization process. The flaring light behind the armaglass dimmed, as did the keening wail of the gale-force wind.

He stepped to the platform and heaved up on the handle of the jump-chamber door. It opened easily. Spark-shot tendrils of white mist curled within it, and Lakesh narrowed his eyes, trying to see through the vapor.

Then Kane plunged through the billowing clouds and collapsed as limp and as cold as a corpse into his arms.

Chapter 12

Brigid opened her eyes, striving and straining for inner balance as always after a mat-trans jump. From the hyperdimensional nonspace through which she had traveled, she seemed to fall through vertiginous abysses. There was a microinstant of nonexistence, then a shock and her senses returned.

Brigid had read the accounts written by Mildred Wyeth when she and her companions had been forced to jump blind, without the knowledge of how to program specific destination points. She described the symptoms of jump sickness, the pain and nightmares she and her comrades had suffered while traversing the Deathlands via the mat-trans network.

Even now, with all of the hyperdimensional pathways routed and the destination codes preprogrammed, jumping was still not the most comfortable way to travel. It felt like a fleeting brush with death.

Brigid struggled against a spasm of nausea and blinked. She saw the silvery shimmer fading from the hexagonal metal disks on the floor. As she tried to focus through the last of the mist wisping over her helmet's faceplate, the radio transceiver accurately transmitted the rasp of DeFore's labored respiration into her ears.

She pushed herself up, leaning against the wall, seeing DeFore stirring dazedly beside her. DeFore groaned and muttered, "No wonder Grant hates these damn things."

Brigid looked around the chamber, and for a second the color of the armaglass walls confused her. They were tinted brown, and by the dim overhead light in the center of the ceiling panels, they looked the same shade as the Cerberus unit's. On closer inspection she realized the brown was darker and deeper, not the rich earth tones of the chamber in Montana but the color of swamp mud.

"Appropriate," she muttered.

"What?" asked DeFore hoarsely.

"Nothing."

The six-sided chambers in the Cerberus mat-trans network were color-coded so authorized jumpers could tell at a glance into which redoubt they had materialized. It seemed an inefficient method of differentiating one installation from another, but Lakesh had once explained that before the nukecaust, only personnel holding color-coded security clearances were allowed to make use of the system. Inasmuch as their use was restricted to a select few of the units, it was fairly easy for them to memorize which color designated what redoubt.

Brigid arose, swaying slightly on unsteady legs. DeFore slowly climbed to her feet, her respiration less strained now. She glanced down at the rad counter and announced. "Midrange green. Safe enough."

Going to the door, Brigid threw her companion a reassuring smile. "Here's the part I like best... opening a chamber door into God knows what."

Unlike DeFore, Brigid had materialized in a number of redoubts over the past year and she knew pretty much what to expect. Most of the installations that she, Kane and Grant visited had been built to standard specs. Generally, the gateway chamber of the complex was situated in the deepest, most reinforced section, as far from the main entrance as possible. Once she opened the door, Brigid expected to see an anteroom opening onto a control room and then a passageway, with the sec door either open or closed. While the jump chambers were self-enclosed, the designers had built a smaller room and a wall between the master controls and the gateway units themselves. These provided something of a buffer zone between the forces unleashed by the mat-trans and the software of the complicated computer system.

Heaving up on the wedge-shaped handle, Brigid disengaged the lock solenoid and shouldered the door open. To her surprise, not only did it require more effort than usual, but she also heard the screech of rusty pivot hinges, a sound she had never heard before in any jump chamber.

When she pushed the door open enough to see past it, she beheld a sight she had never seen in any redoubt—or anywhere else for that matter.

She could see clear across the antechamber into the comp-controlled room, with its rows of consoles and desks. Colored indicator lights danced on the hard-drive bays, and autocircuitry still clicked and whirred purposefully, but those were the only sights similar to the redoubts she had seen before.

Seated in plugs of melted wax atop the control panels, votive candles shed a sputtering, sickly illumination, winking like demonic, flickering eyes from the shadows.

Brigid and DeFore stood in the open door of the gateway chamber, one of the highest and greatest of mankind's technological achievements, and looked at a place torn from the Dark Ages, born from ancient nightmares.

Where the ceiling met the walls, drapes of thick gray cobwebs hung. All the tables and shelves and consoles were state-of-the art, but they groaned beneath the impediments and tools of forgotten black sciences. There were glass and clay jars, some packed with what looked like wads of dried human flesh, others with cloudy liquids in different shades of pink and yellow.

Yellowed skulls, some animal, some human, grinned down from the higher shelves. Intertwined braids of herbs, moss, desiccated birds and mummified reptiles dangled from hooks in the ceiling.

The floor and walls were crisscrossed with pentagrams and confusing designs drawn in a dull, rusty red. Small bones lay scattered within them.

To Brigid's shocked senses, the redoubt had been turned into a combination of cathedral, sorcerer's den and trash dump. She could think of nothing to say.

DeFore found her voice first, though it was tight and breathless. "I thought this redoubt was supposed to be a medical facility."

Brigid nodded absently, realized DeFore couldn't see her head movement inside her helmet and replied, "Apparently somebody decided to redecorate."

"Who?"

"I don't know." She didn't add that getting into Redoubt 47 from the outside—any redoubt for that matter—wasn't as simple as opening a door and strolling in. The sec doors required the entry of a three-digit access code, 3-5-2, input into an electronic key pad. Although it was conceivable some swamp dweller had devoted the time to experimenting, punching in the myriad combinations, she experienced the shuddery feeling that wasn't what had happened here.

The two women stepped down from the platform and moved through the antechamber, toeing aside debris and being careful not to tread on the intricate designs drawn on the floor.

They passed through the control room and out into the main corridor. The floor was just as littered with rubbish as in the antechamber and control room; and the walls were painted with the same whirling symbols. Open doors lined the passageway, and a couple bore plastic signs bolted to the bulkheads beside them. In faded print they read Biohazard Area.

The women entered several rooms at random, finding most of them bare and stripped, dusty and dirt encrusted. One of the rooms seemed to be a central barracks, with the detritus of the culture that had thrived before the bombs fell and destroyed everything in a matter of days. Empty soda cans and disposable cups, candy wrappers, jackets on the backs of chairs, browned photographs on desktops and crumbling paper memos tacked to bulletin boards— all undisturbed, all telltale signs of men and women who had been forced to leave in a hurry. Within a partitioned alcove, they saw a whirlpool bath, the sides of the tub rising three feet from the floor.

On the far side of the living area, they found a heavy door with a simple steel push-bar release. It bore a sign that declared Entry To This BioHazard Section Absolutely Forbidden To All Personnel Below B12 Clearance.

"Vitamins," commented DeFore.

"What?"

"That B12 security clearance always makes me think of vitamins."

Brigid chuckled, just to be polite.

Pushing open the door, they stepped into an adjoining chamber. They saw the carcass of a mainframe computer and rows of chemical-analysis machines. Fetishes and totems of human hair and animal carcasses hung from the ceiling.

"What do you make of all this?" asked the mystified DeFore.

"My best guess is a form of purification, according to voodoo or some other tribal rites."

"How did anybody get in here to do all of this?"

"I can't even guess at that."

"I'm glad we're wearing the suits and helmets," DeFore muttered. "Something tells me the smell in this place is really ungodly."

Brigid felt the same way, but she didn't say so. They walked between two long trestle tables bearing a large glass filtration and purification system and circled around a stainless-steel liquid-nitrogen tank. The lid was open, revealing the honeycomb pattern of individual containers that had once held blood samples.

The women went through a door on the far side of the room and found themselves in a side corridor. The overhead neon strips were unlighted, but dim sunlight was finding its way somehow into the hall, filtering down a stairwell at the end of the passageway.

"Some part of this redoubt is open to the outside," she said.

"Then it seems like there should be vermin in here," DeFore observed. "Bugs, bats or rats."

Brigid pointed toward the skull of what appeared

to be a muskrat lying in a corner. "Maybe they know better."

Unleathering her blaster, Brigid led the way up the stairs, the heavy treads rasping on the metal serrated risers. Looking up, she saw the steps terminating less than fifty feet above. Beyond, she saw a greenish-yellow glimmer, as of milky sunlight suffused through dense foliage. As she climbed, she debated with herself about retracing their steps and going back to the jump chamber to return to Cerberus. Taking samples of the organic tissue in the jars might suffice for testing for the plague bacillus.

But she continued climbing up the stairs until she reached the top. It was there she found the man, and a glance told her he was dying.

Lying on his side on the floor, he was dark skinned and haired. A dew of agony glistened on his face. He wore only a ragged loincloth and a small crucifix of hammered silver, set with tiny beads, around his neck. His limbs were like sticks. His eyes were milky and suppurating in their sockets. His lips had peeled back from blackened gums and discolored, rotting teeth. Several of them looked loose in their sockets.

His body was pocked with inflamed lesions and eruptions, and from these leaked a pale thin fluid. The skin beneath his armpits was swollen so taut it was splitting. The flesh was a purple-black in color and shone with little poisonous beads of moisture.

Brigid gazed in horror at the man, her throat constricting. She noted his shallow, rapid rate of respiration. He coughed rackingly, and crimson tendrils spilled from his slack lips.

When DeFore joined her, she muttered, "Dear God."

Immediately, she went to her knees beside the man, placing her medical kit on the floor and raising the lid. Brigid expected her to fill a hypodermic from one of the bottles of medication, but instead DeFore removed a small culture dish and a tiny needle.

"Aren't you going to inject him with one of the antibiotics?" Brigid asked.

Grimly, DeFore answered, "No point. He's too far gone, in the last stages of pneumonia. All I can do is take blood and sputum cultures."

Pinching the ball of the man's left thumb, DeFore pricked it with the point of the needle. A pearl of scarlet oozed out, and she swiped it over the layer of gel in the culture dish. The man was completely oblivious to what she was doing. A shudder worked along Brigid's spine, and a sense of enormous peril settled over her. It seemed to her that black blotches spread across the man's face even as she watched.

Quickly, she turned away and strode toward the open sec doors.

The light peeping in over the threshold was suffused with shifting green shadows. Brigid cautiously stepped to the open doors and looked around. Thick tropical foliage rose on all sides, turning the late-afternoon sunlight to little more than a dull greenish haze. Cypress trees loomed high, as well as nut-laden pecan trees and sycamores, all of them nearly smothered by tangles of Spanish moss and snarls of creeper vines. Just looking at the humid emerald hell made her break a sweat, despite the internal thermostats of the environmental suit.

Examining the sec doors, she concluded they hadn't been forced open, but she saw how damp earth, mold, leaves and twigs had accumulated between the double-walled thickness of the frame. Obviously, the doors had been open for quite some time, perhaps a very long while.

She returned to the head of the stairs just as DeFore ran a cotton swab over the man's lips. When the tip had absorbed bloody spittle, she put the swab in a culture dish, sealed it and returned it to the medical kit. Gently, with thumb and forefinger, she closed the man's eyes.

"He's dead," she announced regretfully. "No amount of antibiotics would've done him any good."

Closing the case, she stood up. "We got the samples we came for, but they're probably superfluous. It's the Black Death, sure enough."

Brigid and DeFore went back down the stairs and began to retrace their steps. They had walked only a few yards when Brigid became aware of a strange surging motion in the shadows ahead of them. Clicking on her Nighthawk, she directed the amber beam forward. It glinted from moving specks of light. They were like tiny red sparks, but they moved in pairs, seeming to ooze out of the murk.

The flashlight beam illuminated gibbous shadow shapes shuffling and extending claw-tipped, hairless paws toward them. Whiskers twitched and saliva-damp incisor teeth champed.

"Rats," hissed DeFore in an aspirated voice.

"*Lots* of rats," Brigid replied flatly. "Big ones, too."

Sweeping her microlight back and forth, she noticed how the rats were bloated, almost lethargic except for the questing movements of their snouts and forepaws. One of the creatures, the size of a terrier, turned its head directly into the fanning glow of the microlight. Where its eyes should have been, there were only slime-covered purplish patches of wet, scabrous tissue. The rat didn't react to the light.

"And diseased," she added unnecessarily.

"What are we going to do?" DeFore asked fearfully.

"I don't think they can bite through the suits, but I don't want to have them crawling all over us, either."

DeFore shivered at the notion. "They're between us and the gateway. We'll have to go through them."

Brigid extended the pistol, drawing a bead on the blind rodent. "Maybe I can scare them off."

She squeezed the trigger, and the head of the rat burst like a water balloon, spraying blood, fur and brain matter in all directions. The helmet muffled the sharp report of the blaster, and Brigid waited to see how the rats would react to it.

Rather than scampering away, they rolled forward in a wave, hairless tails thrashing, claws ticking on the metal-sheathed floor. They squealed in unison, making a cacophony like one hundred teakettles on full boil, so loud the high-pitched sound penetrated the helmets. They champed their teeth together in rage as they rushed the two women.

Brigid stood her ground, firing the autoblaster. The rounds struck the rats with pile-driver force, obliterating heads and bodies in clouds of gore. The rodents continued to sweep forward. Brigid tried to tell herself that the rats' teeth couldn't penetrate the tough fabric of the suits she and DeFore wore, but the sight of the fur-covered swarm triggered an instinctive, atavistic reaction in her. She stopped shooting and ran back toward the steps. DeFore was at her side. Neither woman screamed, but that was because they knew they needed their breath for running.

The two of them pelted up the stairway, their rasping breath and gasped curses echoing within each other's helmets. Because the helmets reduced peripheral vision, Brigid couldn't tell the toe of her boot had snagged on the jutting edge of a riser until she stumbled forward. She caught herself on the steps with both hands.

A weight slammed into her upper back before she recovered her footing. Even through the multilayered fabric, she felt claws seeking to secure a hold. Brigid didn't frighten easily. In fact, she was outwardly phlegmatic even when internally consumed with fear.

But now she felt the cold sweat of irrational terror literally burst from her forehead, right at the hairline. She tried to clamp her jaws shut on a cry of loathing rising from her throat, but she failed.

Another weight latched on to her lower right leg, and she could feel the pressure of razor-keen incisors trying to gnaw through the suit at the center of her calf. Trying to rise and twist at the same time, Brigid flailed behind her with the barrel of the autoblaster. The metal connected solidly, but the squirming weight remained on her back.

She caught a blurred glimpse of the rodent horde streaming and scampering around her like furry floodwaters, then a rat launched itself from the heaving mass. It slapped against her faceplate, the impact staggering her sideways. All she could see was a bloated, naked underbelly acrawl with black fleas and shockingly humanlike paws scrabbling for purchase on the Plexiglas. DeFore's wordless scream of panic nearly deafened her.

Hammering with her fist, her gun barrel, Brigid rose to her feet, kicking and stamping, feeling bodies squash and break beneath her heavy boot treads. Gritting her teeth, she closed her gloved fingers around the rat on her helmet and pried it off. It snapped viciously at her hand before she flung it away.

DeFore stood at the top of the steps, slapping and beating at the rats climbing her legs. One clung to her bosom, its snout buried in the Suprotect3 weave, teeth worrying at it.

Heart pounding, Brigid stomped and waded through the boiling mass of hair, claws and lashing tails. "Run!" she shouted. "They can't hurt us."

If DeFore comprehended her words, she gave no sign. She screamed, batting at the rodents scaling her like a tree. Weighted down with rats, Brigid fought her way to the top of the stairs, grabbed DeFore by the arm and pulled her out of the redoubt.

They plunged through the foliage. Brigid had no idea of a destination, only that they needed some maneuvering room. She was sure they could outrun most of the rats, as sick as they were. As their feet pounded on the marshy ground, Brigid used the barrel of the Iver Johnson as a bludgeon, whacking the rats clinging to DeFore, knocking them writhing and broken into the overgrowth.

DeFore squeezed the creature hanging on to the front of her suit until it opened its jaws to snap at her hands, then with a half-hysterical cry, she hurled it as far away as she could.

Brigid pushed ahead of her companion, leading with her blaster, clearing a path through the tangle. Trying to see if the rats were in pursuit was a chancy proposition. Because of the helmet and zippered collar, Brigid couldn't swivel her head for a quick, over-the-shoulder glance—she had to more or less pivot at the waist.

She did so awkwardly, trying not to break stride.

She saw nothing behind them but foliage whipped by their passage. She could still feel the weight of the two rats tenaciously hanging on to her, and DeFore carried an unwanted passenger, as well, between her shoulder blades. It clung tenaciously by its teeth, body bouncing and tail lashing in rhythm to her sprinting footfalls.

Then Brigid felt her feet give away beneath her. In an instant, before she could even yell out a warning, her boots seemed to adhere to the ground and jerk her to a violent, staggering stop. Reaching out as she stumbled forward helplessly, she dropped her autoblaster while her hands sought something, anything to grab on to and halt her fall, but no stopgap was to be found. She fell headlong into the morass.

DeFore managed to keep her balance, but she also started to sink into the thick, semiliquid mud as quickly as Brigid. Directly in front of her, the face-down form of Brigid thrashed, struggling in the mire.

"Stop moving!" DeFore cried, her eyes darting around, searching for any fallen piece of wood or vine within reach, but finding none.

The tepid mix of soil, water and other foul-smelling liquids was now up to their waists, and they continued to sink steadily. "This shit is like quicksand," continued DeFore. "The more you struggle, the quicker you go down."

Brigid managed to raise her head clear, but the faceplate of her helmet was occluded with slime and trying to wipe it off only smeared it further. She noticed that the rats on both their bodies had scampered as far as possible from the gelid surface of the bog, perching atop their helmets. The two women took turns swatting the rodents off. They fell into the mire with splats and struggled only briefly before sinking out of sight.

Neither Brigid nor DeFore was concerned by the fear of drowning, but the prospect of sinking farther into the quagmire, trapped at the bottom in the darkness until they exhausted their individual air supplies, was so terrifying as to be paralyzing. The last to suffocate would have to listen to the death gasps and rattles of the first to go.

"What are we going to do?" asked DeFore in a trembly contralto, crossing her arms over her breasts as if she were cold.

Before Brigid could formulate even an inane answer, the mud and debris on the upper layer of the quagmire began to froth and foam. From the midst of the muddy maelstrom, a human head thrust up. Despite the sludge and slime streaming down the man's face, the women saw the intricate network of raw red cuts around both of his eyes.

The man's lips stretched in a smile and he spoke. Neither woman should have been able to hear through the walls of their helmets, but somehow they did.

"My name is Doyle," the man said. "We've been waiting for you."

Then more scarred heads began rising from the muck.

Chapter 13

Kane was falling, and as he plummeted, faster and faster, he knew he was dreaming.

How many dreams in a lifetime? Kane wondered aloofly. One, two, three per night? How many forgotten in the light of day? More unconscious journeys than could ever be remembered upon awakening—that was for damn sure. And were daydreams included? How many dreams over a span of decades then? No, they couldn't apply to the tally. Not daydreams, for they allowed the dreamer to possess at least a modicum of control.

After all, rarely did anyone daydream a nightmare when more pleasing fantasies of power and sex were but a thought away. Amazing the kinds of fused-out thoughts flew through a man's mind when falling in a dream.

Time seemed to hang still and motionless, even while racing forward like a runaway war wag with the pedal bolted down hard to the metal...even as the entire vehicle went crashing down and over the precipice of a sheer dark cliff. It was a queer kind of out-of-control stability.

As for this kind of dream, the answer was held in

the exact number of mat-trans jumps Kane had taken. There were times when he felt he spent more time caught on the cusp of infinity than in his own conscious form.

He tried to call out into the dreamscape surrounding his falling body, but no sound would come. The only noise he could hear was inside his chest; the oxygen within his lungs was echoing heavily with the dull thud, thud, thud of an infinite number of air sacs expanding open and slamming shut. With each new open-and-closing sound, he felt his lungs constrict. One would think falling across the sky would provide him more than enough air, yet for some reason he was unable to catch a single breath.

Overhead, the world was filled with stars. His vision blurred and he wondered to himself which would kill him first—a lack of air or the impact of the fall. He managed to twist his neck and look down below. There was no horizon, no land, no earth, only stars, and he realized he was surrounded by an inky black curtain dusted with a million sequins of starlight.

Suddenly, he was more than merely Kane, a hardened, bold survivalist eking out a day-to-day existence in a world where civilization died in the opening month of the new millennium. No, now he was a man ready and able to defend flag and country as an astronaut in a faceless helmet and bulky spacesuit.

He wasn't sure where that imagery came from. He retained splinters of memory from the third Lost

Earth he had visited, the parallel casement where his alternate-world self commanded a spaceship named *Sabre*.

Again, Kane grinned bitterly at the silliness of dream logic. In the time he'd spent falling, he should have either stopped falling, for there was no gravity in outer space to fall against or exploded into a visceral mass of red blood and white tissue. None of which had occurred as yet—ergo, welcome to Dreamland.

The depths of outer space, at least in this dream, were colder than any of the previous bleak environments he'd been forced to slog through. Logically, the exposed flesh on his face should have gone slack and black and dead.

He gritted his teeth. At least that part of his body seemed to be working, so he tried to speak once more and felt a wisp of precious oxygen escape into the void. The thudding in his chest seemed to grow louder in his ears. No need to waste what little air he had left calling out for help, Kane thought wryly, for in space, no one can hear you scream. His vision blurred, and the stars seemed to streak across the blackness.

He blinked, squinted, blinked again and took in the sight of the universe that surrounded him. If he hadn't been falling, if he hadn't been dreaming, if his heart and soul weren't pounding throughout his body, Kane might have found beauty in the sight of such pristine openness.

The stars were everywhere at once and most distracting.

Concentrate. That was one of the best defenses against a nightmare. Concentrate on the here and the now, the real and the solid, the true and the whole. The last thing he could recall before falling was the tingling sensation of having all of the hair on his body stand up on end right before the electronically charged mist of the mat-trans chamber had crept into his very being, like the absorption of a small silent thunderstorm.

Then came the falling and the stars and the dream, and now it was time to wake up. Kane breathed in, breathed out. Time to wake up.

"He's waking up," a faraway, rumbling male voice said. "I don't think he's feeling any pain."

"He shouldn't be feeling much at all," said another man's voice. "Not after the way I juiced him up with sedatives. He's probably had some vivid dreams, though."

His eyelids lifted. The lighting was muted, diffused, and the world looked strange. Shadowy figures moved, wavered back and forth. The walls were white, the ceiling lit by a neon strip.

Kane opened his eyes fully and tried to sit up. The bed spun. He grasped the high rails on the sides and squeezed his eyes shut again until the spasm of vertigo passed. He asked, "I'm guessing we made it."

One of the shadow shapes shifted close and coalesced into Grant. He came to the bedside and gently pushed Kane back onto the mattress. He held up a slender dart, revolving it between thumb and forefinger. "Barely. You got this in the ass right before we closed the sec door."

Kane became aware of the remote stinging sensation in his right buttock and grimaced. It all came back to him in a rush—the mad, stumbling flight through the jungle, dodging among trees, trading the Indians' blowgun shots with those from their Sin Eaters. Just when they thought they had either eluded the Amazonians or they had given up, a new storm of darts would hiss their way.

Dawn had just colored the sky with pastel hues when they finally caught sight of the small installation. As soon as they approached it, a howling mob of Indians had erupted from the jungle in a final do-or-die frontal assault.

"Shit," Kane said, softly and disgustedly. He hiked himself up to his elbows. "How long have I been out?"

"Seven hours," Grant answered.

Kane winced. A rest of sorts.

"You were exhausted and dehydrated," a new but familiar voice said from behind him. "I gave you a sedative so your system could metabolize the narcotic while you slept."

Kane turned his head to see Auerbach standing in the doorway that led to the laboratory. Narrowing his eyes, he demanded, "*You* gave me a sedative? Who put you back on duty? Where's DeFore?"

Auerbach didn't meet his slit-eyed gaze. He replied, "Away. In Louisiana, I'm told."

"Brigid, too," Grant said.

Memories of being stalked by swampies crowded into Kane's mind, and he sat straight up in the bed. "Why would they go to that hellzone?"

"Lakesh said they went to recce a redoubt down there," replied Grant sourly. "To identify the disease that Samariumville reported. Remember that?"

Kane remembered and he scowled. "How long have they been gone?"

"A little over seven hours. They jumped out maybe a minute before we jumped in."

Auerbach offered quietly, "They weren't supposed to be gone this long."

"And so you just took over from DeFore?" snapped Kane.

In that same quiet, subdued tone, Auerbach responded, "I'm the most qualified."

Impatiently, Kane tossed the sheet aside and swung his legs over the side of the bed. His head spun dizzily for a moment, then it passed. "Get me some clothes."

Grant fetched him a white bodysuit, saying, "I told Lakesh what happened to us, what was done to Domi."

Kane thrust his arms into the sleeves. "And?"

"And the highest of those Indians' gods is Kukulkan, a plumed serpent. Blue and white are his holy colors."

Kane nodded in understanding. "So that's why they painted up Domi."

"Yeah. They thought she was pure of heart and soul, if you can imagine that."

Kane smiled wryly. "It's beyond my ability. So what—when those poor stupes found a mutie snake, they rigged it out in feathers and kept it like an earthly manifestation of their god?"

Grant nodded. "Right. They weren't going to so much sacrifice Domi as marry her to it." A corner of his mouth quirked. "Of course, once the marriage was consummated, she would've ended up in the damn thing's digestive tract, but all in all it would have been a great honor."

Kane zipped up the front of the suit. "And what role were you playing? Maid of honor?"

Grant gingerly touched his left shoulder. "Something like that, I guess."

"Did you get that cut treated?"

Grant nodded toward Auerbach. "He sterilized and stitched me up."

"I've dealt with worse," Auerbach said diffidently.

Kane favored him with another narrow-eyed glare, almost but not quite reminding him of a similar wound he had suffered—when Domi planted her favorite knife in his shoulder.

"Anyway," Grant went on, "it's no wonder the Indians were so pissed off at us. Not only did we bust up the wedding, but we chilled the groom."

Kane shrugged. "It wouldn't have lasted anyway."

Grant smiled ruefully. "Kind of funny when you think about it. Those Indians thought they had a god in the bowl. To us, it was just a monster."

"I guess the difference between gods and monsters is only a matter of perception." Kane started for the door, noting a little weakness in his legs and a bit of light-headedness. "Let's find out what's going on with Baptiste and DeFore."

Grant walked beside him down the corridor and tersely brought him up to date. The news wasn't encouraging. The two women's visit to Redoubt 47 shouldn't have taken more than two hours, three at the outside. With the Comsat relay system off-line, there was no way to monitor their biosigns.

By the time Grant had finished his account, they strode into the ops complex. Farrell, Cotta and Bry were there, manning various stations. So was Lakesh, pacing back and forth beneath the Mercator map, eyeing all the glowing lights and lines as if they were the source of his agitation.

Domi stood nearby, gnawing nervously on a thumbnail. She wore her usual redoubt ensemble of short, sleeveless red jerkin, belted at the waist, which left her gamin-slim legs bare to the upper thigh. Her skin, scrubbed clean of the blue paint, gleamed like polished porcelain.

As Kane walked past her, he commented offhandedly, "You decided to go back to the original color scheme, I see. Too bad. You looked good in blue."

Sullenly, she murmured, "Kiss my ass."

At the sound of his voice, Lakesh turned quickly to face him. "Friend Kane, up and about at last." Worry shadowed his eyes, deepened the seams and creases in his face. "I have some unsettling news—"

Kane gestured to Grant. "He already briefed me. Why didn't you tell DeFore and Baptiste to wait until we got back?"

Lakesh's retort held a bitter, acidic undertone. "I can't tell anyone to do anything any longer, remember? You were instrumental in that."

Kane understood the old man's resentment at his self-perceived authority being usurped, but he also knew it was misplaced. The cooperation among the Cerberus exiles was by agreement; there was no formal oath or vows like the ones he and Grant had taken upon admission into the Magistrate Division. There was no system of penalties or punishments if cooperation was not given, nor was there a hard-and-fast system of government within its vanadium walls.

There were security protocols to be observed, certain assigned duties that had to be performed, but anything other than that was a matter of persuasion and volunteerism. Lakesh had never truly held the reins of power in the first place. Rather than bring up that topic again, Kane opted to remain silent.

Lakesh sighed and said, "Frankly, I expressed my

doubts about the value of their mission, but my protests were disregarded.''

''But for them to jump into the middle of a possible biohazard—'' Kane began.

Lakesh broke in harshly. ''With the environmental suits, they could materialize into a giant petri dish full of the Ebola virus and still be safe.''

''Then why haven't they come back?'' Grant demanded.

Wagging his head in doleful frustration, Lakesh waved to the map over their heads. ''I can't even speculate. The jump line to Redoubt 47 still reads active, so it's not a malfunction in the gateway unit down there.''

''I hope they weren't stupid enough to expand their recce out of the redoubt,'' said Kane grimly. ''Those bayous are triple-dangerous places. I should know.''

Lakesh acknowledged his reference to his own experiences down south with a fleeting smile. ''You were many miles from Redoubt 47, in the vicinity of Redoubt Delta.''

''So? The place was still crawling with carnivorous plants, mosquitoes the size of Grant's head…not to mention swampies.''

''You were in one of their settlements. Boontown, right?''

''Right.'' Kane repressed a shiver when he recollected the zombie-like swampies who, with their double circulatory systems, were virtually unkillable.

"They must have run into something," Grant argued. "Or they would have been back here by now."

Lakesh nodded in reluctant agreement, although he said, "There are any number of possibilities for their delay."

Kane snorted. "Too damn many." He cast a glance toward Grant. "I think we should go count just how many."

Grant's eyebrows drew together, a deep vertical furrow forming above the bridge of his nose. "Are you sure you're up to it? The stuff on those darts really packs a wallop."

"It sure as hell does," Domi piped up. "I still feel wobbly."

Kane regarded Grant keenly. "How about you? Are you wobbly?"

"A little bit," he admitted. "I didn't have the benefit of sedatives and sleep to counteract the effects of the toxin. I had to bleed and sweat it out."

Kane ran a contemplative hand over the three days' worth of beard stubble on his chin. He cast an expectant glance toward Lakesh. "What's your opinion about going after them?"

Lakesh feigned shock. "*You're* asking *me* for my input, actually soliciting an opinion?" He put a hand to his chest. "I may need a second transplant."

Bry and Cotta turned their faces away to hide their smiles. Even Domi couldn't help but grin.

Kane growled, "Old man, I don't recall saying

that all of your ideas were lousy, or that your particular take on something was worthless.''

"You implied as much," retorted Lakesh stiffly.

"You may have interpreted it that way due to your ville-sized ego," Kane countered, "but I never meant it that way. The question still stands—should we or should we not give Baptiste and DeFore more time before we jump after them?"

Lakesh surprised him by actually hesitating to answer. He ran his hands over his sparse hair before saying lowly, "Just before dearest Brigid made the mat-trans jump, she tried to ask me something. I couldn't hear her very clearly because of her helmet. Later, I understood what she asked. I took the liberty of reviewing her last activity in the database."

"What's that got to do with—?"

Lakesh cut him off with a sharp, peremptory gesture. "Hear me out. After accessing the same files she accessed, I suspect—no, fear—something is going on down in the swamps that may portend something other than an outbreak of the plague. In fact, the epidemic may be only an outward manifestation of something far worse."

"You mean it was deliberately released?" Kane voiced an old fear of the ville bred, of manufactured diseases getting loose from buried installations, either by accident or by design.

Lakesh inhaled very slowly, as if he were steeling himself for an unpleasant task. "Yes and no."

"Goddammit," Grant bit out impatiently. "What's

Brigid's computer activity got to do with the bubonic plague?''

Lakesh gave him a frosty stare. ''I'm getting to that.''

''Then get to it already,'' urged Domi irritably.

''My interest in physics always superseded my interest in everything else—except, as you know, for mythology. My grandfather instilled in me a fascination for it with his tales of Ravana and his Rakshashas—''

''Rak what?'' interrupted Domi.

''The Rakshashas are the unholy family of Hindu myth,'' Lakesh explained. ''Their lord is Ravana. They were dedicated evil-doers who strove to defeat the gods, sometimes winning, sometimes losing.''

''Hell of a family,'' Grant muttered disinterestedly.

Lakesh ignored the jibe. ''There is Pischasas, who functions like a vampire and spread foul diseases like leprosy. Bhutas, his kindred spirit, can actually force the dead to rise from their graves and attack the living. Grachas is a demon of disease who infects humans by penetrating orifices. This is the family of the Rakshashas. In other languages, they were called the old ones.''

Kane knuckled his eyes and with a weary sarcasm he said, ''There's a point to all of this, I'm hoping.''

''There is, but I don't know how to begin to explain it all to you. How can I tell you with any conviction of all the things crowded into my mind as result of my grandfather's strange tales? Of powerful beings of unbelievable evil, old gods who once inhabited the Earth, driven away yet returning, becoming manifest briefly, horribly, to the world of men?''

Unperturbed by Lakesh's flight into melodrama, Grant commented, ''And once again, I still don't see what this has to do with Brigid's last activity in the database.''

Lakesh explained to them as quickly and as clearly as he could. Kane, Grant and Domi listened attentively, silently throughout. When he was finished, Grant and Kane exchanged long, searching looks but said nothing.

Folding his arms over his chest, Lakesh tilted his head at a defiant angle. ''You may dispense with the aspersions you're planning to cast on my sanity or lack thereof. I assure you I am not, to employ your quaint vernacular, 'fused-out.' I merely related to you the files Brigid accessed and how they relate to my own knowledge of similar phenomena and entities.''

Kane pursed his lips. ''For the sake of clarity, let me go over this again. Feel free to jump in if I get any of the details wrong. We've got an old one down in Louisiana who may or may not be a vampire or a rakshasha, who may or may not be somehow related to Enterprise Eternity and who may or may not have been killed over 175 years ago by a soldier of the SCOU, and who may or may not be back spreading the bubonic plague.''

Grant turned to him and said with mock severity,

"You know, it sounds like *such* bullshit when you put it that way."

"It sounds like bullshit any way it's put," declared Kane. "But the problem is, if you look at the possibility objectively, it makes as much sense as some of the ops we've already been on."

Grant frowned at him. "Are you really buying into this?"

Kane gestured helplessly. "Until we know otherwise, why the hell not?"

Quickly, but with a great deal of vehemence, Domi said, "I'm sitting this one out, if you don't mind. Or even if you do."

Grant's frown became a reproachful glower. "Don't tell me you believe this crap."

She shook her white-haired head. "Had enough truck with gods lately. Besides, I've seen a lot of strange things in the Outlands. Things I've never told you or anybody else about."

Lakesh angled an eyebrow at her. "Indeed? Like what?"

Grant waved an arm angrily. "You two can compare your strange tales later. There are still two environmental suits in the armory, right?"

"Three, actually," replied Lakesh.

Kane clicked his tongue absently against the roof of his mouth, glanced up at the Mercator map, shrugged then started walking toward the door. "Let's suit up."

After a few seconds, Grant followed him. With a studied lack of enthusiasm, he muttered, "I can tell this is going to be *another* long night."

Chapter 14

The thunder of drums and the incessant chanting filled Brigid's ears as a cacophonous clamor without meaning. Opening her eyes, she saw that she lay inside a lean-to made of lashed-together saplings, but the sounds and movements from outside impinged upon her senses only as confused and faraway noise and motion.

The glare from the bonfire peeping in through rents in the square of cloth hanging in the front of the low entrance hurt her eyes. She squinted, blinked and squinted again. Black figures, backlit against the crimson tongues of flame, shifted in and out of her limited field of vision.

Memory and awareness returned simultaneously in a rush. She lay on her right side on the marshy ground, wrists bound behind her. Her fingertips were numb, and she couldn't tell by touch the material of her bonds. Folding her fingers into fists, she strained against them, but she felt no slack, no give whatsoever. Still, she felt a dull wonder that she was still alive.

After a couple of false starts, she managed to sit up. Pain thumped at the back of her head. Nausea assailed her, and she fought the desire to vomit. She could taste the tang of blood in her mouth, felt and smelled it caked in her nostrils. She twitched convulsively when, by the firelight flickering in through the tears in the hanging, she saw she was naked. Blue-and-black bruises showed on her thighs, reddened welts marring her legs.

She remembered hands lifting her from the quagmire, then ripping the environmental suit from her body, as well as the one-piece garment she wore beneath it. She also remembered fighting, punching, kicking and gouging for eyes.

She glimpsed DeFore doing the same thing, at least for a few seconds. Then a fist fell onto the back of Brigid's neck, and the impact jarred all the way down her spine, blurring her vision. A torrent of blows fell. There had been nothing fancy about a close and personal beating, and that was what she'd received. She'd swung her own fists during this, or at least she hoped she had. By then, all her actions were nothing but a blur of agony, and for every blow she landed, three more crashed into her body. Brigid told herself that she put up a damn good fight. But ultimately, it wasn't good enough.

DeFore wasn't in the lean-to with her, but Brigid refused to surrender to the fear the woman was dead. Inching around, she leaned forward, peering out through a rip in the drapery.

At first she could make nothing of what she saw. All was shadowy and chaotic, shapes moving and

mingling, writhing and twisting, black formless figures etched starkly against the leaping flames of the
bonfire. The whites of rolling eyeballs, the flash of
grinning teeth reflected the firelight.

She saw short people, broad shouldered and deep
chested, naked except for ragged shorts, some little
more than loincloths. The firelight sculpted their
swelling muscles and their dark scarred faces. Beyond them, the ribbon of a wide stream glimmered
in the moonlight.

Her eyes watered in the steady glare of the flames
and she glanced away, then repressed a cry of horror.
A few feet away rose a low pyramid built of gory
human heads. Dead, glassy eyes stared up at the
black sky.

Twisting her head away from the ghastly specta-
cle, Brigid again struggled with the urge to retch.
Shuddering and shaking, she swallowed down the
acid bile that rose in a burning column up her throat.
Since joining the Cerberus exiles, she had witnessed
torture and torment all over the world, but she had
never grown accustomed to it or accepted it. She
never would.

The hanging was roughly thrust aside, and a man
shape blotted out the firelight. Brigid instinctively retreated backward, bare heels digging into the ground.
She pressed against the rear sapling wall. She waited
for the man to speak. He didn't. He whistled.

Brigid was taken aback. She hadn't heard a wolf
whistle in a very long time, not since her early twen-

ties when she walked the promenade of the Enclaves in Cobaltville. Since her exile, she was usually next to Kane in any given situation when other men were present, so admirers tended to keep their expressions of interest in her to themselves.

Ducking his head, the man entered the lean-to, crouching. She recognized his freshly scarred face. Doyle looked to be in his early thirties, and no more than five foot eight. His eyes were tiny bits of black tinged with hints of piercing cobalt blue, which added to his sinister appearance.

He was dressed in denim of different colors and textures, the pants blue and the jacket light tan. He wore a red flannel long-sleeved shirt missing a few buttons, and the gaps showed off the tight T-shirt he wore underneath. On his feet were basic combat boots. He kept the cuffs of the denims tucked into the tops, giving his lower legs a puffed-out look.

"Hello, gorgeous. What's a nice girl like you doing in a hellpit like this?"

Brigid gave him a look of disbelief. "You have got to be kidding."

"What, I'm not good enough to answer questions?"

"Exactly."

"That's not very friendly."

"Neither were you or your swampie friends, as I recall."

"You and your friend are our guests. If I were

you, I'd be a little more receptive of our hospitality. Ocajnik sets great store by it.''

Brigid did not allow the surge of relief Doyle's remark about her friend triggered to show on her face. ''Where's my friend?''

Doyle snickered. ''Here, in another guest accommodation.''

''We're not your guests,'' Brigid snapped. ''We're here because we were attacked and abducted. If you don't like my attitude, then that's too bad. Excuse me all to hell. I hate hurting such a big man's feelings. If this Ocajnik has a problem with my attitude, I'll be glad to take it up with him personally.''

Doyle didn't seem offended by her sarcasm. He chuckled, but it sounded forced. ''I don't think you'd like that.''

Suddenly, a scrabbling was audible from several directions. Skin crawling, Brigid looked around and saw tiny eyes gleaming between the saplings.

''They don't like it, either,'' Doyle said casually.

''Rats,'' she breathed.

''Rats,'' Doyle confirmed. ''A whole army of infected rats.''

With effort, Brigid let steel slip into her voice. ''How did you train them?''

Doyle made a sound between a sob and a laugh. ''They aren't trained. They're controlled.''

''By who? You?''

Doyle shook his head. ''No.''

''By Ocajnik?''

Doyle winced as if in pain, and his right hand flew to his throat, gingerly touching it. "Who else?"

Brigid eyed him dispassionately. "Did he mutilate you like that?"

Doyle's hand crept up almost involuntarily from his throat to the raw scars on his face. "These are his marks. He marks all of his beasts like this, so we'll know one another. You'll wear them, too, soon enough. And like it."

Despite the ragged clothes he wore, Brigid could tell by the man's way of speaking and his face that he was not bred in the backwoods. "Where are you from? Samariumville?"

The question seemed to startle him, as if it had never occurred to him before. Doyle nodded slowly. "Yes. Samariumville. Yes. Historical Division."

"You're an archivist?"

"Yes. An archivist. Yes."

"Like me. That's what I was, in Cobaltville."

In a tight voice, almost as if he were straining to get the words out, he replied, "Looks like we both chose the wrong time and place for a career change."

Striving for a note of nonchalance, she asked, "How did you know we were coming?"

"We have… sources."

"Someone watching us, watching the redoubt?"

"Your arrival was foretold."

"Foretold by who?"

"There is a woman in these swamps. She inherited certain abilities."

Brigid frowned. "Are you talking about a doomseer, a doomie?"

Doomies weren't necessarily psi-muties, but normals with true clairvoyant or telepathic abilities were extremely rare. Extrasensory and precognitive preceptions were the most typical abilities possesed by muties who appeared normal.

"All I know is she foretold your coming. She has great gifts."

"Speaking of gifts, why didn't you sink and drown in that bog?"

He grinned crookedly. "Is that important?"

"I can understand it from the swampies, with their double circulatory systems," Brigid said reasonably. She was trying to think of anything to distract the man. "When they hold their breaths, carbon dioxide builds up in their blood and when it dissolves and forms bicarbonate ions, the ions probably bind to their red blood cells that carry oxygen. Like in crocodiles."

Instead of replying, he coughed—a deep racking cough from the bottom of his lungs. He put his hand to his mouth and when he opened it, a bright pink glob of sputum gleamed in his palm.

"You've got the plague," Brigid said. She didn't ask a question; she made a declaration.

"All of us have it." He jerked his head backward toward the fire. "All of his beasts. But it won't kill us."

She narrowed, then widened her eyes. "Why not?"

"Ocajnik kissed us. Immunized us."

"What?"

Doyle waved her words away impatiently. "I didn't come here to talk about that. You'll find out all about it soon enough. Just like I did."

"Then why did you come here?" she demanded. "To whistle at me?"

"Yes." He blinked rapidly. "No."

At first Brigid thought his eye blinks were due to confusion, then she realized he was trying to stem the tears brimming in his eyes. Tears of shame.

In a faint, aspirated whisper, he said, "I've been sent to defile you. It's my duty as a beast." He paused, then added, "Help me."

Fear leaped through Brigid, but it was a different kind of fear than she had ever experienced before. It was mixed in with a soul-cringing horror and sympathy even as Doyle began to unbutton the fly of his trousers with shaking fingers.

In a kind of groaning mutter, he said, "It's a compulsion, caused by the kiss, the sting. Biochemical imbalance? Maybe. Endorphins and hormones all out of whack? Probably."

Brigid drew up her legs, bending them at the knee. Doyle shuddered, hands frozen at the waistband of his pants. "Makes us act like beasts. Guess that's why he calls us his beasts. Makes sense. No, it doesn't make sense."

"What are you going to do?" she asked quietly.

Doyle's face flushed and contorted. "All the new beasts will take turns with you and your friend. After you've been defiled, you'll receive the kiss. And you'll live forever."

"As beasts?"

Doyle's face suddenly hardened. He jerked down his pants and moved toward her on his knees. Brigid didn't have much leverage with which to kick, but she tried, straightening her legs out and up like springs.

Doyle caught her by the ankles and wrenched her violently forward. Her back scraped along the rough bark of the saplings, her elbows digging little grooves in the soft ground. She managed to keep her head up.

"It's not me," Doyle whispered over and over, as if reciting a mantra. *"It's not me."* He pulled her legs apart.

Arching her back, Brigid twisted her body to one side, freeing her right leg with a fierce tug. She kicked him with all of her strength in the lower belly. Doyle grunted—she could tell it pained him—and she kicked him there again, this time pistoning her heel into his pubic area. Again Doyle grunted.

Panic overwhelmed Brigid, causing her to freeze momentarily, then to thrash and flail madly at him with her free leg. She smashed the sole into his face, felt his nose collapse and raked his eyes with her toes. At least a dozen times she drove her foot into his body and face.

Doyle took it all, grunting softly with each blow. He let her kick and foot smash him until she was utterly exhausted, panting and covered with sweat. She barely mustered up a feeble foot nudge, much less another kick.

Blood trickled from his nostrils, oozed from split lips, crimson threads dripping from a lacerated eyebrow. His mouth opened and his tongue lolled out, the tip tentatively touching the scarlet stream from his nose. His tongue was dead white, as dry as sandpaper.

Carefully, Doyle recaptured her right leg and again spread her legs apart. "It's not me, it's not me...."

A tremendous shout suddenly went up from the swampies around the bonfire. An undulating wail burst from a hundred tongues. Doyle looked over his shoulder, sighed and said, "Here he is. He wants to meet you and your friend."

The chant began slowly at first. "Ocajnik! Ocajnik!"

Doyle released Brigid's legs and joined in with the chant. "Ocajnik! Ocajnik!"

He backed out of the lean-to, pulling his pants up. Brigid managed to sit up, breathing heavily. The wolfish howling of the swampies rose in volume and exultation. They surged and milled about eagerly.

A figure strode into the firelight and at the sight of him, Brigid started violently, her heart seemed to skip a beat, then began to pound again. Against the dancing flames, surrounded by the small, dark people, he stood out with vivid distinctiveness.

The man smiled with a terrible beauty, repellent but magnetic. He wore black leather knee boots, black leggings and a red shirt with billowy sleeves. He smiled broadly, his white teeth gleaming against his pale skin, contrasting with a fall of black hair. His yellow-green eyes were magnificent and invoked in Brigid a desire to please him.

The swampies crowded and clustered around him, and he reached out and touched and patted them as if bestowing benedictions—or stroking his pets. He radiated more than charisma; he exuded an aura of evil—absolute, unregenerate, charming and desirable *evil.*

Chapter 15

For the past twenty minutes, Grant and Kane had been alternately bemused, amused and irritated. The jump from Montana had been clean, causing them to suffer only a few moments of disorientation.

Their true disorientation didn't begin until they left the mat-trans chamber and started touring Redoubt 47. They found no clues that DeFore and Brigid had been there, but judging by the symbols painted on the walls and the hanging fetishes, someone paid regular visits to the installation.

Most of the redoubts they had visited were in near-perfect condition, with just occasional mechanical failure or circuit malfunction. The original comp-controlled nuke-power sources always seemed to work reliably, maintaining temperature and air circulation. They were designed to control every aspect of their underground environments, in the event of the worst-case scenario coming to pass.

The redoubts stayed quiet and still, their automatic cutoffs and bypass arrangements taking care of the rare malfunction as the computer brains waited for the human masters to return.

This redoubt was the proverbial pigsty. Outside of

the control room, the overhead lights didn't work, so they were forced to rely on the amber beams provided by the Nighthawks.

The mysteries posed by the totems and painted sigils bewildered both men. And since neither one enjoyed walking around in a state of bewilderment, they quickly grew tense and annoyed. It took them only a couple of minutes to establish that Brigid and DeFore weren't in range of the UTEL helmet comms, but reaching that conclusion induced more anxiety.

The environmental suits served as another source of irritation. The helmets reduced their field of vision, seriously impaired their hearing and limited all of their senses. As former hard-contact Magistrates, Kane and Grant were accustomed to relying on all of their finely honed instincts when entering a potential killzone. Walking around in a high state of alert while wearing the suits was an exercise in futility since they were essentially cut off from all external stimuli. All they could see was what lay directly ahead of them, all they could smell was the compressed air provided by their tanks and all they could hear was each other's respiration.

Both men carried Sin Eaters strapped to their forearms, and long combat knives were scabbarded in web belts at their hips. The stripped-down subguns known as Copperheads dangled from shoulder straps. The blasters were barely two feet in length. The magazines held fifteen rounds of 4.85 mm steel-jacketed rounds, which could be fired at a rate of 700 per minute. Even with their optical image intensifiers and laser autotarget scopes, the Copperheads weighed less than eight pounds.

Out in the main passageway, Kane and Grant checked each door, scanning the rooms that lay beyond. Most of them were completely bare, stripped of anything useful long ago.

They entered a central barracks area, equipped with bunks, a few tables and chairs, a whirlpool bath, not to mention half a ton of ancient garbage. They crossed the large room to a door bearing a sign that read Entry To This BioHazard Section Absolutely Forbidden To All Personnel Below B12 Clearance.

Grant rapped it with the barrel of his Copperhead and growled. "Every time I'm on the verge of taking off this damn helmet, something like that reminds me of where we are."

Kane smiled ruefully. "I don't need the reminder. But if we leave the redoubt, I think we can take them off."

"Providing we can find our way out of here," Grant replied gloomily.

"Baptiste and DeFore obviously managed it."

Grant turned away from the door. "Some of these places have maps showing the layout. We need to find the— *Ow!*"

Kane gaped as Grant spun in an awkward circle like a dog trying to catch its tail. He let loose with a stream of profanity as he pirouetted, slapping at his back.

"Something hit me!" he shouted half in anger, half in fear.

Kane saw nothing, then directed the microlight to the floor. The beam haloed the eight-inch arrow lying on the floor and glinted dully from the sticky substance smeared over its sharp point. With a cold rush of recognition, he said flatly, "We've got swampies in here."

Sin Eaters sprang into both men's hands at the same time, and they swept the barracks room with their Nighthawks. Kane realized the arrows couldn't penetrate the tough layers of the environmental suits, but that wasn't much of an advantage. He knew from past experience swampies were exceptionally strong, and since neither he nor Grant could see where they might be hiding in the shadow-shrouded area, they could easily be overwhelmed.

Standing back to back, they shone the microlights all around, their ragged breathing resounding in each other's ears. Grant held his Copperhead in his left hand, with his Sin Eater hanging at waist level in his right. Both weapons were ready to unleash twin songs of doom at anything foolish enough to challenge him.

They stepped carefully toward the partitioned corner that held the whirlpool bath.

"See anything?" Grant demanded.

Before Kane could reply, he felt a stinging blow

against his chest, directly on his left pectoral. He caught only a glimpse of the arrow bouncing away before he depressed the Sin Eater's trigger stud, aiming at the partition enclosing the whirlpool. The weapon responded with a stutter, as six 9 mm rounds flew through the door effortlessly, the thin wooden barrier serving as no deterrent.

At least three of the rounds found their target, and a muscular swampie woman dressed in brown burlap dropped a crossbow. Her fingers tried to hold in her rapidly spilling guts. The driving force of the bullets easily flipped the woman backward, but she didn't fall. She struck the raised rim of the tub and used it as a brace to fling herself forward again. She shrieked in agony, in fury, in hatred.

"What the fuck?" roared Grant. He fired the Copperhead in a short burst.

The woman screamed, smacked her hands over the new wounds and fell writhing to the floor. Almost immediately she began struggling to her feet again.

Kane fired three more rounds from his Sin Eater. The bullets slammed into the swampie woman's forehead, tearing half-inch-wide holes through her skull. She went down again, but this time she didn't rise.

"What the fuck?" panted Grant a second time.

"Double circulatory and cardiovascular systems, remember?" Kane said. "Aim for the head."

Grant nodded, giving a grunt of disgust at the primitive condition of her weapon. Like most outlanders and mutie peoples, swampies weren't keen on blasters, finding it difficult to keep them in good condition and, since the Program of Unification, much too hard to find the proper ammunition.

Hunched in a tight posture, Kane narrowed his eyes and peered inside the partitioned enclosure, glancing long enough at the zone to assure himself the swampie was indeed dead before scanning the rest of the area.

Behind him, Grant whispered, "Clear?"

Kane nodded as he started to step back. "Good thing they've—"

Then a stocky figure rose from the bottom of the large round whirlpool tub. The compact crossbow in the man's hands flung an arrow in his direction. The bolt punched Kane in the diaphragm, its stinging impact knocking air from his lungs. He started to double up.

The swampie launched himself from the tub, mouth opening in a screech of hatred and triumph that Kane could barely hear. The mutie held a notch-bladed knife in both hands. He yelled something indistinguishabale to Kane, then he was on top of him.

Kane felt the knife blade drag along the front of his suit, and he slapped the weapon aside with the barrel of his Sin Eater. Forcing himself to carry on against the burning pain in his solar plexus, he whipped around with his Copperhead, squeezing the trigger at point-blank range. The swampie toppled over backward, most of his face dissolving in a welter of blood, bone and brain.

Kneading his midsection, Kane glared down at the dead man. "Bastard."

Grant murmured, "You were saying?"

"I was saying it's a good thing they've only got crossbows and knives."

The sound of rapid firing was muted for a split second. Neither man was sure of its source or what it was. Then Kane saw pinpoints of flame flickering from behind the tub and his helmet literally seemed to jump beneath a shuddering drumroll. Bell-like chimes reverberated painfully against his eardrums. At the same time, a spiderweb pattern of cracks spread across his faceplate.

Kane and Grant dived, tucked and rolled in opposite directions.

"Son of a bitch!" Grant's outraged bellow smothered the echoes of the chime vibrating inside of his head. "They've got *blasters!*"

NEITHER MAN KNEW if the material of his garments was dense enough to turn bullets, but neither was particularly inclined to put them to the test. The tall, shadowy blasterman behind the tub tracked them with streaks of full autofire, and even over the hiss of air escaping from the breach in his helmet, Kane recognized that staccato roar. The man was using a Sin Eater.

The stuttering hail of bullets came ripping toward

them, starting low and going high like rockets taking off in flight. Kane felt a numbing blow across his right hip as he came out of his roll.

Extending both blasters, Kane pressed the triggers, smearing the shadows with dancing tongues of flame. The Copperhead sprayed a steady stream of bullets with a sound like the prolonged ripping of silk. Little flares flashed sparks on the sides of the tub as bullets ricocheted from the steel.

Kane knew that sustained full-auto bursts only wasted ammunition, but his focus was on driving the gunman to cover, not scoring lethal hits. Though he emptied both of his weapons, he achieved his objective—the gunman dropped out of sight behind the whirlpool.

Grant threw himself in a reverse somersault, and he struck back first against the legs of a table, nearly overturning it. He saw the swampie horde appear first, looming out of the darkness. He counted six, seven, no, eight of the shuffling muties. Centering the red dot of the Copperhead's autotargeter on the swampie who appeared to be more or less in the lead, he held the trigger, squeezing into the little subgun's recoil.

The rounds nearly took the top of the head off the swampie. His eyes bugged out at the sound, and his throat seemed to open with crimson lips. Blood pulsated outward in an angry gusher.

The other swampies scattered, running in a peculiar scampering gait. He had about half a second of triumph before he felt an agonizing viselike grip on his upper left arm. He felt the stitches and edges of his knife wound pull apart.

Grant glimpsed the scarred, silently snarling face just as the mutie yanked his 230-plus pounds up from the floor. With a ripping of the nearly indestructible fabric, the swampie tossed him across the barracks room. He slapped the concrete floor chest-first, and all the air went out of his lungs in an agonized bellow. The Copperhead went skittering out of his left hand.

The helmet comm transmitted the bellow to Kane. He rolled back up on the balls of his feet and turned to see swampies crowding in around Grant's body, thrusting down at him with knives.

Dropping the empty Copperhead, Kane ejected the Sin Eater's spent clip with his right thumb and snapped in another with his left, making both actions appear to be one smooth motion.

His first two shots struck a swampie full in the face. The next one caught a smaller man in the left side of the head. The fourth shot was a little low, blowing a piece out of the shoulder of a woman. Kane instantly corrected his aim and put another round through her forehead. The back of her skull vanished in a haze of red. Hair, brain tissue and bone settled around her ears.

Voicing raucous cries, the muties scattered again into the murk, not wanting to face another volley.

Grant, dragging in great gasps of air, forced himself first to his hands and knees, then he staggered erect. He surveyed the room with ferocious eyes, then they flashed with fear. "If Brigid and Reba met up with those things—"

Kane turned back to the partitioned whirlpool enclosure. "Reba?"

"That's DeFore's first name. If these swampies were in here when they arrived—"

He didn't finish. There was no need to, nor did he have the opportunity. The blasterman behind the tub opened up again. Kane's Sin Eater blazed in reply. Grant squeezed the trigger of his own handblaster, shifting position so his and Kane's barrage constituted an improvised cross fire.

By the strobing effect of the muzzle-flashes, they saw the man throw up his right arm and clutch his throat with his left hand. He collapsed out of sight.

Grant and Kane ceased firing, though Kane kept his blaster trained on the tub as Grant came toward him, swinging the smoking bore of his Sin Eater in short back-and-forth arcs. He retrieved his Copperhead, and the two men cautiously approached the whirlpool from opposite directions. By the illumination of their Nighthawks, they saw a thick pool of blood, almost black in the dim light, spreading out across the floor.

A man wearing black molded body armor lay on his back between the tub and the rear wall. Blood from a throat wound pulsed up and over his gloved fingers. The red-tinted visor of his helmet glinted in the amber beams of the microlights.

"Fucking fireblast," Grant husked out. "It's a Mag."

Kane blinked in shock and groped for a response. Finally, he said lowly, "Mebbe it's a swampie in Mag's armor."

Grant knelt beside the dead man, gingerly reaching for the underjaw locking guard of the helmet. A lucky bullet had ripped open the man's jugular vein, in a tiny portion of his neck unprotected either by the high collar of the Kevlar undersheathing or the base of the helmet.

"No," he said. "Look at his size, his build, the color of his skin. He's not a swampie."

He undid the lock on the helmet and pulled it from the man's head. An unfamiliar face stared up at them. Fresh red cuts crisscrossed the flesh around his eyes.

"He's scarred like the swampies, though," Grant grunted. "What the hell for? Where's he from?"

"Samariumville is the best guess," replied Kane, glancing around anxiously. He saw nothing but murk.

Grant stood up, lips tightly compressed beneath his mustache. "This makes no damn sense at all."

He grimaced in pain and glanced down at his left arm. A flap of the suit's material hung loose. In an astonished voice, he said, "That swampie bastard ripped this stuff. Lakesh said it was supposed to be indestructible."

"I guess it's proof against anything but swampies." On impulse, Kane unzipped the seal of his suit's collar.

"What are you doing?" demanded Grant.

Kane tapped the cracks in his helmet's faceplate. "I'm losing air. And if good air gets out, bad air comes in."

Grant eyed him doubtfully. "What about bacteria?"

"A chance I'm willing to take. Besides, with the way those swampies move, it's easier to hear them before you see them."

After a thoughtful few seconds, Grant nodded in reluctant agreement and unzipped his own seal. Lifting their helmets off their heads, they both cautiously sniffed the air and Kane made a face.

"What is it?" Grant asked.

Kane looked at him, surprised that Grant couldn't smell the scent of rotten eggs, of sulfur. Then he remembered that Grant's nose had been broken three times during his Mag days and always poorly reset. Unless an odor was extraordinarily pleasant or virulently repulsive, he was incapable of detecting smells unless they were right under his nostrils. A running joke among his fellow Magistrates had been that Grant could eat a hearty dinner with a dead skunk lying on the table next to his plate.

For the first time, Kane envied this impairment. However, Grant could feel the high temperature, at least in the mid-eighties, and feel the fetid, sticky atmosphere. Sweat sprang out on their faces almost instantly.

Generally speaking, the air inside a redoubt wasn't the freshest in the world, but the interior temperature, humidity and air quality always seemed to be at the proper comfort level for humans.

"Let's try to find our way out of here," Grant said. "It's a sure bet those sons of bitches won't let us get back to the gateway."

Kane moved quickly but cautiously across the room, to the door bearing the biohazard sign. Softly, he said, "This looks to be the only way out of here."

Grant hesitated, gritted his teeth, then nodded. Kane used the barrel of his Copperhead to push the bar down while Grant palmed the door to one side. The chamber beyond held an old computer and medical equipment. After listening for any sound for a few moments, they entered, walking quickly through it, paying no attention to the animal carcasses hanging from the ceiling.

The two went through a door on the far side of the room and found themselves in a narrow corridor. At its end, they were just able to make out the foot of a stairway, lit very feebly by light from somewhere above it. The air was moister and warmer, and the stench of sulfur was now so strong, even Grant fingered his nose. "Pew."

"Yeah," Kane said dryly.

They made their way down the passageway and

up the stairs, pausing every few seconds to scan ahead and behind them.

"You think they gave up?" Grant whispered.

"Did those snake-loving Indians give up?" Kane countered.

"Point taken."

They reached the top of the steps and came to a dead stop, first looking at each other, then out. The sec door stood open, showing off a night sky filled with starlight. There was a nearly full moon hanging low in the sky, and the lack of cloud cover allowed it to shine down at full wattage, so while their vision was limited, they weren't out for a blind stroll, either.

The two men inched out of the redoubt door, looking and listening for any sort of threat, but none appeared to be forthcoming. They did a quick look of the grounds surrounding the redoubt door, gazing out at the cypress, live oak and sycamore trees, their leafy branches reaching high into the night sky.

Glancing down at the ground, Kane saw the imprint of a treaded boot sole in the marshy ground, a match for the pattern on the boots they wore.

"One of them came this way," he murmured.

Grant nodded. "I wonder who."

Leaving their helmets just inside the open sec door, they followed the tracks into the undergrowth. There was an eerie lack of insect or bird sounds. All they heard was the squish of the muddy earth beneath their boots.

The swamp was thick all around them, the deep

green fronds, the heavy-leaved interlocking branches pressing in everywhere. Even the moonlight that filtered through the branches held a queasy green tint. Still, combined with the beams of their Nighthawks, there was sufficient light to follow the trail.

Kane, taking point as always, used his combat knife to slash branches that blocked their way. The tracks were intermittent, but there were enough footprints or smeared impressions thereof to provide a trail to follow. Every few minutes, he'd hold up his hand for a brief stop so they could listen for any sounds of pursuit.

They entered a small clearing, and Kane started to walk across an open patch of ground. Then his pointman's sixth sense rang an alarm, and he came to a full stop in midstride. He stopped so suddenly that Grant, wiping sweat from his face, bumped into him.

Kane lurched forward, stumbled and his right leg sank up to the knee in a thick mingling of mud and water. Grabbing him by the arm, Grant pulled him backward. His leg came free with a sucking sound.

"Sorry," Grant muttered.

Kane scanned the area with slitted eyes, shining his microlight around the foliage bordering the quagmire. The beam struck an object that reflected the light. Moving cautiously, walking heel-to-toe, they skirted the edge of the bog and saw a helmet from an environmental suit lying in the shrubbery.

Neither man said anything for a protracted period of time. Then, trying to tamp down his rising fear,

Kane picked it up, looking inside of it. A small spattering of dried blood showed on the interior of the faceplate.

Dropping the helmet, Kane looked around. On the far side of the bog he saw flattened grass and broken foliage, the only signs that even remotely resembled a trail. Without a word, he moved forward.

They walked into an almost perfect ambush.

Chapter 16

The full moon shone like a polished silver medal when Doyle brought Brigid from the lean-to. He didn't escort her across the camp; he half dragged, half carried her. She closed her mind to her nudity since most of the swampies were as naked as she, and she paid no attention to their jeers and catcalls. Whenever she stumbled, Doyle would murmur, "Sorry, sorry, it's not me."

A toadlike chunk of a man, reeking of a cesspit, capered before her, his stubby callused fingers reaching out for her breasts. With a curse, Doyle kicked out at him, and the swampie melted back into the throng.

"They're happy tonight," he said, indicating the heap of decapitated heads. "They killed six members of the Moudongue cult today. Not to mention capturing you and your friend."

As they circled the bonfire, Brigid saw DeFore was as bound and as naked as she was. Like Brigid, she had a few cuts, bruises and scratches but nothing worse. The intricate braids she affected had come loose, and her hair hung in wispy strands over her upper shoulders. The face she turned toward Brigid was expressionless, her eyes dull. She looked more than fatigued—she looked exhausted from enduring too many hours of terror.

DeFore's escort, though taller and sturdier of build, bore a resemblance to Doyle in that he also appeared out of place. And like Doyle, the ugly cuts inscribed around his eyes were fresh and unhealed.

They faced the man Doyle had called Ocajnik. He sat on a rattan stool, flanked by a pair of swampies. On his lap rested DeFore's open medical kit. He poked at its contents, and when Doyle pulled Brigid to a stop in front of him, his eyes flicked up and down her form and he smiled. His smile was pleasant, as if he were being introduced to her at a social function.

When he spoke, his smooth, melodious voice, touched by a hint of an accent, cut through the clamor of the camp like a hot knife through butter.

"Reba here tells me your name is Brigid."

For a second, she was confused and embarrassed by her confusion. She wasn't sure who Reba was supposed to be, then realized DeFore had told him her first name—a revelation that had never been shared with Brigid.

"It's been a very long time since I've met such charming and refined women. I doubt you'd believe me if I told you exactly how long it's been."

The pitch, timbre and vibrations of his voice gently caressed her inner fear, like a soothing touch. She felt her fear begin to ebb, but at the same time her skin crawled beneath his intense yellow-green stare.

Ocajnik removed a small glass ampoule filled with a clear fluid. He studied it, revolving it between thumb and forefinger. Brigid noticed his fingernails were at least two and a half inches long, tapered to sharp points, and were exceptionally clean. "She further informs me that these liquids could cure the Black Death."

Brigid did not respond until Ocajnik angled a questioning eyebrow toward her. She ducked her head, saying breathily, "Yes."

"I'm always impressed by the advances in science made by man during my sleeps. Every time I awaken, there seems to be a new one. But how little man changes."

He turned to the swampie standing on his left. "LeGrand, please relate your tale."

LeGrand closed his eyes, and his swart face took on a studious air.

"They come for him. They come from the sky. They come from within, without, without shape, without form. Across the sky and back again. Across the world over and over. A patchwork, a joining of lands...thread through a needle, the pathways hidden. They travel by lightning, by thunder, through the magic of the storm. Harnessed in the caves, the energy electric, the energy forbidden."

Both Brigid and DeFore were able to read between

the lines of the man's recitation. What he described sounded suspiciously like a mat-trans jump.

"There are two men, brothers in all but blood," continued the swampie. "Brothers in arms and in souls. They will seek two women who possess healing knowledge. They will come from the pathways hidden and arrive at the forbidden place of dead science."

Brigid felt a chill go up her back and across the nape of her neck as LeGrand stopped speaking and cast expectant eyes toward Ocajnik.

The man on the stool glanced from Brigid to DeFore. "You have to admit, that certainly describes you two ladies."

Brigid showed no emotion. "Perhaps. There is a lot of room for interpretation."

Ocajnik tapped the medical kit. "Judging by this, I'd say the prediction was correct."

He returned the ampoule to the case, closed and latched the lid and handed it to LeGrand. "Take this and dispose of it."

The swampie bowed and scurried away into the shadows.

Ocajnik stared directly at Brigid without speaking. She tried to avert her gaze, but found herself compelled to meet his eyes. Impressions filled her—not images, but whispering touches of emotion, of abandoned passions, of wantonness, of unbridled and utter release from rules, morals and inhibitions.

She felt her respiration increase, her heartbeat

speed up and with a great, conscious effort, Brigid tore her gaze away from his beautiful eyes. She cleared her throat and asked, "What are you?"

The man seemed a little startled, not only by the question but by the fact she had even asked it. "I presumed you would have been told by now. My name is Ocajnik."

"That's not a proper name," she replied in a challenging tone. "It's an old Serbian word that means 'he who walks in darkness.' There are other derivations."

Ocajnik's eyes flickered in fleeting appreciation, and he laughed. "Very good, Brigid. That name was forced upon me many years—many centuries—ago, so I simply adopted it. I've had other names, in other lands."

"Like Orlok, Nygotha and Rakshasha?"

He nodded. "Not to mention Vlad Tepes and Gilles de Rais."

"You still haven't answered my question. What are you?"

"Would it make any difference to you in your present situation?"

"It would," she retorted stolidly.

Almost apologetically, Ocajnik said, "Not everything in existence can be slotted into scientific niches. You want to explain me, is that it, and therefore diminish what I am—or what you fear me to be?"

"And what is that?" she asked, despising the rising tremor in her voice.

He shrugged negligently. "A Nygotha, a Rakshasha, a vampire. An entity who lives by an entirely different set of laws than any conceived by your kind's scientists."

DeFore spoke for the first time, her voice a thin, dry whisper. "There's another possibility."

Ocajnik threw her a patronizing smile. "And that is?"

"You're a mutie, like these swampies of yours."

The condescending smile didn't falter. "A mutie?"

Trying to overcome a slight stammer, DeFore replied, "Products of genetic engineering. We call this bunch swampies. They're descendants of a genetic manipulation program called the Genesis Project. You probably had something to do with Enterprise Eternity—perhaps you're the source of the chimeric cells that bred human vampires."

Ocajnik chuckled warmly. "Do go on, Reba."

"The more I think about it," she said, an edge entering her voice, "the more likely that seems. You're probably a natural-born mutant, exceptionally long-lived, and your genes provided the jumping-off point for twentieth-century scientists to tinker, splice and eventually make more muties."

Ocajnik listened attentively, still smiling. "Mutie," he echoed, rolling the word around on his tongue, as if testing the taste and texture of it to see if he liked it. "Mutie."

Then he moved. He was so fast, to Brigid's eyes it was as if he had simply vanished from the stool. She felt the rush of air past her cheek. She heard the meaty smack of the blow, as sharp as a gunshot, and DeFore fell heavily onto her back. Brigid cried out as she saw blood springing from the woman's nostrils. Her eyes rolled back in their sockets, showing only the whites.

Ocajnik towered over her, roaring in a maniacal rage. "*Mutie?* You dare to presume I am some offal spewed from your kind's experiments? *Mutie!*"

He screeched words in an unintelligible, hissing tongue, and though Brigid struggled to understand, the blazing fury he directed at DeFore's presumption hammered at her, and she flinched back. At the periphery of her vision, she saw Doyle swallowing hard, turning away, fixing his eyes on anything other than the raging monster standing over DeFore.

Ocajnik returned to English and snarled, "Do you truly think you can apply your beast's reason to a *god?*"

Kneeling, Ocajnik flipped DeFore roughly onto her face and ripped away the bonds at her wrists. He performed both motions with such savage economy and blinding speed, his movements were a blur. Under his hands, she seemed to weigh no more than a child, and the thongs around her wrists parted as if they were rotten string.

He rose to his full height, dragging DeFore with him. Her head lolled back on her neck, her arms dangled limply behind her. With one hand supporting the small of her back, Ocajnik squeezed the hinges of her jaws, forcing her mouth open. In a thick, guttural croon, he said, "Now thee will learn the wisdom of the old ones."

Ocajnik put his lips close to DeFore's face, and his black tongue slithered from his mouth, coiling and questing. Brigid cried out in revulsion. She made a move as if to lunge toward him, but Doyle restrained her.

Turning his head toward her, voice slurred but serene, Ocajnik said, "Make no move or outcry, else I shall rip thy beast's heart from thy chest and force it down this slut's throat."

Doyle covered Brigid's mouth with a hand and whispered desperately in her ear, "Do as he says. It's so very important *you do as he says.*"

Brigid swallowed hard, almost overwhelmed by the realization she had never felt so terrified or helpless in her entire life.

She could only watch, engulfed by soul-searing horror, as the tip of Ocajnik's tongue dabbed delicately at the blood streaming over DeFore's lips. Though the wavering firelight provided uncertain illumination, Brigid was sure she saw a tiny barb right at the end of Ocajnik's inhumanly long tongue.

"Kiss me and live forever," he whispered.

And his tongue disappeared between DeFore's

parted lips. Her body convulsed; her arms shook in spasms, trembling fingers spread wide. She moaned and made muffled cries. She came to semiconsciousness, struggling, trying to push Ocajnik away, but he only tightened his grip around her waist, pressing her closer.

Her frantic struggles weakened, then ceased altogether. After a moment, her ample hips began to undulate.

In an instant, Ocajnik released her, his tongue withdrawing with a snap, a tiny thread of crimson trailing from its tip. DeFore collapsed bonelessly, shuddering, to the ground. Her limbs shook violently as if she were suffering a seizure. She rolled onto her side and retched, vomiting out a jet of blood. Gasping and gagging, she lay in a fetal position, eyes squeezed shut.

Ocajnik knelt beside her, speaking in a low, gentle voice. "A healer thou claim to be, a scientist who travels the pathways invisible. But still only a beast. This is not a penalty for insulting thy master, but rather a gift.

"There are no universal laws of what is considered to be right and to be wrong. Such definitions are truly subjective. Man has always acted like a savage. It is twined in thy very nature, and to attempt its removal would leave thee mewling in the dust.

"Therefore, I am permitting thee to unleash the savage within thee, to free the animal of the constraints thy false civilization has put upon it. I will allow thee to be thy true self. What other god would do that?''

As he spoke, he lovingly caressed her thighs and DeFore moaned softly at the touch. Her moan became a deep groan. As Brigid listened to the sounds rising from her throat, she slowly understood the vocalizations were not of pain, but of arousal.

Ocajnik continued to touch her, to stroke her carefully, and DeFore jerked, finally rising to all fours, head bowed, abasing herself before the beautiful man with the beautiful eyes and the maddeningly exquisite touch.

She was weeping though, and said in a sob-choked voice, ''Please don't make me—''

''Hush,'' Ocajnik said softly, and touched her again.

She called out wordlessly, her body rocking back and forth. With a flourish, Ocajnik swept the flat of his hand over her body. ''There, now. Thy leash is loosening. Can thou not feel it? Free the beast.''

Animal cries of release burst from DeFore's lips. Nausea roiled in the pit of Brigid's stomach, and she feared she would throw up while Doyle had his hand clamped over her mouth. She fought down the sickness and watched and listened.

The worst part was that interspersed with DeFore's primal screams, Brigid heard her sobbing, ''This isn't me. *This isn't me!*''

THE NEXT HALF HOUR passed for Brigid as a blurred tapestry of horror and perversion.

As the moon reached its zenith, the camp of the swampies reddened into a crazed, shambling, open-air madhouse. Brigid stood frozen, her eyes dilated, her entire body frozen.

Ocajnik left DeFore writhing on the ground and shouted in a language full of liquid consonants and harsh syllables. The swampies swarmed around him, and one brought forth a rolled tarpaulin. He spread it out on the ground, and four scar-faced muties positioned themselves at each corner, holding them clear of the ground.

Ocajnik mingled among the swampies, the beasts, petting one here, kissing another one there, laughing, making them laugh in return. They danced and capered around him in mindless adoration, trying to catch his notice.

At length, Doyle removed his hand from Brigid's mouth and he said softly, "You must watch this. If you resist, if you try to escape, you will become the object of the game. It will be a far worse fate than your friend's."

Looking at DeFore stirring fitfully on the muddy earth, Brigid found that hard to conceive. "Game?" Her voice seemed to echo from the vast gulfs of space. "What game?"

"Something the master created to entertain his beasts."

Since Ocajnik showed no more interest in DeFore, the swampies acted as if she weren't there, either.

They stepped on her, stumbled over her, trampled on her.

Hot tears stung Brigid's eyes, and she stepped toward the woman, but Doyle pulled her back. He said, "She's a beast now. Let her lie."

DeFore finally raised her mud and blood-spattered face, looking around unfocusedly. Her lips moved as if she were talking to herself. A swampie woman nearly tripped over her, looked down and spit on her bare back.

"Is this the defilement you were talking about?" Brigid asked hoarsely.

Doyle started to snicker, but it stuttered into a whimper. "It hasn't even begun."

After a couple of false starts, DeFore managed to totter to her feet, raking her disordered hair out of her eyes. Brigid watched her, nerves wire-taut and trembling as the woman stumbled blearily, first a few paces backward, then lurching forward.

DeFore had been more than humiliated and debased. Her dignity had not only been stripped from her, but it had also been crumpled and contemptuously tossed away, like a soiled tissue. Her identity, her crisp, efficient manner, had been tossed away with it.

"DeFore," Brigid called.

She acted as if she hadn't heard, or if she had, she didn't recognize the name. Brigid called to her twice more, then shouted, "Reba!"

Her head jerked around, brown eyes covered with a wet, glazed sheen.

"Over here, Reba."

Mechanically, like an automaton, DeFore walked toward her. Her lips still moved and finally Brigid understood she was chanting, but without any emotion or conviction, "This isn't me, this isn't me."

Brigid couldn't look into her eyes and so she fixed her gaze on Ocajnik. She had known anger before, even a wild fury. But never had she felt drowned in hatred, so intense it seemed to flow almost tangibly along the line of her vision.

I will see you die, she vowed silently, fiercely, if it is possible for you to die. I will be there to watch you die!

Two swampies surged from the shadows, carrying between them a squirming, naked girl. She was dusky of complexion, with long straight black hair. By the contorted expression on her face, she was nearly insane with fear. She uttered little wordless screams.

They hurled her unceremoniously onto the center of the tarp. Laughing, the swampies at the corners lifted the big square of canvas, bagging the girl at the bottom. In unison, the four of them began jerking the tarpaulin up and down until the girl flew straight up, arms and legs flailing, hair all a tangle.

The swampies set a steady rhythm and with each bouncing ascension, the crowd hooted and yelped. Ocajnik stood beside the makeshift trampoline following the girl's up-and-down trajectory with a studied, smiling interest.

Then his right hand shot out, fingers slashing, and slit a neat gash across her throat. Blood literally fountained from severed arteries and veins, driven by her wildly pumping heart. Brigid felt warm liquid drops splatter across her face like a brief rain shower.

The blood misted across the upturned faces of the swampies as the dying, hemorrhaging girl continued to bounce up and down. Ocajnik's tongue darted out to catch a few flying droplets. He spoke a word, and the swampies stopped propelling her upward, allowing her body to huddle at the bottom of the canvas. They kept the edges upturned so the blood formed a pool.

Ocajnik knelt down and plunged first his tongue, then his face into the rising puddle of crimson and began to feed. A beastlike howling arose from the spectators, a wailing primitive shout of exultation.

After only a few seconds, Ocajnik raised his head and grinned directly at Brigid. He had changed. Despite the scarlet glistening on his face, Brigid saw the parchment-yellow skin, the ropy veins pulsing at the sides of the hairless head, just above the malformed batlike ears. Sharp, twisted teeth showed in his mouth. But the eyes still glowed yellow-green, the color of the walls of hell. They were not even remotely human.

Brigid's overwrought nerves gave way. She cried out, her voice lost in the roar of approbation for the slaughter. Her reason tottered, staggered and changed her cry to a shrill peal of hysterical laughter.

Then, for the first time in her life, Brigid Baptiste fainted.

Chapter 17

The ambush was well planned, an explosion of organized chaos that would have closed like the jaws of a steel trap if one of the swampies hadn't tripped over a root and fired his crossbow prematurely.

The bolt flew short and buried itself in the earth between Grant's feet. His reaction was immediate. The Sin Eater flashed into his hand, and his index finger depressed the trigger stud. Flame and thunder gouted from the barrel as he loosed a long, stuttering, full-auto volley into the woods. The 248-grain rounds crashed into tree trunks, peeling away bark and slashing through leaves.

Jamming the Copperhead against his hip, Kane pressed down the trigger, firing in the opposite direction. Even over the double jackhammer roars, they heard rising-and-falling howls, like banshees riding the wind. Wavering spear-points of orange flame smeared the gloom, smoking shell casings spewed from ejector ports. The fusillade of full-auto fire whipped the foliage with the fury of a gale-force wind.

Swampies launched themselves out of the brush, defying certain death. Blood spurted and chunks of flesh gouted into the air, intermixed with splinters of bone. They retreated, wailing, melting back into the swamp.

Kane and Grant relaxed the pressure of their respective trigger fingers before they emptied both their blasters. For a long moment, they heard nothing but bullet-shredded twigs and leaves showering down in a rustling rain.

Quietly, Grant asked, "Has it occurred to you that these bastards expected us?"

"That occurred to me at least half an hour ago," Kane replied in the same subdued tone.

"How could they know we'd show up?"

Then swampies rushed them like shadows, pressing in from all sides. Kane and Grant fired their Sin Eaters. Flame wreathed the muzzles, casting an unearthly strobing effect on the scarred faces snarling before them. The bayou became a babel of shouts and screams, punctuated by the stuttering roar of the blasters.

Bodies slammed into Kane, nearly bowling him off his feet, fetching him up hard against a tree trunk. He directed a final triburst from his Sin Eater and saw a mutie stagger backward, most of his face vanishing in a bubbling fountain of blood. He used the Copperhead as a bludgeon, clubbing away hands clawing for his face.

Lit by the Nighthawk microlights, the battle in the jungle took on a nightmarish, hallucinatory quality.

Other than their crossbows, the swampies were

armed with crude knives and machetes. They hacked and slashed and thrust at the two men, howling and swearing in Creole. Kane felt the chopping impacts against the tree trunk at his back. Several of them shrieked, "Oka-jee-neek!"

In close combat, there was always the temptation to hose bullets around indiscriminately, but both Grant and Kane knew that wasn't always the best option. Not only would each be in danger from the other man's barrage, but blasters were useless when it came to hand-to-hand fighting.

Letting the Copperhead dangle by its lanyard, Kane swung out with his combat knife, his arm curving up, then down and across a swampie's throat. The razor-sharp blade went into the flesh as if it were damp brown paper, ripping across with no resistance.

Blood sprayed out and over Kane's arm. The mutie stumbled backward, careening off one of his fellows. He was clutching his throat, babbling French words in a wet whisper. Crimson seeped out from his fingers as he finally fell on his side, his legs spasming.

Two of his companions tripped over his legs, and they stumbled directly into a pair of knife strokes from Kane. Using the tree at his back as a brace, he swung the knife in a fast, glittering arc, wheeling on the balls of his feet. The blade slashed through throats, plunged into bellies, withdrew to chop at arms and hands.

The swampies crowded Grant fiercely, one of them

slashing at him with a machete. As short as he was, he tried to cut Grant's legs out from under him. But the big man had expected it, weaving away, pivoting to his right and stabbing at the mutie's neck. The mutie was quick, hunching his head between his shoulders so that he took only a shallow flesh wound on his scalp.

Still, blood rivered into his eyes, blinding him momentarily. Uttering croaks, the swampie lifted his hands to staunch the flow and clear his vision. Grant drove the knife halfway to the hilt into the side of his throat.

A swampie chopped at Grant with a machete, its thin blade chiming on the honed steel of the big combat knife, deeply notching the metal. Blue sparks briefly lit up the darkness.

The mutie swung the machete again, slashing sideways this time in an effort to shear his adversary's head from his shoulders. Grant ducked under the effort and kicked at the swampie's knee from a crouching position.

The sound of the kneecap breaking was like a mushy crack. The swampie didn't fall, swinging the machete again as Grant came back up to a standing position. He parried the blow and slashed out with his knife in a lightning countermove. The knife ripped open the man's belly, but he didn't fall, even after half of his intestines fell in blue-sheened loops nearly to his knees.

Screaming and holding in his guts with one hand,

the swampie raised the machete over his head, preparing for a cleaver blow. Stomach boiling with nausea, Grant swung his knife from the shoulder, powering it with every bit of his weight and every iota of upper-body strength.

The shock of impact jarred up his right arm into the shoulder, and the mutie's body reeled to the left, while his head tumbled to the right.

A snarling swampie lunged forward, grabbing at the front of Grant's suit. Unbelievably powerful fingers found a grip on the fabric and gave a terrific yank. Grant's legs bent at the waist, his chin hitting the top of the mutie's upthrust kneecap.

The top layer of the garment tore in the swampie's fingers, and Grant pushed himself erect and toward the mutie in a single whip-fast movement. The swampie bounded forward headfirst to meet him, driving the top of his skull into Grant's gut. He exhaled loudly with a whoof and staggered back on his boot heels. Only a tree trunk kept him from falling.

Another swampie delivered a kick to Grant's unprotected belly.

There was the explosive sound of a single shot, and the mutie who had kicked him took a faltering step back. Then his lips opened and a stream of vermilion spilled out.

As the mutie tipped forward and fell onto his broad chest and face, Grant glimpsed a tendril of smoke curling from the bore of the Sin Eater in

Kane's hand. "Last round until I reload!" he shouted hoarsely.

Grant didn't respond to the comment. Taking a deep, raspy breath, he fisted his knife tighter and closed in with another swampie.

Back and forth the battle rolled, blades slashing and chopping, scarlet streams spurting, mouths screaming, feet stamping the fallen underfoot.

The attack ended with the same abruptness with which it had begun. The swampies did not so much engage in a retreat as melt back into the shadow-splotched foliage, cursing and spitting in rage.

Kane and Grant leaned against trees, trembling with sick weariness, knives dangling from their hands. "You hurt?" Grant asked hoarsely.

Kane shook his head, and the swamp spun around him. He winced at the stabbing pain of the arrow strike, an injury he'd forgotten during the adrenaline rush of the battle. "Don't think so. You?"

"Don't think so. We were damn lucky." He added dourly and unnecessarily, "This time."

Grant examined the rips in his environmental suit with disbelieving eyes. "How can those little sons of bitches be so strong?"

Assuming Grant's query to be rhetorical, Kane responded with a question of his own. "Did you catch that word some of them were screaming, 'Oka-jee-neek'? What does that mean?"

Grant hawked up from deep in his laboring lungs

and spit into the shadows. "How do I know? I don't speak swampie."

Kane palmed away sweat from his hairline. "Swampies speak Creole, a sort of French dialect. That word didn't sound like French to me."

Irritably, Grant replied, "I don't give a shit whether they speak French or Russian. Which way did they go?"

Kane shook his head. "Doesn't matter."

Both men quickly reloaded their blasters. Pushing himself away from the tree as he took in a lungful of the humid, fetid air, Grant coughed and said, "Whichever direction we're going in, let's get moving."

They heard a prolonged rustle from the underbrush, as if a wind shook the leaves, but they felt not so much as a hint of a breeze. The sound made the flesh creep along the spines of both men. They shone their microlights toward the foliage, and the beam reflected off a constellation of tiny sparks at ground level.

"What the fuck—?" began Grant softly.

Then a rat launched itself from the ground at his face, and his Sin Eater blasted deafeningly. The rodent was hurled upward by the impact of lead and thudded to the ground. A chittering squeal arose, high-pitched and angry. It wavered up to a nerve-stinging crescendo, then died into a minor note.

Suddenly a black mass swept toward them, like a

thundercloud scudding only inches above the ground, blotting out leaves, twigs and creepers.

A shudder shook Kane violently. The sight of those hundred deadly little beasts with teeth whose bite meant death turned his stomach as no mutie ever had.

"Which way?" asked Grant tightly.

"That doesn't matter."

They began a shambling run through the morass, ducking and dodging along paths that zigged and zagged like the trail left by a brokenbacked snake. The ground became marshier until at every step their boots sank ankle-deep into the muck. The farther they ran, the more the bayou closed in.

The two men waded through many shallow pools and avoided equally many deep ones. It was necessary to swim on two occasions, since channels that cut across their path couldn't be circled. In the first one, nothing occurred except Kane's briefly choking on a mouthful of rancid water. As they left the second, and the dripping Grant hauled himself out onto the bank, Kane saw the black water roil and bubble ominously, as if something large moved off the bottom toward the surface. They moved on, stopping periodically to rest and pick off huge brown leeches, nasty things six inches long that clung to their one-piece garments.

"Hospitable place, Louisiana," growled Grant, gingerly inserting the point of his knife between a sluggishly squirming leech and the crotch of his environmental suit.

They heard a distant, ululating cry, which was answered several times over. The howls met and echoed in the dense foliage. The swampies were still tracking them. The two men started moving again, away from the calls.

"How many of these slaggers are we going to have to chill before they give up?" Grant demanded in exasperation.

"As long as one of them can walk," replied Kane grimly, "they won't give up."

Grant recollected what Kane had told him of his prior encounter with swampies, and how he had only managed to escape through trickery by turning the lethal bayou flora against them.

Even as Grant recalled this, a hideous croaking bellow rang out somewhere in the moist dark ahead of them. With it came a splashing splat, as of something extremely heavy slapping the mud.

"What the hell was that?" Grant asked.

Kane shrugged. "It could be anything in this place."

They had no choice but to keep moving forward, but they'd gone less than a hundred yards before they were forced to stop at the edge of a big patch of open marshland. The area was well lit by the bright stars and full moon. The mud shone silver in places.

Humping up out of the middle of it they saw a small island made of partly dead, partly growing plant matter. Grant pointed to it. "That might make a good place to hide out until morning. We'd be able see and hear the swampies before they could get to us."

Kane eyed the stretch of muddy marsh to the island and shook his head. "We'd leave a trail."

Grant nodded in agreement and turned away. The reeds on the far side of the marsh suddenly parted, and four swampies materialized from the shadows. He bit back a cry of disbelief and horror.

The four swampies were more than the walking wounded; they looked like walking autopsies. One had half of his hip and thigh shot away, exposed bone and muscle glinting wetly. The right arm of another man dangled by strings of gristle and muscle tissue. The third swampie bled from several bullet holes in his chest. Only the fourth mutie displayed no apparent injury.

He spoke when he saw them, extending his loaded crossbow. "Good sport, ville men. You're tough. But de game is over now."

Kane raised his Copperhead, setting the butt against his shoulder. He gauged the range at around eighty feet and he switched the selector switch to single shot. "I'm down to my last full magazine for the Copperhead. How about you?"

Grant shouldered his subgun. "I've got less than half a full load. We can't afford to miss with these head shots."

"There's probably more behind them, you know," Kane commented.

"I have that very same impression," retorted Grant dryly. He watched the swampies shamble toward them. "I'll take the two on the right. You take—"

A deafening bellow exploded from the marsh. The island of vegetable matter rose, heaving itself out of the mud. Filthy water streamed and splattered down.

The creature dimly resembled a turtle, but the great opalescent eyes were set three feet apart on the blunt, beaked head. Its monstrous, scaled, bowed legs were like tree trunks, supporting a huge, horny shell the size of a Land Rover. Foot-long, scimitar-curved claws tipped the webbed toes.

Grant and Kane froze, and the swampies came to a shambling halt. The two men didn't bother to aim their weapons at the vast, wet bulk rising from the mud. The blasters in their hands felt like toys. They simply weren't designed to deal with a threat on the scale of the creature.

The creature extended its massive head from beneath the overhang of the shell, its plate-sized nostrils quivering. Cold eyes fixed on the swampies standing at the edge of the marsh.

"It smells their blood," Grant breathed. "They're bleeding into the mud and that's what roused it—"

Whatever else he intended to say was drowned out by a grunting roar. Propelled by its gargantuan legs and flat feet, the creature lunged out of the marsh like a coiled spring. Before Grant and Kane could even blink, the weight of what must have been ten tons hit the mucky ground of the bank. The impact sent mud cresting in a wave, drenching the two men with filthy water and bits of plants.

A blood-chilling roar of screaming and bellowing arose. The creature's great limbs kicked and flailed, and its beaked snout opened, then closed with a snap. A swampie writhed between the huge jaws. He had time to scream once. Bones crunched, and the lower half of the man fell to the ground while his torso slid down the monster's gullet, swallowed in a single gulp.

At that, Kane and Grant turned and ran in the opposite direction.

"He's not going to regenerate from that," Kane panted.

"No shit," wheezed Grant.

As they struggled through a copse of ferns, Kane said, "I thought the giant variety of mutie animals were extinct."

"So?" asked Grant disinterestedly.

"So, over the last couple of months we've run into a sand worm, a giant snake and now that thing."

Tersely, Grant replied, "Under the circumstances, you should be more concerned about *us* becoming extinct."

After wading hip-deep across a scum-filmed stream, they reached high ground and paused to catch their breath near a high-rooted mangrove. Although they saw no sign of the rodent or the swampie horde, they heard a dog bay, and what sounded like the distant whinny of a horse.

Neither man commented on the sounds, but when they moved on, they did so at a cautious walk. They hadn't advanced more than a few yards when they saw the man's arm.

Dusky of complexion, it was wrapped in the bloody tatters of a shirtsleeve. At one end a hand contracted around the wooden handle of a machete; at the other end was a mess of splintered bone and hacked flesh.

Kane stooped over it, poking at the hand with the tip of his combat knife. "Whoever it belonged to wasn't a swampie. He's got fingernails. It's not more than a few hours old."

Grant played his microlight along the muddy trail. "There's the rest of him."

They went to the corpse and realized quickly that Grant's assessment had been wrong. The man's body had two arms, but he was missing his head. A few yards away, they found the man who'd had his arm lopped off. Lying beside him was another decapitated corpse, and next to him was a dead swampie with a hole in his forehead.

A bullet had struck the mutie just above the left eye, leaving a neat dark hole from which blood still seeped. The exit wound was huge—a portion of skull the size of Grant's fist had been blown out, bone, blood and brain matter mixing with the ooze of the ground.

"Somebody's got blasters around here," Grant murmured. "Looks like a thirty thirty might have done that."

"Yeah," Kane agreed. "That somebody doesn't seem to like swampies any more than we do."

Straightening up, Kane splashed his light around and saw more corpses, at least six of them minus their heads, and unlike the severed arm, the heads were nowhere in sight. His pointman's sense rang a faint alarm, but he wasn't sure of the trigger.

"Hell of a fight here. Looks like the swampies were collecting heads."

"Whose heads?" Grant asked.

A lilting voice floated through the darkness. "Ours, *mes amis.*"

Chapter 18

"Hold it there," said the throaty voice in a thick Creole accent. "Drop the blasters. Keep your hands in the air now and turn around slow."

Kane's keen ears had heard not a single sound until the commands had been given. However, even if the words were hard to understand, the intent and delivery were unmistakable.

Grant and Kane did as they were told, letting the Copperheads fall from their fingers into the dirt. Weary and winded, they needed time to size up the situation, and they couldn't think of any better way to do so than turning around.

Surrounding them in a semicircle was a group of half a dozen men. A seventh person was mounted on horseback. Kane saw it was a woman, a girl really. Her skin was a warm chocolate in color, and her dark eyes were only a shade lighter. Her nose was very straight, her nostrils flaring widely out, and her lips were full and pouting.

Her great mass of dreadlocked hair tumbled in thick braids to her waist. She wore jeans, sandals and a man's ragged, buttonless flannel shirt. The tails were knotted at her midriff and barely covered her breasts. Silver glinted at her bosom, bright against the darkness of her skin. Her eyes were cold and strange, yet gleaming with intelligence and resolve.

She wasn't beautiful in the conventional sense, but there was a wild loveliness about her that held the eyes of both Kane and Grant.

Beside her horse crouched a four-legged, black-and-tan shape. It was the biggest dog either man had ever seen, with a huge head and a shovel-shaped underslung jaw from which dark ivory fangs protruded.

The woman's male companions had also been on horseback, three per side. Some of them were Caucasian, while others looked as if they were a mixture of Indian and black.

The woman stayed in the saddle of the dun mare, perched in the stirrups, peering down at them in the moonlight. Every man there had a gun trained on Grant and Kane, a lethal mix of rifles and pistols. One man aimed a lever-action Winchester at Grant's chest.

"Like I said," he sidemouthed to Kane. "A thirty thirty."

Kane didn't respond. Regardless of their weaponry, there were too many to outshoot, and nowhere to run except into the arms of swampies or the teeth of rats.

"Those big-ass blades, *mes amis*," the woman said. "We'll take them off your hands, as well."

One of the men claimed Kane's combat knife, sliding it into a sash. He gave a quick pat-down to check for other weapons, and pronounced Kane clean. He moved on to Grant.

"What evil path brings you into this land?" the woman asked in an arrogant tone.

"We seek missing friends," Grant replied.

"You are in trouble," the woman said in a gentler voice. "There are powerful enough problems here yet to come without outlanders like you showing up to muddy the waters."

"Like what?" Kane asked. "The plague?"

Grant indicated the bayou with a jerk of his head. "Or the shitload of swamp muties creeping around here collecting heads?"

The woman and several of the men reacted with uneasy surprise. They engaged in a hurried whispered conference in Creole. After a couple of minutes, Grant cleared his throat noisily.

The woman gave them an annoyed look. "What are your names?"

"Kane."

"Grant."

"Who are the friends you seek? Two women?"

Now it was their turn to react with uneasy surprise. "Yes," Grant answered. "Have you seen them?"

The dark woman responded with another question. "Does one of them practice the healing arts?"

"You might say that," Kane said.

"Did you travel by the pathways invisible?"

Kane and Grant hesitated before replying, exchanging a brief glance. Knowledge of the mat-trans gateways was one of the most ruthlessly guarded secrets in postnuke America. However, it was obvious the people who lived in the region had been inside the redoubt many times.

Kane repeated slowly, "You might say that. Would you mind telling us who you are?"

The young woman sat up straighter in the saddle. "I am called Mama Esther."

Grant smiled. "You don't look old enough to be anybody's mama."

Esther looked slightly offended. "No, M'sieu Grant, it is a title, bestowed upon me by the people of Moudongue. I am the high priestess of *vaudaux*, although I don't expect you to understand what that means."

"Voodoo?" ventured Grant.

Mama Esther nodded. "I am impressed. Now both of you will come with us."

Kane and Grant didn't move, and gun barrels snapped up. Caught in a bad situation that looked to be deteriorating, Kane cursed himself for a number of reasons—first and foremost for getting caught flat-footed by a bunch of mush-mouthed Cajuns. He was so exhausted and wrung out, he hadn't responded to the alarm triggered by his pointman's sixth sense.

Grant made a dismissive gesture with his upraised left hand. "As much as we appreciate the invitation, we should find our way back to those pathways invisible."

"I don't think you understand," Esther said mildly. "Your arrival was foretold."

"Foretold by who?" demanded Kane.

"By me in a vision. Therefore, you're coming with us."

"That's what you think," Kane said softly as the queerly silent Cajuns moved in to flank him, the closest ones holstering their guns so their hands would be free.

The two largest men took the lead positions, both wider and taller than Kane, but there was nothing about them that could be considered flabby or fat. They were lean, hard men, much like Grant and Kane themselves. All muscle. Both had dark, bony faces and flashing dark eyes. There was no malice in their faces, only calm resolve. Two more men bracketed Grant.

Each of them took an arm and a wrist, clamping down firmly with their strong fingers and hands. The result had Grant and Kane feeling that they were in the grip of mighty steel talons. They didn't bother to struggle or prevent the Cajuns from stripping their Sin Eaters from their forearms. They conserved their flagging energy and their fading strength. Esther still had talking to do; that much the two men could discern from the woman's placid demeanor.

"If you take us by force, other people will come after us," Kane said with as much menace as he could muster. "By those pathways invisible. And they won't be as friendly as we are. That's not a threat, but a cold hard fact."

"I don't believe you, M'sieu Kane," retorted Mama Esther. "I did not see any others arriving by the path but you and two women. They are with the old one, and you will be with us. A balance of assets."

"What if we say no?" Grant rumbled dangerously.

The girl fluttered a hand through the air. "You may say no all you wish. It might amuse the *loa*. Regardless of how many times you say it, you will still be coming with us. If you choose to do so unwillingly, then you must pay the price."

Then Kane lost what was left of his frayed temper.

THE TWO CAJUNS BEGAN dragging Kane forward, and he practiced a simple and time-honored move. He lifted his leg and stomped down as hard as he could with his boot heel, mashing it into the instep of one man's foot. Since the Cajun wore only sandals, Kane felt the delicate metacarpal bones break beneath his heel.

The sudden, overwhelming pain caused the man to involuntarily release his upper arm, freeing Kane to deal with the second captor. Kane fell back, snaking his upper body to the left and swinging out with his right fist. A good solid impact ran up his arm when his knuckles connected with the man's jaw, snapping his head over with a small spray of spittle and blood.

Kane stayed balanced on the balls of his feet, raising his hands for protection and keeping Grant to his back. The man he had stomped lurched forward and brought up his knee, smashing it into Kane's crotch.

Kane didn't give the attacker the pleasure of hearing him scream, although both testicles were singing a duet of white-hot agony. The environmental suit had cushioned the impact, but still he staggered and deliberately dropped to his right knee. The man, favoring his injured foot, tried driving his knee into his face.

With his left arm, Kane deflected the knee and reached out, palm up, and clutched the man's testicles, which he squeezed as hard as he could. The Cajun screamed in pain, but Kane maintained the hold as a form of payback. His Mag martial-arts instructor called it Monkey Steals the Peach.

The men flanking Grant, paralyzed by the sound of the shrill screams ripping out of the throat of their companion, were almost motionless. Grant decided to move, yanking free of the Cajun on his right and shooting his left elbow back into his throat.

The man staggered backward, holding his throat in both hands, his tongue protruding from his mouth. Mama Esther shouted something. She sounded very angry.

With wild whoops, all of the Cajuns converged on

Kane and Grant with fists, feet and gun butts. Even the dog joined in, baying and barking.

To both Kane and Grant, it was as if they were reliving the day of their final examinations when they were sixteen, their last day as recruits and their first as badge-carrying Cobaltville Magistrates. There was no such thing as failure of the examination—those who survived it were the ones who didn't fail.

The test had no true name, but everyone called it Blood Stomper. Kane in particular remembered that day, nearly seventeen years later, with a painful vividness. Already possessed with a near inhuman drive to win, the young Kane had been a ferocious opponent. Even the larger recruits tended to give him his due, and tried to keep from being run down when Kane had the ball.

Blood Stomper mixed elements of predark American football with European soccer, but what few rules were in place served to drive home the object of the game—get your team's ball from one end of the playing field to the other, and damn the consequences. The ball was only out of play when it went out of bounds, or the carrier was stopped in his tracks by almost any means possible.

The concept of being fouled wasn't one of the rules. Also missing from Blood Stomper were protective helmets, padding and gear. The recruits played in little more than loincloths. There was no protection. Rarely did an examination end without multiple injuries, ranging from bloody noses to fractured skulls. Deaths, although not commonplace, weren't rare.

Kane had taken the ball that day and run like the hell winds of Texas, face flushed, feet pumping, the sound of his overtaxed lungs rasping in his ears. Blockers on his side did their best to clear the way, but Kane was moving too fast and dealing with his encroaching foes in two ways—he either outmaneuvered them and kept moving forward, or he went right through them. He was confident in his speed and reflexes and so became careless, if not downright cocky.

That day his drive and speed were not adequate to keep him safe. He took an elbow to the throat and fell down fast and hard, flat on his back, gagging from the blow and gasping to regain the wind that had been shoved out of his lungs when he slapped down on the hard ground beneath the grass.

The opposing team then used their fists and feet to keep him from ever getting up again. There wasn't anything personal in trying to beat him to death—it was part of the examination. He would have done the same to a fallen member of the opposing team.

The pain induced by the flurry of kicks and blows had been incredible. Kane had never forgotten the sensation of smothering and choking mixed with being slammed by a convoy of sledgehammers.

The sledgehammers of Kane's youth were back in full force, each of them thudding down against his skin—hitting bone and muscle. What the Cajuns did to him out on the bayou brought all those memories back in a rush. His vision blurred, and he felt vomit rise into the back of his throat. His mouth was hit by a fist and his teeth cut his lower lip, bringing salt and blood. His own sweat blinded his vision, but he caught a blurry impression of Grant going down under two rifle butts.

There was no way to prepare for the pummeling he received. Open and closed hands smashed into his face, while feet drove into his belly. He managed to get off a vicious kick of his own, very well placed, and had the satisfaction of seeing a man rolling in agony on the ground, clutching his groin and wailing.

For his effort, the kick was returned twofold. Kane's head fell forward, facedown. A heavy foot landed on the back of his neck, mashing his face into the moist earth. He struggled and managed to turn his head to one side to keep his nostrils and mouth clear. He screwed his eyes shut and then blinked them open, trying to stay conscious.

He thought he had succeeded until he realized he was being pushed out of inky depths by waves of pain. Those waves were expanded by the jostling of the trotting horse he was tied to. At least the pain meant he was still alive, and he could use it to keep his mind centered.

Kane opened his eyes and looked into a red-tinged darkness. Blurred trees were whipping past, their barren branches framing an equally out-of-focus moon. For a quick second, he feared permanent damage might have been done to his vision, but clarity returned.

The sledges were still hammering along, hitting him in time with the sound of the horse's hoofbeats as it galloped on the old scrub path. The world around him was gray in the night. He wanted to curse, but lacked the necessary strength to open his mouth and form the words. All he could do was breathe, and even that was labored and painful through an aching rib cage.

His hot breath whistled in and out of his nostrils, which were caked with dried blood. He resisted the urge to sneeze. A sneeze at this juncture might blow his head clean off his shoulders, if a stray tree branch didn't knock it off first.

From the jostling and the confusing mess of dimly moonlit ground and sky, Kane realized he was tied over the saddle of the horse belly down, legs on one side and arms on the other. Draped over the saddle leather like a sack of potatoes, and feeling about as lively, he was seeing the world upside down. His ankles and wrists were bound to the stirrups, and he wondered if Grant was enjoying the same travel accommodations.

And with every step the animal took, the sledgehammers came calling. Kane felt his conscious mind slip away, into sleep, into a retreat from the agony he was experiencing. If only the horse would stop moving, just for sixty seconds, he could deal with his predicament. But the damn nag kept running at a gallop. Kane wondered what had been done to the animal to make it react so spooked, then decided he didn't want to know.

The horse ran and bounced and moved with apparently no intention of stopping anytime soon. Each jostle created a new explosion of pain at the end of each and every nerve ending in Kane's bruised and battered body. He licked his lips, feeling the split in the lower one, and tried to work up enough energy to call out a command. He was rewarded with an arid rasp that was so faint he knew the horse would not have heard even if they were standing still, which they decidedly were not. With the noise the beast was kicking up Kane doubted he would have been heard with a bullhorn.

He knew that unless he came up with something, and triple fast, he was a passenger until the horse decided to stop running. Kane tried to move, wiggling his lower body where it rested across the horse's back. The end effect was to make his guts feel as if they were going to fall out of his mouth, and the horse still kept running. He was grateful he hadn't eaten anything solid in more than a day.

Kane clenched his teeth and prayed he would pass out again. He didn't, but the horse's gait faltered and its pace slowed to a merciful walk. He heard it blowing noisily, snorting as if irritated. He tried to lift his head, but he felt the pressure of a hand on the back of his neck, holding him down.

Over the hoofbeats, he heard Mama Esther say, "We're almost home, M'sieu Kane. I regret bringing you in such a fashion, but it was your choice. Every choice has a price."

Chapter 19

The cobwebs stretched over Brigid's eyes were too thick to see through at first. She could see only patterns of light, some dark, some bright, moving around slowly. She heard vague sounds that resolved into a voice, whispering in her ear, urging her to wake up.

Then she felt someone systematically slapping her face. The cobwebs parted, and she saw Doyle looking down at her. She lay in his lap, his head and shoulders silhouetted by the bonfire flaring madly behind him.

"You've got to wake up," Doyle whispered. "I can't protect you if you don't wake up."

Brigid blinked, craned her neck and saw a swampie grinning lasciviously down at her, the one Ocajnik had addressed as LeGrand. His lips glistened with blood, his teeth red-filmed. He had pushed his loincloth to one side and rubbed his half-erect and uncircumcised penis vigorously.

She tried to rise, hampered by her bound hands. Her surroundings slowly came back into focus. Swampies clustered around the tarp on their hands and knees, drinking the blood, gorging themselves on it. She was irresistibly reminded of a clump of ticks, sucking on blood until they were bloated.

They laughed, voices slurred. Ocajnik stood and watched, eyes dreamy, the handsome host again— except for the wet scarlet coating his face and staining his clothes and hands. The sexual tension was as rich and thick as the coppery tang of fresh blood.

Doyle helped Brigid to her feet, and as she swayed unsteadily, temples throbbing, she saw DeFore standing close by, head bowed, eyes open but not seeing.

Ocajnik beamed at Brigid. "Hast thou realized the arrogance of human reason now? What does humanity know of the mysteries of this Earth?" His tone became oily with mock sympathy. "'Tis a terrible shock to come to the understanding that common human laws have no validity or true significance. Thou needs time to rest, to come to terms with what thou has learned. Later, thou will learn more."

He gestured dismissively. "Thou may contemplate all of this in the pit. Doyle, take them."

With hands on both women's shoulders, Doyle guided DeFore and Brigid through the camp. DeFore shuffled along sluggishly, barely lifting her feet more than an eighth of an inch above the ground. She moved like a somnambulist.

Most of the swampie men and women had consumed large quantities of home brew and were stumble-footed drunk. They passed several who were violently ill, vomiting copiously. Others lay passed out and snoring. Children wandered around, helping themselves to pots of food.

Bless the beasts and children, Brigid said to herself bitterly.

A thought occurred to her, and she asked, "Did Ocajnik kiss all of them?"

Doyle murmured, "He didn't have to. They've been waiting for his return for a long time, since skydark. They're part of him—they always have been."

"How can that be?" she demanded. "They're products of genetic engineering."

He nodded dolefully. "Yes."

He pulled the two women to a halt before a pallet of crudely nailed wooden slats. He lifted it away, revealing a cisternlike pit.

"You must go down there," he directed.

Brigid eyed the edge of the hole and involuntarily drew back. "What's down there?"

"Nothing…yet."

Doyle stepped behind her and Brigid felt a pressure between her wrists. Then her hands were free. Doyle surreptitiously pocketed the knife as Brigid raised her hands, looking at the rawhide thongs half-buried in the flesh of her wrists. She tried to flex her fingers while hiding the agony of returning circulation from Doyle.

"Why must we go down there?" she asked, peeling away the leather strands embedded in the skin.

"Two men, brothers in all but blood, will come

looking for you," Doyle answered quietly. "If they cannot see you, they cannot find you."

With that, Doyle put a hand on the small of her back and propelled her over the edge of the hole. Brigid did not allow a cry of fright to escape her lips as she plummeted into the pit. The fall was short, less than ten feet, and cushioned by the thick mud at the bottom. She landed on all fours with a splat. She felt small things wriggling beneath her hands and feet.

DeFore landed awkwardly, nearly on top of her. Doyle placed the pallet back over the opening. Some pale moonlight spilled down between the slats. She and DeFore crouched in the mud, not speaking or moving, just listening to the rasp of each other's breathing.

By any sane measurement, Brigid knew she should be terrified and despondent. Ocajnik's power over the swampies seemed absolute, and it required a conscious effort for her to keep from surrendering to utter despair. She glanced over at the mud-smeared DeFore, who sat hugging her knees, her eyes darting wildly like some trapped animal.

The woman's external identity had been peeled away—doctor, scientist, rebel, exposing the naked beast within. Silently, Brigid Baptiste vowed she would not allow that to happen to her. She had been taken prisoner several times in the past, but never had she felt so helpless. She forced her intellect to battle the terror clouding her mind and she sought to establish a balance between analysis and horror.

"DeFore—"

The woman twitched as if the sound of her name were like the sting of a whip against her bare flesh.

"Reba," Brigid began again. "Kane and Grant, maybe even Domi, will come after us. They may be close. We've got to be ready."

DeFore didn't answer.

"We've got to think our way through this," she continued in a low, calm voice. "We've got to come up with something to change the set of variables."

DeFore inhaled sharply but still didn't respond.

Brigid fell silent, then clumsily moved over to sit beside DeFore. She tried to edge away, but the damp walls of the pit kept her from moving too far. Brigid put an arm around her shoulders. DeFore's muscles were so locked, so rigid, it was like trying to hug a bronze statue. Calmly, softly, in the scholarly tone she had perfected during her years as an archivist, Brigid began talking. To survive, one needed a clear head. She worked hard to keep hers that way, and now she tried just as hard to clear DeFore's.

"I think your hypothesis that Ocajnik was the source of the chimeric cells used by Enterprise Eternity, which created the Cornelius family, may be dead-on. Of course, that doesn't explain exactly what he is or where he came from, but it gives us a jumping-off point for some halfway educated guesses."

She paused and added wryly, "I know speculating

and theorizing gets on your nerves, but just bear with me. It helps to talk this out.''

DeFore half closed her eyes, face impassive.

"Let's proceed from the assumption that all folklore has a basis in fact," Brigid continued. "Distorted and disguised, but that legends are indications of actual occurrences. Over time, the true historical connection is lost or forgotten.

"Perhaps thousands—maybe even tens of thousands—years ago, a race of entities existed that were feared both as demons and gods. Elemental spirits, maybe. Creatures made primarily of energy. Ocajnik may be one of them. His powers are inherent and natural, seeking control by a form of mental and emotional parasitism, as a vampire sucks blood by instinct rather than by any conscious design. Maybe he and others like him became the source of all vampire legends.''

The metallic tension in DeFore's body relaxed a bit. Just a little, almost imperceptibly, but it was enough to encourage Brigid to go on.

"Furthermore, like all parasites, Ocajnik must give something back to his host, a beneficial side effect, even if it is superficial and transitory. He can project feelings of pleasure at the same time he's draining his victims of energy, giving a sense that all is good, tricking the host's physical and spiritual senses. There's an actual biological side effect, sexual in nature. Doyle mentioned something about the release of endorphins.''

DeFore's lips stirred slightly. In a dull, strained whisper, she said, "Endogenous morphine controls the body's reaction to pain…it plays a role in pleasurable activities like eating…and sex."

"Exactly." Brigid did not allow the relief at DeFore's participation in the discussion, as subdued as it was, to register either in her voice or manner. She acted as if she had expected it all along.

"It's possible Ocajnik adjusts the release of endorphins in the human body," she said. "He does this instinctively. Vampires are popularly believed to be addicted to blood. Maybe it's not just the blood that causes a habitual reliance, but the pleasure-inducing chemicals produced by our own bodies. He can tamper with the systems governing the internal production of endorphins.

"This works out for him because the critical, reasoning parts of the brain move slowly. Erotic thoughts and a fixation on physical sensation become dominant. It's a form of biochemical mind control.

"It's significant that both you and Doyle used the same phrase—'it's not me'—to describe how you felt. The higher brain functions, though impaired, still operate on a nominal level so you can at least understand what is happening."

DeFore stirred slightly, her muscles losing a bit more of their rigidity. Quietly, she said, "Maybe critical enzyme activity is inhibited, as well, causing the neurons to fire repeatedly."

"Yes," said Brigid. "That seems likely."

"Then that means—" DeFore's words trailed off. She bowed her head and bit her lip.

Brigid pulled her closer and whispered, "That means what happened to you wasn't your fault."

DeFore lost what little control she had left then, bursting into tears. She wept openly, keening, shaking and crying, rocking to and fro. Brigid held her tightly, letting her pump out every drop of shame and humiliation. Tears flowed from her eyes, cutting runnels through the grime caked on her cheeks.

"It wasn't your fault," Brigid crooned to her over and over. "It wasn't your fault. It wasn't you."

Finally, the tears slowed. Shivering and sniffing, DeFore husked out, "How can we stop him?"

"I don't know," Brigid replied flatly. "But he's flesh and blood, and therefore he can be hurt."

"But if he's not human—"

"In mythic lore, if a demon assumes the attributes of mankind, then its flesh can perish. Even if he is an old one, a vampire, he has the limitations of a human body. He's vulnerable."

DeFore swiped a hand over her running nose, further smearing mud over her face. "But what about the plague? The rats? How does he control that?"

Brigid was silent for a long, contemplative moment, then sighed heavily. "I don't know. Traditionally, vampires are able to control the meaner things in nature, the vermin, the scavengers. There could be a form of telepathy at work here, a psychic interdependence."

"Or it could be there is no explanation," DeFore said in a small, little-girl voice. "It could be just what it looks like—supernatural, demonic—and Ocajnik has nothing to do with stimulating endorphins or body chemicals."

Brigid compressed her lips as a shiver shook her. "I won't accept that. I *can't* accept that."

DeFore said nothing for a long stretch of time. Then she asked, faltering, "Do you really think Grant and Kane will come for us?"

"That's about the only thing I'm sure about," she replied confidently.

DeFore snorted with a touch of her old imperious manner. "With the risks they take, we don't know that they didn't get themselves chilled in South America."

"I know they didn't. Just like I know they're somewhere out in the swamp already, looking for us."

DeFore looked at her skeptically. "How do you know that?"

Brigid groped for an answer, then shrugged. Lamely, she answered, "I just know."

The head ruled the body, thinking came before emotions, but Brigid always shied away from trying to explain the bond between she and Kane. Logically, there *was* no explanation. They were bound by spiritual chains, linked to each other and the same destiny.

She recalled another name she had for him: *anam-*

chara. In the Gaelic tongue, it meant "soul-friend." Dreams they'd had during a mat-trans jump suggested that not only had they lived past lives, but in all those lives they were continually intertwined with each other in some manner. The idea that she and Kane had existed at other times in other lives had seemed preposterous to her when it had first come up. Maybe it still would have if she hadn't experienced those jump dreams herself.

Resolutely, Brigid pushed the conjectures away. What mattered most was survival until Kane and Grant arrived. She knew they would, because believing anything else would have been intolerable.

It seemed as if hours passed in the pit. Brigid wondered why sunrise didn't come. At other times, she felt that time was not moving at all, and it had been only minutes since they were placed in the hole. Time became immeasurable. Finally, she dozed off, but she awoke in what felt like seconds. It was still dark, but she heard a scuff and scrape of feet above her.

She looked up, but quickly looked away as loose dirt from the edge of the hole sifted down into her face. Someone was lifting away the wooden pallet, and fear and hope warred in her mind.

Then a rat landed on her lap. She didn't scream, but her body thrashed with utter loathing and she kicked the little thing hard. It screamed.

DeFore echoed that scream as another rat plunged down from above, then another and another.

"Hey, yo' bitches," said a laughing voice above

them. "We t'ink yo' need some company down dere!"

Brigid felt leathery paws touch her bare shoulder, and she tore a rat from her back and smashed it head-first against the wall of the pit. Her breath came hot and short in her throat.

"Anam-chara," she whispered in an aspirated voice. "Where are you?"

Chapter 20

The ville, if it could be called that, was set in the center of a bowl-shaped hollow, a natural amphitheater. It wasn't more than a jumble of tar-paper shacks and reed-roofed huts built around a large concrete structure, probably an old outbuilding from a predark estate.

Like everywhere else Kane and Grant had been that night, the main thoroughfare of the ville was choked with mud. A row of public outhouses lined the bank of a wide stream. Judging by the stench collected around them, they hadn't been attended to a long time. A string of small fires burned along the rim of the hollow, casting a greenish flame and a nauseating odor. Evidently, they were kindled from wood that had been treated with sulfur, which only added to the vile effluvium provided by the outhouses.

Rows of flat-bottomed, sharp-prowed boats were tied to the posts of a splintery wharf stretching out over the stream.

The people, for the most part, were swarthy of complexion, although it was hard to ascertain whether their skin tone came naturally or was just residue from living in the swamps.

The makeshift settlement was like dozens Grant and Kane had seen over the years in the Outlands. Villes like this, far from the authority of the baronies, were used as refuges by slaggers, men and women who lived outside the law, often with a blood price on their heads.

After Kane and Grant were untied from the horses, they entered the concrete block building, wobble-kneed and bleary-eyed, behind Mama Esther. A brass bell and striker hung by the door. She opened it and waved them in. The first thing they noticed was the coolness of the room. The interior was air-conditioned, and the temperature difference was akin to walking facefirst into a glacier.

They saw a black-and-gray metal box humming peacefully in the far window pumping out chilly air from a front grill. The building had electricity, at least in the form of some kind of on-site generator. Luxuries like this were almost unheard-of in the Outlands. That meant at least one person in the ville was competent with writing and machines. Techies were worth their weight in ville scrip, and got the best rates on the open market for their talents.

The cool air was such a blessed relief, neither man was inclined to protest the rough treatment or the manner in which they had arrived in the ville for fear of being booted back out into the humid hell. Also, the two men shouldering Winchesters were strong inducements to keep their tongues curbed.

Floor-to-ceiling shelves lined the walls, and many of them held small metal cans with faded paper labels. Kane and Grant realized the building had once been a shelter, stocked with emergency foodstuff.

They knew that predarkers gleefully consumed anything out of a tin can as long as it was sealed, never dreaming the food within might actually spoil after a time—or, even worse, the foodstuff might break down and mutate into something that would give the consumer a raging case of the trots, a blinding bellyache or a deathly dose of food poisoning.

Following the directions of the riflemen, they went into a small bathroom and stripped off their mud- and blood-encrusted environmental suits. With water that flowed from the spigot, they did what they could to clean themselves. Both of them moved stiffly because of pain from their beatings. Kane's vision was still slightly blurred.

They dressed in ragged shirts and patched jeans provided by one of the men. They kept the boots from the environmental suits.

Mama Esther guided them to a wooden table and gestured for them to sit down at the benches. "Now, let me look at you."

To their surprise, she examined them quickly, professionally and thoroughly. Her long, beringed fingers probed and prodded their bodies expertly. At the end of it, Esther told Kane he probably had a mild concussion, and she was concerned about the possibility of internal bleeding from some of the kicks to the gut Grant had taken, but there was nothing that could be done except an extended period of bed rest.

"And that," she announced, "we cannot afford. Not until tonight's business is done. Now you must eat to regain your strength. I'm sure you're hungry."

From an adjacent doorway, two barefoot girls wearing thin cotton dresses of dirty white brought them dishes of turned wood with bent and rusty metal knives and forks. The food smelled enticing and sharply reminded Grant and Kane how long it had been since they had last eaten. Still, they exchanged wary glances.

Mama Esther caught the brief eye exchange. "Eat now," she said sternly. "We'll talk later."

They ate a hearty meal of corn bread, black-eyed peas, spiced crayfish and rice, washing it all down with clear, clean, cold water. Mama Esther waited until they were almost finished before starting to talk. She did so tersely, matter-of-factly, although her lilting Creole accent made her story difficult to follow in some areas.

"I am a *vaudaux* priestess," she announced. "A *houngan*, as was every member of my family going back hundreds of years. Do either of you know what the practice of *vaudaux* entails?"

"You make dolls and push pins into them?" Kane ventured.

"Black magic?" offered Grant.

Mama Esther's lip curled in a sneer. "I'm surprised you ville men know even that much, no matter that it's wrong. It's the practice of white and black magic. It originated in the ancient religions of western Africa, brought here by people sold into slavery.

"Like all magic, *vaudaux* depends on the cooperation of spirits, demons and deities. We call these spirits the *loa,* and *houngans* such as myself are their intermediaries.

"*Houngans* have many responsibilities, not just to the *hunsi,* the congregation, but to the *loa.* We undergo a long training and initiation period, all in absolute secrecy. Mine began when I was but six. Fully initiated *houngans* have what you call magic powers. I can see things that are about to happen. All of us wear symbols of the *loa* from whom our powers derive. This is mine."

By thumb and forefinger, Esther lifted a small silver cross that dangled by a thong from her neck. The crucifix was of hammered silver, set with tiny beads. At the ends of the traverse arms, small feathers fluttered.

"This is the cross of Saint John the Baptist, handed down from the first *houngan* of my family, Daddy Lefevre. Saint John joined the ranks of the *loa* when he was decapitated two thousand years ago. There is a huge assemblage of *loas,* and they choose certain *houngans* to watch and help, like guardian angels.

"But the goodwill of the *loa* is not obtained for

nothing. The *houngan* upon whom he smiles must not fail to oblige him in his wishes. If we contact our *loa* for help, and we disregard what they tell us, they take away our powers, mebbe our souls. My *loa* tell me about you, about the women you seek. So now you understand why I had to bring you here. I had no choice. Not only are lives at stake, but souls.''

She looked speculatively from Grant and Kane, waiting for their reaction. Finally, Grant asked, ''Do you know where the women we seek can be found?''

Esther nodded vehemently, her dreadlocks bouncing. ''I do indeed. The swampies have them. And Ocajnik has the swampies.''

Kane held up a hand, saying irritably. ''Back up a little. What do you mean the *loa* told you about us?''

''Your coming was foretold,'' she answered curtly.

''By whom?''

''By me.'' Her lips creased in a half smile. ''Neither of you put a lot of stock in prophecy, do you?''

Grant said smoothly, ''It's plain you do.''

''I use any and all tools at my disposal, M'sieu Grant,'' the woman replied. ''Wouldn't you?''

Kane fixed his most stony glare on her. ''So you and your slaggers nearly beat us to death because of a prophecy?''

Esther shrugged. ''You had the choice of coming of your own free will.''

''I hate mind readers,'' growled Kane. ''Rather

have a stickie at my throat. At least with them you know that you're getting in the way of a mutie."

"A mutie? You've gotten me confused with someone else," Esther retorted in an amused tone.

"What was the prophecy?" Grant asked. "How can you be so sure it pertains to us?"

Esther closed her eyes. In a soft voice, she said, "They come for him, they come from within. They come across the sky and back again. Across the world over and over. A patchwork, a joining of lands...thread through a needle, the pathways hidden. They travel by lightning, by thunder, through the magic of the storm. Harnessed in the caves, the energy electric. Worse, the energy forbidden, explosive, destructive. Yet still they come, they still come.

"There are two men, brothers in all but blood. Brothers in arms and in souls. They will seek two women who possess healing knowledge. They will come from the pathways hidden and arrive at the forbidden place of dead science."

Kane felt a chill go up his back and across the nape of his neck as Esther stopped speaking. It was obvious "the forbidden place of dead science" was Redoubt 47.

Grant cleared his throat and looked toward Kane. "You have to admit, that certainly describes us."

Kane showed no emotion. "Mebbe."

"There is no 'mebbe,'" Esther said fiercely. "Otherwise, I never would have gone out to find you. If the *loa*'s words were true, and they have never proved wrong before, I knew you were on the way."

"So why not wait until we got here?"

"Because time was running out. What I saw is a danger to both of us. My foes are your own."

"What foes?" Kane demanded. "Swampies?"

Esther nodded. "*Oui.* Those you call swampies were created by unnatural means, the forbidden science. They are an affront to God, to the *loa*. They were spawned by a residue of the old one, Ocajnik."

"I don't understand," said Grant hesitantly. "Swampies are muties."

"From what we know of them," Kane put in, "they were created by something called the Genesis Project. We're not quite sure why, but since they have double circulatory and cardiovascular systems, it's pretty apparent they were bred for war."

Esther nodded in agreement. "That is the legend among my people, too. Black sorcery mixed with even blacker science, an old one's essence mingled with human blood. We have lived in peace with them for many years, though they are not to be trusted. Long ago they swore their allegiance to Ocajnik. They waited for his return. And now, at last, he has come."

"Who's this Ocajnik?" Grant asked, stumbling a bit over the pronunciation.

"He is a *what*, M'sieu Grant. An old one, one of the last of the elder things to stand before the tide of man and reason."

"That's not very precise," Grant pointed out broodily.

Esther shrugged. "How can one be precise about the nature of evil? Pure, unadulterated evil, not leavened or weakened by any emotion. He is Ocajnik, a creature who has never died. He woos all the darkness within the human soul like a lover. He knows the wisdom that has lasted out the aeons in the blackness beneath the earth.

"He is the king of the those shadowy hordes that revel among the tombs of the ancient dead when night veils the swamps and the rats flit among the offal. Those he kisses live forevermore in the darkness of the spirit."

Kane turned toward Grant and asked sarcastically, "Did that answer your question?"

Calmly, Esther continued, "Daddy Lefevre was the first of my line to contain Ocajnik, nearly three hundred years ago."

"So opposing this old one is like what," Grant inquired, "a family business?"

Her full lips pursed with distaste. "Over a century later, his work was undone by one of your white coats. The old one was found here in the bayou and revived by scientists who were obsessed with violating the fundamental will of God by finding a means to make man immortal.

"The old one, ever the deceiver, the trickster, went along with them in their hidden bunker, amused by their clicking computers, their vials of fluids, their hypodermics. They thought he was the answer to their mystery.''

She barked out a harsh, contemptuous laugh. ''Blind fools rushing to their doom. Ocajnik saw the whitecoats as a means to an end, to create a ready-made slave race.''

Kane grunted and turned toward Grant. ''The chimeric cells Lakesh told us about must have come from Ocajnik.''

''Is that possible?'' Grant asked doubtfully.

''Why not? And if his cells were spliced to swampie DNA, that might be how he controls them...a genetic link.''

Esther seemed uninterested in their input. ''Then came the nuke.'' She waved her hands and imitated the sounds of explosions. ''Cataclysms rocked the world, tore it asunder. Sections of America vanished under the waves. Whole nations were blotted out. The sky became dark, the world was hurled back into savagery. For a century and a half, Ocajnik ruled this land and those you call swampies. They marked themselves with a brand to show who was their master, and by this mark they might recognize one another.''

With a finger she traced lines around her eyes. ''It looked for a time as if he and his children might prevail and plunge the world back to the primordial horrors of the ancient times. But my great-great-grandmother, Mama Minuit, and her *hunsi* were able to contain Ocajnik yet again.''

"Contain him?" echoed Grant skeptically. "What's with all this containing shit? Why didn't she just chill him?"

Esther favored him with a pitying smile, as if he were a backward child failing to reason out a simple problem in arithmetic. "The old ones cannot die, M'sieu Grant. Though when they assume the form of a human, they are subject to many of the limitations of humanity.

"All men know this of the ancient gods, who often appeared in the guise of mortals. In human form, they can only use human faculties. They can be wounded by certain weapons."

"Like what?" Kane asked.

"Silver, for one," she replied. "Salt for another."

"Silver and *salt?*" Kane's tone was incredulous.

"Providing they're both properly blessed and purified, of course."

"So now this Ocajnik is back?" inquired Grant.

"He is awake and walking the shadows again, *oui*. He has already gathered his followers. This night they set upon my people, slaughtering many, taking their heads as trophies. Soon they will come again, to murder us all. If we cannot be made Ocajnik's slaves, then we will die."

She paused for a moment and added grimly, "If we do not stop them, the plague brought forth by Ocajnik will spread, killing everyone who lives in this land, mebbe the whole world."

"That's a pretty tall order," Grant observed dryly.

"Ocajnik has plenty of time. He has already enslaved four ville men."

Kane nodded. "We met one of them in the redoubt. Was it your people who opened up and redecorated the place?"

"Oui," she confirmed. "A very long time ago. It was where the whitecoats spawned the monsters from Ocajnik's essence. His evil aura haunted it, so we tried to bless it, to sanctify it, to let the light and air of the world into it."

A line of consternation appeared on Esther's forehead. "It was in vain. Once Ocajnik was resurrected, and he heard my prophecy, he dispatched his minions to lie in wait for you and the women."

"How did he hear your prophecy?" asked Grant suspiciously.

Stolidly, Esther answered, "I told LeGrand, one of his minions. I had no choice."

Grimly, Kane said, "It sounds to me like this is your fault."

Esther gestured angrily, spitting a few words in Creole. Then, in English, she grated, "How can I make you understand? This is all about preordainment, about fate, the road of destiny. About the powers of darkness swallowing the light of reason!

"When the rats appeared and the plague broke out, the swampies knew it was a sign of their master's imminent return. They could not release Ocajnik himself because they could not touch his sepulchre. It was sealed by silver, by the cross of Saint John.

But they knew ville men, descendants of the white-coats who created them, would come here. History would repeat itself, and Ocajnik would bestride the bayou again.''

Grant scowled. "Then why didn't you stop the ville men from releasing him?"

"It was the will of the *loa!*" Esther cried in exasperation.

"Right," Kane drawled.

He stood up so suddenly from the bench that the men with the rifles fumbled to bring them to bear. Kane ignored them, saying, "Give us back our weapons and point us in the direction of the swampie settlement. We'll find our people and be on our way."

Esther shook her head, her coiled tresses bouncing like springs. "No."

"No?" Grant pushed back from the table and assumed his full, formidable height.

"No," she repeated coldly, firmly, not in the least intimidated. "The time is not yet nigh. We strike at sunrise, at the first cock crow, when his powers weaken."

"What's with this 'we' shit?" Kane growled.

She affected not to have heard him. "The *loa* will be with us. He will incarnate in my body during the *humfo* ritual. The *loa* will mount me and ride me as his horse. During the ceremony, you will be purified."

Grant and Kane said nothing for a long tick of time, first glancing toward each other then toward the

bores of the rifle muzzles staring at them like hollow
eyes.

At length, Kane muttered, "Why do I have the
feeling that being purified won't be a simple matter
of letting us take baths?"

Esther grinned, her white teeth flashing bright
against her dark skin. "Your instincts serve you well,
M'sieu Kane."

She went to the door and opened it. She struck the
bell twice. The sound was ringing and sharp. "I call
the *hunsi*. Your purification begins."

Chapter 21

The drumming was steady and regular, almost like the muffled beating of a huge heart, echoing all around the hollow, seeming to come from all sides at once. The sulfurous smoke of the many fires drifted around on a light, eddying breeze.

In the center of the natural amphitheater a bonfire blazed, only a few yards from the stream bank. High flames licked from rough-hewn logs, and people danced around them in time with the throbbing drumbeat. There seemed to be an equal number of men and women, most of them naked but for knotted loincloths. Sweat glistened on their bare flesh. Their bodies jerked in rhythm to the drums, as though the measured beats inflicted muscular convulsions.

Numerous goat-masked figures danced near the outer ring of fires, leaping and spinning like dervishes. The people who sat around Kane and Grant moved their shoulders with the drumbeats. From time to time, they uttered howling chants.

Gourds were dipped into a troughlike hollowed-out log filled with a greenish liquid. The congregation sipped from the gourds, shuddered and passed them along. Grant and Kane abstained, but they found themselves unpleasantly affected by the cease-less cadence. Kane found his shoulders moving to the barbaric rhythm and he swore.

"I saw a ceremony like this once," Grant mut-tered. "In a triple-poor Outland settlement, every-body dancing to bring rain. It gets into your bones after a while."

Kane nodded. "Where's Esther? I thought she was running this show."

As if on cue, the onlookers at the edge of the hol-low parted and a naked girl leaped nearly into the fire. It took both men a moment to recognize Esther. Her long dreadlocks were bound up in a multicolored scarf, and her body was painted bright yellow with bands of red over her breasts, back and belly. In her right hand, she held a yellowed human skull. In her left, she whirled the silver crucifix by its thong.

As if by its own accord, her slender body re-sponded to the rhythm of the drums, propelling her around the edge of the bonfire in a jittery, jerky, arm-flailing dance. Her eyes appeared to be closed, but somehow she managed to skirt the flickering flames. She danced through the billowing clouds of smoke, through showers of embers.

Esther circled the fire, then around the perimeter, whirling the cross over her head. The other dancers joined in, and Esther threaded her way among them, now and then facing one of the men, placing the skull between her thighs. The man would bend and bestow a kiss upon it. The onlookers bellowed out an incomprehensible song, interspersed with yips and yowls.

Kane watched, trying to fathom as much meaning out of the ceremony as he could. The drums continued to thunder, but now much faster and louder.

Esther twirled madly on the balls of her feet. Sweat pebbled her flat-muscled body where it wasn't covered by paint. Her pirouettes brought her closer and closer to where Kane and Grant sat on the ground. With a piercing, panting cry, she came to a stop before them.

Stooping down, Esther opened her eyes. They gleamed with a wild, deranged light, and her lips peeled back from her teeth in a grin. Both Grant and Kane felt an inward cringing at the grin—it was demented, mocking and superior all at the same time.

Mama Esther raised the skull to her lips, pressing them against a small hole bored in the rear of the cranium. She took a deep breath and exhaled into the hole. Whitish-gray powder, like ash pulverized to the consistency of dust, puffed out of the eye sockets in a cloud. It settled on the two men's faces. They sputtered, resisting the urge to sneeze.

Kane began to flick dust from his eyelashes when he experienced the bizarre sensation of ghostly fingers caressing his mind, as if they were probing something hidden, something valuable.

In a hoarse, altered voice, Mama Esther said, "Now you will be cleansed and reborn."

Kane and Grant allowed themselves to be gently

lifted to their feet by a pair of masked men and guided to the bank of the stream. Esther capered before them, chanting in a singsong cadence. All of Kane's instincts yelled at him, but it was as if his mind were shrouded in several layers of thick, soft velvet.

The two men were led down the bank and into the warm shallow waters. Mama Esther left the skull and the cross on the ground and, standing hip deep in the stream, she lifted both hands, palms outward. A goat-masked man slashed the edge of a curve-bladed knife across the flats of her hands, two bisecting strokes for each one. Superficial cuts in the shapes of crosses oozed bright red blood.

Esther chanted in a guttural, harsh whisper, employing a language that didn't sound like Creole. As she did so, the man clasped Grant's and Kane's left wrists, and deftly cut the same cross into the palms of their hands. Kane felt no pain whatsoever, not even dismay when he saw scarlet drops dropping into the brackish water.

Moving between the two men, the *houngan* clutched their hands tightly, squeezing so that trickles of intermingled blood streamed down her wrists and forearms and fell into the stream. They spread out in dark, wavering patterns.

Mama Esther continued to chant, squeezing their hands as if they were sponges until muscles stood out in stark relief on her slender arms and her entire upper body trembled with the exertion. Then the words ceased issuing from her throat and she relaxed her grip.

Still holding their hands, she murmured to them softly and they lay down in the stream, immersing their bodies in the water. Somehow, Kane understood the act was a symbolic drowning.

When they were hauled back up, soaking wet, Mama Esther drank a mouthful of water, then spit it directly into their faces. Their hands were bandaged with strips of gauze that smelled strongly of unguent.

Esther proclaimed, "You have been baptized in the name of Saint John. You are now purified. And we must get on with what must be done."

Wiping at the muddy mixture of ash and water on his face, Grant asked, "Which is…?"

"Salvation or damnation," Mama Esther replied. Her macabre grin widened. "Both will carry a heavy price."

IT SEEMED TO BRIGID that she and DeFore had fought for days against the rats. Her arms became leaden with the ceaseless flailing against the fur-covered bodies. Her upper body was bleeding from a score of tiny claw-inflicted wounds, but as yet none of the rats had bitten her or DeFore. Both women panted through constricted throats.

"Can't keep it up much longer," DeFore groaned beside her. The bodies of dead rats lay in heaps at the bottom of the pit. The few that she and Brigid hadn't killed feasted on the corpses, chewing their way through the soft underbellies.

The ceaseless whipping of her arms lagged, and a brown furry beast darted up her body toward her face and throat. DeFore shouted, seized it in her fists and beat at others with it, using it as a bludgeon. The captured rat squeaked and squealed, and the other rodents drew back, scrabbling just out of reach. They chittered in fear.

"Make it keep squealing," Brigid said breathlessly.

DeFore did, and while the rat shrilled in fright and pain, the others held back. "It won't last long," she panted.

"No," Brigid agreed. "And there's no way out...unless Kane and Grant come."

DeFore shook her head. "We'll have to get out of this ourselves."

Brigid said nothing, feeling a sickening despair fill her. At least the swampie had stopped dropping rats on them from above. He was content to stand around and shout encouragement to the rodents. She wasn't sure, but she thought he had a few favorites, ones that he singled out as the rats most likely to deliver the deadly bites.

Already the truce of fright seemed to be ending and the rats were scuttling back over the bodies of their dead brethren to the attack again. As she had since the first half-dozen rats had been dropped on them, Brigid dug her fingers into the moist wall of the pit and broke off a fist-sized clod. She hurled it with all her strength at a brown-and-white-spotted rodent, catching it full in its pointed snout. It twisted over backward on its hind legs and lay writhing with a broken neck.

DeFore broke the back of the rat between her hands over her knee and hurled its corpse among the survivors. The rats continued to circle them, but with regular sweeps of their arms and shouts the women were able to drive them back.

Above them, Brigid heard the murmur of another voice, the scuff and scutter of feet. She couldn't look up, as the rats wouldn't permit any distraction. Metal rasped overhead, followed by a sound like an ax chopping into wet wood. She heard a gurgling cry. A second later, she felt warm liquid sprinkle her bare back and shoulders. She thought at first the swampie was urinating down into the pit. Then she saw a speckling of blood on her upper arms.

An instant later, a round object plunged down from above and landed among the rats. It rolled briefly, and both women bit back cries of horror. It was the head of a swampie, the one Ocajnik had called LeGrand.

Doyle's urgent whisper filtered down. "Hurry up. I had to kill him. He wouldn't let me bring you up."

The rats, first frightened by the arrival of Le-Grand's head, became enthralled by the blood oozing from the ragged stump of his neck. They paid no attention as the women scrambled to their feet.

Doyle lay on his stomach at the edge of the hole, arms outstretched. "Hurry!"

"You go first," Brigid said to DeFore.

"No!" said Doyle sharply. "Not her. She's been kissed. She's one of the beasts. Leave her to the rats. She's immune to the plague now."

Brigid glared up at the man, raking her tangled, dirty mane of hair out of her eyes. "Both of us or neither of us."

Doyle hesitated, raised his head to glance around then nodded. "All right. Just hurry!"

Making a stirrup with her linked hands, Brigid heaved DeFore up into the arms of Doyle, who lifted her out of the pit. She heard a scrabbling behind her and saw several rats crawling over LeGrand's head, creeping toward her feet. She gathered herself and leaped straight up, clasping Doyle's forearms. With a grunt of exertion, he swung her up and out.

They crouched down in wedges of shadow, seeing no swampies nearby except for the headless body of LeGrand. With the blood-smeared machete in his hand, Doyle pointed to their bodysuits, which lay wadded on the ground. "I've brought your clothes...what's left of them."

The two women quickly donned them, finding them not impossibly torn, though the sleeves were rent. Chafed by the fabric, the scratches inflicted by the rat's claws began to pain Brigid.

Staring directly at her, Doyle said, "If you want to live, we'll have to get you out of here."

"How?" DeFore asked.

"Not you," he retorted. "You've been kissed. You're a beast now."

"She's not marked, is she?" Brigid realized Doyle was mad—not raving yet, but insane nevertheless, so she spoke to him quietly and reasonably, trying to appeal to the shred of rationality choked by the clouds of dementia.

Doyle squinted at DeFore, examining her closely. "No."

"Then she's not a beast, is she?"

Licking his lips uncertainly, he murmured, "No, I suppose not."

"All right, then," Brigid declared breezily, as if the matter were settled to the satisfaction of all parties. "Are there any weapons we can use?"

He shook his head slowly, waggling the machete. "Only this, which I took from LeGrand."

"Give it to Reba."

As he passed it over to her, DeFore asked, "How do we get out of here? By the stream?"

A line of concentration appeared in his forehead. "No, it's too well-guarded. If there's retaliation from the Moudongue congregation, it'll come from there. You'll have to go through the bayou."

Brigid and DeFore exchanged fearful glances. The torn bodysuits were not suited to braving the swamps. The boot socks weren't fitted to that kind of walking, either.

Doyle stood up. "Let's go."

He walked ahead, carelessly, with assurance, and DeFore and Brigid made no sound as they followed him through the camp. At its edge, he led them down a barely defined path. Briars snagged at their clothing and scratched at their hands. Brigid had to fight to keep from plunging desperately forward at a mad run that would have exhausted her within minutes.

Doyle stopped so suddenly DeFore nearly trod on his heels. He looked this way and that, murmuring, "Let me think, let me think…which way…"

There was no warning at all, not even a rustle of foliage but suddenly the shadows ahead of them were crowded with the short, squat figures of swampies. DeFore and Brigid whirled to retreat, but that way was blocked, as well, not just by swampies but by Ocajnik.

He smiled, folding his arms over his chest. "A rebellious beast must be disciplined. Doyle, you will go into the pit. The women shall be defiled. If they survive, they'll bear my mark."

Brigid knotted her fists, her jaw set rigidly. Resisting would only bring on her death, whereas if she submitted… She locked her teeth on a groan of despair. It was over and Kane had not come. When a swampie reached for her, she didn't struggle.

If Brigid surrendered philosophically, DeFore did not. She swept raging, screaming, toward the line of swampies around Ocajnik. Laughing, they parted before her and seized her from behind, forcing her to the ground.

She slashed with the machete and hamstrung a swampie so that he dropped to one knee, bleating in surprised pain. She took another swampie in the groin with a sideways swipe of the blade, and he pitched shrieking to the ground, hands clasped over his crotch, blood squirting between his fingers.

Ocajnik laughed with what seemed like genuine amusement.

Snarling in fury, swampies hurled themselves upon DeFore, wresting the machete from her hand. Snarling herself, Brigid threw herself upon them. The hand-to-hand fight was brief—twist, gouge, kick and punch.

The swamp muties seized her arms and legs, yanked her head back by her hair. A man approached her with the bloody machete in his hand. With a gloating smirk, he moved its blade suggestively toward Brigid's throat. Its wet edge touched the side of her neck.

Then somewhere in the darkness came a crack, like the breaking of a distant branch. All the swampies, even Ocajnik, reacted with surprise, eyes widening, heads turning in the direction of the sound. Everyone froze, silent, in attitudes of listening for a long moment. All except Brigid.

She laughed. It was hoarse, but it didn't hold a note of hysteria. Instead, it was a laugh of relief, overlain with a touch of triumph. She'd recognized the unmistakable report of a Sin Eater.

Chapter 22

The dugout canoe rounded the bend. The stream, wide and swift at that point, foamed brown at the boat's prow. The water was black, with wavering white shadows cast by the waning moon. Above the tree line in the eastern sky glowed the faintest salmon-pink sunrise.

Kane looked at the glimmer as he slid his paddle almost noiselessly in and out of the water, in tandem with the other four men in the little craft. He had almost convinced himself he had somehow returned to the days of the skydark, the eternal night.

Floating from upstream ahead of them came shrill cries and yells.

Mama Esther, sitting forward in the boat, said softly, "The beasts are still at their revels." She was dressed in the same clothes as when Kane and Grant first saw her. The only addition to the ensemble was a large leather bag slung over her right shoulder.

Working his paddle, Grant commented quietly, "From what you told us, they have a lot to celebrate."

"Your friends may be part of that celebration," she reminded him darkly.

Grant didn't need the reminder. He paused in his paddling to glance over his shoulder downstream and saw the second of three canoes, loaded with the *houngan's* heavily armed *hunsi*. Ammunition glittered dully in crossed bandoliers, and light glinted from long blades.

Somewhere in the bayou, paralleling their course, another contingent of the Monudongue warriors approached Ocajnik's camp on horseback. Counting himself and Kane, Grant figured there were at least thirty people closing in on the muties, by land and by water.

Mama Esther couldn't provide an accurate estimate of the opposition. She doubted the swampies numbered more than fifty, particularly after the casualties they had sustained in the battles during the night. The odds were unfavorable enough despite the swampies' primitive weapons. And Ocajnik was the most formidable X factor.

Esther suddenly stiffened and hissed a command. Her people obediently rowed toward the right-hand bank, drifting into tall reeds and bulrushes. Wordlessly, she pointed ahead. Kane and Grant leaned forward, peering in the direction of her finger.

About thirty yards away, they could just make out a sagging dock stretching over the stream. They also glimpsed three squat-bodied swampies right at the water's edge.

"It is as I feared," the *houngan* whispered bitterly. "They stand watch for us."

Kane glared, fanning away gnats from his eyes.
"They're standing sentry for an attack force, right?"

Esther's *"oui"* was puzzled and impatient.

"What if they don't see a force, but only one
man?"

Grant and the woman whipped their heads toward
him, startled. Contemplatively, Esther replied, "As
vicious as they are, and they're maybe so drunk, too,
they'd go after him themselves. It would be sport."

Kane nodded in agreement. "That's what I figure."

Swiftly, he unbuckled his Sin Eater from his forearm and removed his thick-soled boots. He whipped
his combat knife from the web-belt scabbard.

"What are you planning?" Grant demanded in a
raspy whisper.

"The old distract-and-conquer strategy," Kane answered blithely. "I'll let them see me splashing
around. If they come after me, the rest of you can
creep up and land the boats."

Grant shook his head in disgust. "What if they
catch your ass? Or worse, instead of coming after
you in the water, they just run back to the camp to
let everybody know there's a suicidal idiot in the
stream?"

"We won't be much worse off than we are now.
We can't go ashore without them spotting us any-
how, right? Besides, I'm counting on you to cover
my ass so they *can't* catch it."

Placing his combat knife between his teeth, Kane

slid his legs over the side of the canoe, brought his index finger to his nose and snapped it away in a sharp salute. Gravely, Grant returned it. It was a gesture the two men had developed during their Mag days and reserved for undertakings with a one-percent chance of success.

There was scarcely a splash to mark his smooth entrance into the stream. Ripples spread quietly, but Kane's head didn't break the surface again. Under water, he stroked for the darkness beneath the dock.

When he rose, it was with his hands against the slime-coated base of a piling. He lifted his head and peered through the shadows. Rays of light escaped from a bonfire burning somewhere inland. By that faint illumination, Kane made out the figures of the swampies on the bank.

He submerged noiselessly, then swam toward them. He took the knife from between his teeth and his head broke the surface. He spit a long jet of water in the direction of the bank, then backstroked leisurely away.

The swampies gaped at him in commingled shock and disbelief. One of them drew a blade from his ragged clothing and bounded into the stream. He vanished beneath the water.

Fisting his knife, Kane dived. There was no visibility under the black surface, but Kane had marked the swampie's course and his knife groped for him. The point touched living flesh and felt it flinch away. He stroked forward, at the same time lunging with his knife as if it were a sword. Its razor-keen point bit deep into the man's back.

Wrenching the blade free, he struck twice more, then swept backward. There was a great kicking commotion that made the water boil. The swampie's head broke the surface, and Kane heard a gasped cry in Creole. Instantly, the other two swampies took to the water, swimming toward Kane, trying to encircle him.

Kane stroked swiftly away, but a round head broke water within a yard of him. He flung himself toward it, his knife flashing in a decapitating swing. The head flinched back out of range and instantly disappeared, but not before Kane glimpsed a knife between its teeth, a knife that would now be seeking his groin.

It was useless to try to back-kick out of range. The swampie had the speed of a dive behind him, so Kane did the only thing possible. He plunged forward and to one side at the same time. He had an impression of two other swampies moving toward him, then he whirled to strike at the closest man. The mutie's knife broke water first, thrusting toward the spot where a moment before Kane had been.

Kane didn't wait for the whole man to show. He dived with the knife aimed directly for the body behind that arm. He felt the blade sink home, halfway to the hilt. He did not attempt a second stroke, but floundered on past the man, dragging his knife with him. There was no telling where the knife had struck, but he knew he hadn't inflicted a fatal wound.

Stroking cautiously beneath the water, knife hand feeling ahead for obstructions, he touched the splintery surface of a piling, circled it and allowed himself to drift upward. His lungs were straining and there was heavy pounding in his ears.

But when his head eased above the surface, he didn't gulp in air. Behind the post, he waited, listening. He didn't push out into the open. Probably the two or three swampies were doing as he did, treading water and waiting for their enemy to betray his position.

Soundlessly, Kane submerged and swam toward the spot where he had entered under the wharf. It was laborious work, pushing off from the base of a piling and groping ahead to keep from ramming headlong into another. Twice he submerged before, in the dimness, he could detect open space ahead of him. Then he exhaled noisily and began to swim with small splashings, deliberately making noise. Behind him all was silence.

He swam on, not too swiftly. When he had gone twenty yards from the edge of the wharf, he peered behind him. With the speed of fish, two swampies were swimming after him. He began to flounder, as if fatigued. The knives in the mouths of his pursuers were visible, glints of silver in the fading moonlight.

From the bank, Grant's Sin Eater spit red flame. There was a thin, inarticulate cry and one of the heads broke apart, then vanished. With the shot and the cry, Kane spun about and sped toward the remaining swampie. The man paused uncertainly, turned and began to swim back toward the wharf but at a pace that was markedly slow and burdened.

Kane swam after him with a powerful overhand, then it occurred to him that seconds before the swampie had been swimming easily. Even fear shouldn't have affected his speed so adversely. In fact, it should have had the opposite effect.

The thought was only half-formed in Kane's mind when he dived to one side, stroking with all his strength. He felt the faint concussion of Grant's second Sin Eater shot and burst above the surface to find another swampie frothing the water in a death flurry, a fist-sized cavity in the rear of his head.

The first swampie was making better time now for the dock. It was obvious the mutie's floundering was part of a trap. He had led Kane on until his companion could dive underwater and knife him from below.

The swampie thrashed and kicked, but Kane overtook him quickly. The man turned and lashed out impotently with his knife. With a quick grab, Kane latched on to his wrist. He wrenched and the weapon sank to the bottom.

Gurgling in anger and fear, the swampie fastened upon him with arms and legs, and black water closed over them as they sank below the surface. Kane struggled to free himself, the swampie clung to him with legs and arms like tempered steel, his head tucked beneath Kane's chin.

Colored lights danced in the blackness of the water, and he knew they signified approaching unconsciousness. Suffocating beneath the stream in the grip of the mutie, Kane had the knife between his teeth as his only recourse, even though he could not free his hands to wield it.

With enormous, tendon-straining effort, Kane twisted his head to one side, to turn the point of the long blade toward the swampie's neck. The noise of his own hammering heart was thundering in his ears. His lungs strained. He blew out a little breath through his nostrils to relieve the pressure. He managed to squirm sideways so the knife turned downward. He jabbed downward with the blade between his jaws.

The point sank into yielding flesh, and the swampie's grip loosened around him. Bubbles flooded from his open mouth, and Kane dimly heard him cry out. Kane wrenched and broke free, then, moving by instinct, he thrust the knife at an upward angle through the underside of the mutie's jaw.

He felt the point grind against bone as the fourteen inches of steel drove through the roof of the mutie's mouth and into his brain.

He whipped the knife free. A ribbon of crimson trailed from the point as the swampie's body went under. Then his head broke the surface, his eyes turned up and red-tinted water poured from his silently screaming mouth. Then the head went under again and there was nothing but bloody froth that slowly seeped away downstream.

Kane stroked for the bank and, when he reached the shallows, he turned and waved his knife over his head. As he did so, he heard in the distance the caw-ing crow of a rooster, then a crash of blasterfire.

Chapter 23

As Brigid laughed, she heard another shot followed by an eerie silence. Ocajnik hissed something in Creole, and the swampies began to mill back toward the camp, dragging her and DeFore with them. The silence was suddenly broken by the crowing of a rooster from somewhere in the bayou, but very close.

Ocajnik visibly blanched and pushed his way roughly through the confused swampies, shoving them out of his way. They made questioning sounds, reaching for him. He slapped their hands away.

The volley of gunfire ripping from the underbrush was not what the swampies or their master expected. Most of the muties were already running slap-footed toward the camp when what sounded like a dozen rifles banged in unison.

A bullet missed Brigid by inches, smacked into the side of a swampie woman's head and swatted her backward. She opened her mouth to scream, but only blood came out.

The muties set up a disconcerted squalling, slapping at their bodies where bullets struck them. The swampie who menaced Brigid with the machete clawed at the base of his spine. She watched the man drop the weapon and fall, kicking in agony.

Within a second of the fusillade, the swampies milled and swarmed like a colony of terrified ants. Shrieking and screaming, they raced blindly back toward their camp, bowling Brigid, Doyle and DeFore off their feet.

With a pounding of hooves, a line of horsemen appeared, crashing through the underbrush and firing rifles as they rode. They swept in like a flesh-and-muscle tidal wave, flame and noise spouting from the bores of lever-action Winchesters.

Brigid could catch only fleeting impressions as they galloped past. The mounted people were dressed in white cotton shirts and ragged pants and most of them were dusky of complexion and dark of hair and eye. They yelled high, strange cries that seemed to frighten the swampies even more than the blasters, cries that belonged far away in another time. A huge mastiff ran among them, baying with a deep-throated, blood-chilling malevolence.

They thundered past and around Doyle, DeFore and Brigid, who scrambled out of their path. The horsemen gave the three people swift, gleam-eyed appraising glances. One of the mounted men, like a casual afterthought, pointed his rifle at Doyle and squeezed the trigger.

The bullet turned his scarred face into a red jelly smear, spinning him around on his heels and dropping him heavily into the brush.

Brigid and DeFore crawled swiftly over to him, turning him over. Despite the round that had cored a path through his head, the man's eyes were open and blinking. He struggled to speak.

"They saw only the beast," he whispered. "And they killed it. Now it's me again. It *is* me."

His eyes remained open, but life eased out of them, leaving them empty and blank.

DeFore sank her teeth into her underlip and gently closed Doyle's eyes. "Maybe what happened to him should happen to me."

Brigid didn't reply, turning her head in the direction of the camp. Gunshots and hoofbeats continued to resound, intermixed with gobbling shrieks of fear and pain. She listened carefully, then heard familiar cracking reports.

"It's Grant and Kane," she said, pulling DeFore to her feet. "They're here."

DeFore gave her a dull, dispirited, almost uninterested look. "How do you know?"

Taking her by the hand, Brigid led her stumbling through the brush. "Two Sin Eaters. Who else would—?"

She bit off the remainder of what she intended to say as two more jackhammer stutters cut through the predawn gloom. A horse, then a man screamed in pain.

Releasing DeFore, Brigid sprinted forward, heart pumping fearfully. When she reached the edge of the camp, she had no choice but to stagger to a halt or be trampled. Figures were locked in a mass of combat, spilling and falling to the ground beneath the impacts of bullets and crossbow bolts. Riderless horses and people ran this way and that, in disorganized clusters of terror and fury.

A man fell off his horse with a wheeze, clutching his hands to his upper body where a feathered shaft sprouted. A spattering of arrows fell. The thrum of automatic gunfire rang out from the other side of the bonfire, and more men fell from their mounts.

Carefully, moving in a crouch, Brigid circled the logs of the fire and saw two scar-faced men standing head and shoulders above the milling swampies. They fired full-auto bursts from big-bored handblasters at a pair of horsemen. The barrage smashed into the animals, knocking them onto their hind legs with heart-rending screams.

The handblasters were Sin Eaters, but the men weren't dressed as Mags. They wore the same motley, mismatched collection of ragged clothes as the muties. But at each of their shots a man either plunged from the back of a horse or the animal shrieked, reared and crashed to the ground.

Brigid stared in dumbfounded shock. She hadn't just assumed Kane and Grant had arrived to rescue them; she had believed it with an almost religious faith. She was still staring when the swampie woman attacked her, lunging viciously with a straight-arm thrust. A long knife, like a thorn of steel, gleamed in her fist.

She reeled back and threw herself sideways to escape, dodging a slash with the blade. She rolled, kicked the woman in the back of the knee and knocked her leg out from under her. As the swampie tried to catch herself, she dropped her knife.

Scooping it up, Brigid stabbed for the woman's throat and missed, but the blade took her in the shoulder. Still, she screamed and scuttled away.

Brigid wasted no more time on her. Her anger was as cold as an arctic night and as black. Head down, she rushed the men with the Sin Eaters. They were so occupied squeezing off one shot after another they didn't see her until she was nearly beside them. One man swung his head toward her a shaved sliver of a second before she stabbed him through the heart, holding the knife point upward. The steel slid smoothly between the ribs, and she gave the blade a twist of her wrist, cutting open the walls of the beast's heart.

He didn't even grunt as his knees sagged and he sank to the ground.

The other man whirled toward her, leading with his blaster. A subgun chattered in a short burst. The beast spun around on his toes, the top of his skull floating away in a red mist.

Brigid pivoted at the waist.

A soaking-wet and ragged Kane marched toward her, his own Sin Eater in hand. A swampie charged him, wielding a machete, and he triggered it, the 9 mm rounds driving through the side of the mutie's head, opening up his cranium like a ripe melon struck with a hammer. The man flopped onto the ground, flat, dirty feet kicking spasmodically.

All the strength seemed to seep out of Brigid's body through the soles of her feet and she sank to her knees. She refused to respond to his calls of "Baptiste!"

Only when she felt his hand close around her wrist and haul her to her feet did she even acknowledge he was there. She tried to fight her way out of his grasp.

BRIGID BAPTISTE'S FACE was like that of a corpse. The flesh was pale, as if drained of blood where it wasn't covered with filth. Her green eyes were dry and bright. Her smile turned into flat, mocking laughter. "Is it you," she asked, "or a beast?"

Kane released her, nearly backing away from the madness in Brigid's eyes, from the fever harshness in her laughter. "It's me, Baptiste. Grant's here, too. Where's DeFore?"

She gestured negligently over a shoulder. "Somewhere."

Kane frowned and demanded, "Somewhere *where?*"

Brigid laughed again, and in her throat it turned into a sob. She choked it down, opened her mouth to speak.

A heavy, solid weight bowled Kane off his feet, cannonading him headlong across the ground. He fought his way to his hands and knees, trying to drag air into his lungs. The swampie loomed above him like a storm cloud, raining blows, hammering the breath out of him. The stink of the swamp clogged his nostrils.

Kane heard the characteristic thunderclap report of a Sin Eater. The mutie jerked violently, and lifeless fingers slid away from his throat. As he collapsed, he saw a fist-sized chunk was missing from his skull.

Brigid crouched beside the man she had heart-stabbed, holding his hand between her own. A faint curl of smoke twisted from the barrel of the blaster. Behind her he saw Grant and Mama Esther rushing toward them, leading a charge of the *hunsi*.

A rush of swampies surged to meet them, grappling hand to hand. Dozens of them scampered around the bonfire. Kane had his Sin Eater set on triburst. He chopped down three of the closest muties, sending them flopping to the ground, spurting blood and bone from devastating head wounds.

The swampies fought with a desperate savagery that surprised even Kane. Fingers gouged out eyeballs, necks were broken between immensely strong hands. They exposed themselves to blasterfire as if they didn't know or care what death was. The swampies courted death to deal death.

Grant opened up with his Sin Eater, and three swampies fell heavily, blood spurting from red-rimmed holes in their heads. Kane shifted position, trying to reach Brigid.

Back and forth the struggle rolled, blasterfire crashing, humans and muties howling. Feet churned the ground to crimson-tinted sludge. The dead, the wounded, the mutilated were stamped underfoot. The killzone was packed and jammed with swampies and *hunsi,* combatants crushed together breast to breast.

The *hunsi* were outnumbered, but the effect of their blasters was devastating. The screaming wave of combat surged and spilled away from the fire, spreading out across the swamp campsite.

The battle stopped. The end was not sudden, but more of a gradual decline, with fewer and fewer shots being fired as the swampies retreated into the foliage. The *hunsi* started to pursue them, but Mama Esther, shouldering her big blunderbuss, called after them, frantically, desperately.

Some of her people obeyed, breaking off the pursuit. Others, caught up in blood fever, paid no attention and ran to the edge of the swamp. Then Ocajnik was among them.

He was a whirlwind, plunging his claws between ribs, ripping hearts from chests amid sprays of blood and viscera. The *hunsi* screeched as Ocajnik pulled their arms from their bodies, flayed flesh from their faces, killed them with openhanded blows to the face that pulverized bones and spewed brain matter from ears in a jellylike mass.

"Get back!" Esther shouted. "It's him! It's Ocajnik!"

Grant and Kane stared, shocked into momentary

paralysis by the handsome, dark-haired man marching toward them, killing and mutilating as he came. They brought his figure into target acquisition and fired all the remaining rounds in their Sin Eaters. They saw him react to the impact of the bullets, which turned him this way and that and brought forth small grunts from his smiling lips, but he remained on his feet. Then the firing pins clicked on empty chambers.

Esther stepped forward, planting the butt of the blunderbuss against her shoulder, bringing it into firing position.

Ocajnik's yellow-green eyes flared at her. His pace slowed, but he didn't come to a full halt. "Conjure woman." His voice seemed to fill them, to make the air shiver. "Thou and thy fetishes and charms cannot slay me. Dost thou truly think that toy will do thee any good against a god?"

"You're no god," Esther replied flatly, thumbing back the lock. "You're a leftover from a time gone by."

"Point that toy at me," Ocajnik snarled, "and I will tear thy tongue from thy head and eat it before thine eyes."

"Fuck you," Esther said quietly, and squeezed the trigger.

The explosion that erupted from the muzzle of the gun wasn't quite as loud as a detonating gren, but it wasn't much quieter. Kane felt his eardrums compressed by the concussion, and his body shook to the jolt. Only a little smoke and flame belched from the barrel.

A glob of white granules, looking almost like a fist-sized snowball, catapulted from the flared bore and struck Ocajnik dead center, bursting in a fine mist of powdery particles. He didn't fall or bleed or even stagger.

Instead he thrashed and screeched and beat at himself as if he believed he had caught fire and was trying to smother the flames. His flesh peeled, blistered and erupted in pustules. They burst like punctured balloons, squirting a thick, foul-smelling mucuslike substance.

Ocajnik roared, consumed with agony and fury. He clawed at himself, his mouth spreading wide and spewing more of the heavy liquid. His long tongue lashed back and forth, like the tail of a lizard in its death throes.

"What the hell?" Grant's tone was hushed, hoarse.

"I loaded it with purified salt, just like I told you," Esther said with savage satisfaction. "And now for the silver."

She dropped the blunderbuss and plucked from between her breasts the cross of Saint John. She held it high in her left hand and approached the hissing Ocajnik, who crouched and watched her approach with wide, staring eyes. All of his human features faded, falling away like a snake shedding its skin.

Around the small silver cross, arcing skeins of

static electricity seemed to crackle and dance. Esther had taken only a few steps when Grant and Kane heard a meaty thud. She gave out a cry of pain and surprise.

Mama Esther stumbled and fell to her knees, her right hand pressing against her chest, just below her left breast. A feathered shaft jutted out between her splayed fingers. She kept her hand there as she eased into a sitting position, as if she were trying to catch the pain.

Two of her *hunsi* shrieked furious words in Creole and fired their rifles blindly into the foliage. Ocajnik laughed, a ghastly rattling of dry bones. He started to straighten up.

Then DeFore was behind him and in crazed motion, whipping the machete in her hands up across the rear of Ocajnik's neck. Roaring in outrage, he whirled, long talon-tipped fingers clawing for her in wild sweeps. One of them tore a rent in her bodysuit's sleeve and the skin beneath it, but she paid no attention.

She chopped at him with the blade, holding it in a double-fisted grip as if it were a battle-ax. The edge sank deep into his oozing belly and withdrew with a sticky smack.

"This is me," DeFore gritted, delivering another vicious slash. "*This is me,* you perverted son of a bitch!"

Pink foam bubbled out from Ocajnik's lips, and he reached for her again, uttering a gargling cry.

Kane and Grant started to lunge forward, but Brigid Baptiste pushed between them, elbowing them aside. She snatched up the crucifix from Mama Esther's slack fingers and dashed directly at Ocajnik.

Fueled by panic, Kane tried to grab her. "Baptiste—no!"

Clumsily, Ocajnik shambled around to face her. Brigid left the ground in a long dive as if she intended to tackle him. A sweep of black-clawed fingers opened up the back of her bodysuit, but she slapped the tiny cross between the leaking lips in Ocajnik's belly. She hit the ground, tucked and rolled.

From Ocajnik's body shot a single shaft of white light, unbearably bright. With a deafening, prolonged shriek, he reeled and staggered, tearing at his belly, ripping out clots of tissue. He shriveled, and then flames roared out of him and around him. His clothes and skin exploded with a blinding, crackling flare.

He screamed and howled and ran, frenzied, a flaming human-shaped torch, every inch of his body spewing fire. Ocajnik's body imploded in a burst of blue-and-white flames. All that was left was a blackened streak of carbonized ash that gave off a few sputtering sparks.

Kane and Grant and all the people watching had no true concept of what they had just witnessed. But all of them felt a surge of relief so great it made them weak.

Numbly, Grant knelt beside Mama Esther,

wincing at how deeply the arrow was embedded in her chest.

Hoarsely, she whispered, "Nothing you can do for me now." Her lips stretched in a grimacing smile. "Even the *loa* don't expect you to fight a devil out of hell and come out with a whole skin. I knew there was a price to pay. And my vision was a true one...you traveled by lightning, by thunder, through the magic of the storm."

Mama Esther closed her eyes and died with the smile still on her lips.

Her *hunsi* waved Grant back and, stone-faced, they claimed her body, carrying it away toward the river. Kane turned toward Brigid and DeFore, who stood motionless, staring at him without really seeing him.

It took him a couple of tries, but finally he spoke. "Whatever was going on here, I suppose it's over."

Neither of the women replied or even acted as if they heard him. They looked toward the eastern sky, at the rising sun. It rose, swimming in cloud shadows the color of blood.

Kane cleared his throat, following their gaze. "At least the sun finally came up."

Brigid eyed him blankly. "Is that supposed to mean something good?"

Taking DeFore by the arm, she walked slowly after the *hunsi*.

Kane looked toward the lurid red sky, desperately seeking an unshadowed sun.

JAMES AXLER

DEATH LANDS ®

Pandora's Redoubt

Ryan Cawdor and his fellow survivalists emerge in a redoubt in which they discover a sleek superarmored personnel carrier bristling with weapons from predark days. As the companions leave the redoubt, a sudden beeping makes them realize why the builders were constructing a supermachine in the first place.

Brutal civil war...

STONY MAN™ 47

COMMAND FORCE

Stony Man is called into action as a rogue party of Albanian freedom fighters attempts to collect a blood debt on America's streets. The Free Albania Party has crossed the line from rebels to terrorists, and their thirst for retribution against the hard-line Western powers has reached crisis proportions.

Available in June 2000 at your favorite retail outlet.

Blood inheritance...

DON PENDLETON's

MACK BOLAN®

STORM FRONT

A homegrown terrorist group lying dormant for more than a decade rises to continue its war against the American government. Revenge against the Feds who stalked and shut down the Cohorts years ago is the first on its agenda of terror. The group's actions are matched bullet for bullet by the Executioner, who is committed to eradicating the Cohorts and its legacy of bloodshed.

Available in July 2000 at your favorite retail outlet.